SAPPHO, by ALPHONSE DAUDET

Alphonse Daudet was born in Nîmes in 1840. Ten years later his father's silk business failed, and Daudet's childhood was spent against a background of financial difficulty. He arrived in Paris in 1857 where, supported and encouraged by his brother Ernest, he sought to earn his living by writing. His first published work was the collection of poems, *Les Amoureuses*, and on the strength of these he obtained a job on the *Figaro*. More importantly he came to the attention of the Duc de Morny, half brother of the Emperor Napoleon III, who offered him a post as his secretary. Daudet now not only had an income and contacts, but time to write.

His literary career was varied. He followed poetry with plays and was a prolific journalist and short-story writer. In 1866 he published *Lettres de Mon Moulin*, a series of sketches of Provence which is his best-known book. His novels include *Tartarin de Tarascon* (1872), a burlesque on French provincial life, and a series of realist works including *Jack* (1876) based on life in a shipyard, *Le Nabab* (1877) which established his European reputation, and *Sappho* (1884).

Daudet became a prominent but independent literary figure. He declined to be categorised with either Flaubert or Zola, although much of his work bears similarities to theirs. He was a leading *naturaliste*, writing with the eye for accuracy typical of the movement, but his work is brought alive by his gift for vivid, impressionistic description and because his naturalism never excluded the warmer side of his character. At Daudet's funeral in 1897 Zola declared: "His eternal merit will consist of this compassionate love for the humble, of this victorious laughter pursuing the fool and the wicked, and all of the extreme kindness and fair satire which impregnate each of his books."

ALPHONSE DAUDET

SAPPHO

TRANSLATED BY EITHNE WILKINS
WITH AN INTRODUCTION BY
NELL DUNN

A NOVEL

PUBLISHED BY THE SOHO BOOK COMPANY
1 BREWER STREET LONDON W1

Published by
THE SOHO BOOK COMPANY
1/3 Brewer Street, London W1R 3FN
1987

First published in France in 1884
This translation first published by Hamish Hamilton in
1951
Passages from the Goncourt Journal by kind permission
of the
Oxford University Press
Walton Street
Oxford

British Library Cataloguing in Publication Data

Daudet, Alphonse
    Sappho
    I. Title   II. Sapho, *English*
    843′ .8[F]   PQ2216.F3

    ISBN 0–948166–12–6

Printed and bound in Great Britain
by Redwood Burn Ltd, Trowbridge, Wilts
Cover design, title page and introductory material
© THE SOHO BOOK COMPANY LTD 1987
Designed by Sally McKay at Graham Rawle Designs
and by THE SOHO BOOK CO LTD

INTRODUCTION

NELL DUNN

Sappho is a modern novel. Tobacco is called by its brand name. The lovers picnic in bed. It is also very thrilling. The end surprises.

Apparently, Daudet wrote it to warn his sons off wild women, but I wonder if it did the trick. Sappho, our heroine, is fascinating and her life is a life of romantic adventure that many women might envy – not for her the kitchen sink or the well-paid career but instead love affairs with artists and poets. And for our young hero from the South, Jean Gaussin, who gets deeply involved with her, she provides, at least, a full sentimental education.

Alphonse Daudet came from Provence to Paris when he was 17 and by the time he was 25 in 1865, was trying to earn his living as a writer. In the Goncourt Journal dated January, 1885, we are told how that came about:

"Daudet went on to say that during all those years he had done nothing at all, that all he had felt had been a need to live, to live actively, violently, noisily, a need to sing, make music, to roam the woods, to drink a little too much and to get involved in a brawl. He admitted that at that time he had no literary ambition, but just an instinctive delight in noting everything down, in recording everything, even his dreams. It was the war, he declared, which had changed him, by awakening in him the idea that he might die without having achieved anything, without leaving anything durable behind him.... Only then had he set to work, and with work came literary ambition."

Sappho was written in 1883 when Daudet was 43 years old. It is almost certainly based on his long affair, as a young man, with a courtesan known as Chien Vert, which he broke off when he decided to get married. However she wasn't the only woman of dubious reputation he had a liaison with. Daudet was fascinated by women of the street and found them sexually far more exciting than respectable women. There is a lovely story in the Goncourt Journal of 1876 told as a conversation between Zola and Daudet....

"'Just imagine', Daudet went on, 'it was our wedding anniversary a few days ago.... Now you know that I love my wife for all sorts of reasons, for fine qualities which I am the only one who knows; and then I don't need to tell you that I worship my child, and that goes with my affection for my wife.... Well I decided to take home some flowers for her. But there I was, in the Rue d'Argenteuil, in that confounded street with the dark doorways in which dirty women stand hitching up their skirts – the sort of women I like when I am excited – with the result that I spent half an hour pretending to be waiting for the bus and not waiting for it at all, but breathing in the smell of prostitution in that street like a bitch on heat. I might still be down one of those alleys now if it weren't for the fact that I am as superstitious as an Italian, and I started imagining frightful diseases, diseases which would be my punishment if I were unfaithful on that particular day. All of a sudden I took to my heels, rushed into Madame Prevost's, threw all the money I had on the counter, and said: "Make up a bouquet of white lilac for me with all that." There were sixteen francs. I hadn't even dared to keep some money for the bus. My wife actually scolded me for arriving home half an hour late; but I have never been so pleased with myself in the whole of my life, and you can't imagine how much it had cost me!' "

There is a wonderfully erotic feel running through the book that French writers are so much better at capturing than English, such as the moment when our hero guesses his mistress has had a night of passionate love-making with another man from the way the bedclothes look. The nature of sexual love is deeply explored and Daudet is accurate in describing the crazy, inspired pain of sexual jealousy. Inspired, because it feeds the imagination in vivid gasping fantasies.

Daudet was living in Paris and writing at an extraordinarily rich period for the arts. He was part of the artistic and intellectual society and knew Flaubert, Zola, Mallarmé, Rodin, Degas and Baudelaire to name but a few. Sappho is part of the naturalistic movement led by Flaubert and Zola. It is a marvellously earthy book, full of sex, drama and domestic bliss. There is a wonderful passage where our hero goes home to the South to visit his family on the lovely wine-growing estate. They greet him and fuss over him and he is enchanted to be back in the beautiful countryside. He goes to bed and sleeps and waking the next day he is overcome with boredom and can't wait to get back to Sappho.

The book tackles that age old conflict, whether to pursue innocence and the respectable life, or to live for our impulses and explore the dead of night. But then the consequences can be grave.

It is in many ways a feminist book. Sappho makes her own decisions, she isn't constricted by social mores and for this I admire her. She is a woman who makes brave choices and draws us in and fascinates us. Both the book, and Sappho herself, are full of the charm and lure of the disreputable and the adventurous.

'COME, look at me. I like the colour of your eyes. What's your name?'

'Jean.'

'Just Jean—nothing else?'

'Jean Gaussin.'

'From the South, of course. I can tell that. And how old are you?'

'Twenty-one.'

'Are you an artist?'

'No, madame.'

'Oh, well—so much the better.'

These scraps of talk, almost lost among the shouting and laughter and the dance-music of a fancy-dress ball, one night in June, passed between an Italian piper and an Egyptian peasant-woman, in a conservatory full of palms and tree-ferns at the back of Déchelette's studio.

The piper's replies to the Egyptian woman's pressing interrogation were given with all the ingenuousness of his extreme youth and the trustful unconstraint of a Provençal who has long had no one to talk to. A stranger in this world of painters and sculptors, he had been lost, the moment when he entered the ballroom, by the friend who had brought him there; and for the last two hours he had been rather hopelessly loitering, entirely unaware that his handsome face, burned dark and golden by the sun, and his tight curly hair, close-cropped as the sheepskin that he wore, were arousing whispers of curiosity and admiration all around him.

He was jostled by the shoulders of those dancing past and was laughingly mocked by these wild young painters because of the bagpipes that he carried the wrong way up and his ragged mountainy clothes, too thick and heavy for this summer night. A Japanese girl with eyes that spoke of the back streets of Paris, with steel daggers stuck through her hair, high-piled in a bun, sang softly, teasingly, at him: 'How handsome, ah, how handsome the postilion is!' while a Spanish *novio* in white silk lace, passing by on an Apache chieftain's arm, brandished her bouquet of white jasmine right in his face.

He did not know what to make of these advances, thought he must be perfectly ridiculous, and took refuge in the cool shadows of the conservatory, which had a wide divan by the wall, under the overhanging greenery. An instant later this woman had come and sat down beside him.

Was she young? Was she beautiful? He could not have told. . . . The long blue woollen dress tightly wrapping the full curves of her figure revealed two slender rounded arms, bare to the shoulder; and her little hands, loaded with rings, and her wide grey eyes, made larger still by the outlandish iron ornaments dangling over her forehead, completed a harmonious picture.

Doubtless she was an actress. Many actresses came to Déchelette's. And the thought did nothing to put him at his ease, for he was terrified of people of that sort. As she talked she leaned very close to him, her elbow on her knee, her chin resting on her hand, her attitude serious, mild, a shade languid.

'So you really are from the South? With such fair hair, too! How extraordinary!'

And she wanted to know how long he had been living in Paris, whether the consular examination that he was preparing for was very difficult, whether he knew a great many people and how he came to be at this party of Déchelette's, in the Rue de Rome, so far from his own Latin Quarter.

When he mentioned the name of the student who had brought him—La Gournerie—a relative of the writer's—she knew him, he supposed—the expression on her face changed, suddenly darkening. But he paid no attention, being at the age when the eyes shine without seeing anything. La Gournerie had promised him that his cousin would be here and that he would introduce him. 'I love his poems. . . . I should so much like to know him.'

She smiled in pity at his frankness and gave a pretty little shrug of her shoulders, at the same time taking the light leaves of a bamboo in her hands, parting them, and gazing into the ballroom to see whether she could find his great man for him and point him out.

The masquerade was now sparkling and swinging like a real fairy festival. The ceiling of the studio—or rather, the hall, for it was hardly ever used for working in—had been carried to the height of the house itself and made it one single vast room; and now all its sheer, pale, summery hangings, its thin straw or gauze blinds, lacquer screens and multi-coloured glass, and the bush of yellow roses standing in front of a tall Renaissance fireplace, were lit up by the bizarre rainbow light of innumerable Chinese, Persian, Moorish and Japanese lanterns, some made of pierced iron-work, cut out in ogives like the entrance to a mosque, others made of coloured paper, in the form of fruits, and yet others fanning out in the shapes of flowers and ibises and serpents. Then suddenly swift, bluish streaks of electric light made all these thousand lamps look pale and cast a frosty moonlit gleam on faces and bare shoulders and the whole phantasmagoria of stuffs, feathers, spangles, and ribbons jumbled together here at this ball and rising, tier on tier, up the broad-balustraded Dutch staircase leading to the first-floor galleries, where one could catch glimpses of the necks of the double-basses and the feverish sweep of the conductor's baton.

From where he sat the young man could see this through a tracery of green branches and flowering creepers that seemed to intertwine with the scene beyond, making a framework for it and, by some optical illusion, falling into the ebb and flow of the dance, casting garlands of wistaria on a princess's silvery train, setting a dracaena leaf in the hair of a pretty little Pompadour shepherdess; and now he found his interest in the scene heightened by the pleasure of being told by his fair Egyptian the names—all known, all famous—concealed by these fancy-dress costumes that were so amusing in their variety and fantastic inspiration.

That whipper-in, with his short whip stuck in his cross-belt, was Jadin; and there, a little farther away, that country priest in the worn soutane was old Isabey, made taller by having a pack of cards in his buckled shoes. Dear old Daddy Corot was smiling under the enormous peak of a pensioner's cap. Others he was shown were Thomas Couture as a bulldog, Jundt as a policeman, and Cham as a stork.

And a number of gravely dignified historical costumes worn by very young painters—a Murat in a plumed hat, a Prince Eugène, a Charles I—emphasized the difference between the two generations of artists: the newcomers were sober, serious, and reserved, their faces, like those of ageing speculators on the stock exchange, furrowed with lines characteristic of preoccupation with money, while the older men were much more truly the lads letting themselves go, boisterous and untrammelled.

In spite of his fifty-five years and the palms awarded him by the Institute, there was the sculptor Caoudal as a down-at-heels hussar, his arms bare, showing his herculean biceps, a painter's palette dangling against his long legs by way of a sabretache, as he whirled round a lone cavalier of the time of the Grande Chaumière, opposite the musician de Potter, a muezzin on high holiday, his turban askew, doing the belly-dance and shrieking 'Allah, il Allah!' in a high falsetto.

These illustrious revellers were surrounded by a large circle of dancers now sitting out and resting; and in the foreground there was Déchelette, the master of the house, puckering up his little eyes under a high Persian hat that well suited his Kalmuck nose and grizzled beard; he was delighted with the gaiety of his guests and, though without showing it, actually having the time of his life.

Déchelette the engineer, a well-known figure in the artistic world of Paris ten or twelve years ago, very kind-hearted and very rich, with faint hankerings towards art and with that airy freedom of manner and disregard for the conventions that comes from a life of travel and bachelordom, was building a railway line from Tabriz to Teheran; and in order to recuperate from ten months of exhausting work, nights passed under canvas, and fever-ridden dashes over sand and swamp, every year he came home to spend the hot season in this house in the Rue de Rome, which had been built to his own design and furnished as a summer palace. Here he gathered together brilliant men and good-looking women, demanding that civilization should in a few weeks give him the essence of all the headiness and sweetness it contained.

'Déchelette is back in town.' That was the news that went round the studios the moment someone noticed the huge canvas awning rising like the curtain in a theatre, baring the great window in the front of the house. This meant that the merry-making was about to begin and for the next two months there were to be musical entertainments and junketings, dances and carousals, slicing through the silent torpor of the Quartier de l'Europe in the season of country holidays and sea-bathing.

Personally Déchelette did not join in the bacchanal rumbling on in his house night and day. This tireless reveller took his pleasures with a chill intensity, a vague, smiling look that suggested a hashish-trance, and yet with unruffled tranquillity and lucidity. He was a very loyal friend, giving without counting the cost, and he regarded women with the contempt of an Oriental, mingled with indulgence and courtesy; of all the women who came there, attracted by his great wealth and the light-hearted fancifulness of the setting, not one could boast of having been his mistress for longer than a day.

'He's a good sort of man, though . . .' added the fair Egyptian, who was giving Gaussin this information. Suddenly she broke off to say: 'There's your poet.'

'Oh, where?'

'Straight in front of you—as a peasant bridegroom.'

The young man uttered an 'oh' of disappointment. So that was his poet! That fat man shiny with sweat, displaying lumpish graces in Hodge's double-pointed shirt-collar and flowered waistcoat. . . . The great despairing cries of the *Book of Love* came to his mind, that book he never read without a faint shuddering of ecstasy. And he murmured aloud, mechanically:

> ' To quicken your body's splendid marble into life,
>   O Sappho, I have poured away my last heart's-blood.'

She turned sharply, her barbarous jewellery clinking, and exclaimed:

'What's that you say?'

They were lines of La Gournerie's. He was surprised that she did not know them.

'I don't like poetry,' she said, curtly. And she remained standing, with a frown, gazing at the dancers and nervously brushing against the beautiful lilac clusters hanging in front of her. Then with an obvious effort she made up her mind, said 'Good night,' and was gone.

The poor bagpiper was quite taken aback. What is the matter with her? What have I said? he wondered. He racked his brains but could come to no conclusion except that he would do well to go home to bed. Mournfully he picked up his bagpipes and went back to the ballroom, less disturbed by the Egyptian's departure than by having to make his way through all this crowd before he could reach the door.

His sense of his own obscurity among so much fame and brilliance made him all the more diffident. The dancing had stopped. Only a few couples swung around, in raptures, to the last bars of a dying waltz, and among them Caoudal, gigantic, magnificent, with head held high, whirled with a little *tricoteuse*, whose coif flew out behind her as he swept her round, borne up in his freckled arms.

Through the great windows at the back, flung wide open, came little gusts of purifying early morning air, stirring the palm-leaves and bending the candle-flames as though to snuff them out. One paper lantern took fire, sconces splintered, and all round the room servants set out little round tables like those outside cafés. At Déchelette's people always sat down to supper in fours and fives; and this was the time when fellow-feeling sorted everyone into little groups.

What shouting there was, what savage yells, the yodelling of the back streets answering the high-pitched 'aie-aie-aie-aie' of the Oriental girls, and what low-voiced colloquies, and the rippling laughter of women yielding to a caress.

Under cover of the turmoil Gaussin was slipping towards the door when his student friend stopped him—streaming with sweat, pop-eyed, a bottle under each arm—saying: 'Where on earth have you been? I've been looking for you everywhere. I've got a table, and women, and there's the Bachellery girl from the Bouffes. . . . Got up as a geisha, d'you see. She sent me to get you. Come on, quick!' and he ran off.

The bagpiper was thirsty. Besides, he could feel the lure of the ball, and he was tempted by the pretty face of the little actress who was beckoning to him across the room. But a grave, gentle voice murmured almost in his ear:

'Don't go. . . .'

The woman who had been with him only a little while ago was close beside him, almost clinging to him, pulling him away; and he followed her without a moment's hesitation. Why? It was not that she attracted him; he had hardly glanced at her, and the other girl, beckoning to him, adjusting the daggers in her hair, appealed to him far more. But he was obeying a will stronger than his own, obeying the impetuous violence of another's desire.

Don't go . . . !

And all at once there they both were out on the pavement in the Rue de Rome. Cabs were waiting, in the wan morning light. Crossing-sweepers, and labourers on their way to work, gazed at this festive tumult over-brimming into the street, this couple in fancy-dress, a Shrovetide carnival at the height of summer.

'Your place, or mine?' she asked. Without really knowing why, he thought that his place would be better, and gave the cab-driver his remote address. All during the journey, which was long, they talked little. All she did was to hold one of his hands between hers, which he could feel were very small and icy cold; and if it had not been for the chill of this uneasy fondling he might have believed that she was asleep, leaning back in the depths of the cab, with the shadow of the blue blind sliding over her face.

They stopped in the Rue Jacob, outside an hotel catering for students. There were four flights of stairs, a long, hard climb. 'Would you like me to carry you?' he asked, laughing, though softly in this sleeping house. She took him in with a slow look, scornful and tender, a gaze full of experience, measuring him up and quite distinctly saying: 'Poor boy. . . .'

And with the lovely fierce energy of youth and of the South he came from, he took her up in his arms and carried her like a child; he was sturdy and strapping, for all his girlish fair skin, and he went up the first flight without stopping for breath, rejoicing in his burden and the two beautiful, bare, rosy arms linked round his neck.

The second flight was longer, less delightful. The woman let herself go, and weighed the more heavily. The iron of her dangling ornaments, which was at first a caressing, a tickling of his skin, began to prick more cruelly and enter into his flesh.

On the third flight he was gasping like a furniture remover shifting a piano. He was too breathless to speak, while she, with fluttering eyelids, rapturously murmured: 'Oh, sweetheart, how lovely . . . how I do enjoy this. . . .' And the last steps, which he climbed one at a time, were like the treads of a giant staircase and the walls, banisters, and narrow windows seemed to be turning in an endless spiral. It was no longer a woman he carried in his arms, but some heavy and dreadful thing that was stifling him, a thing that he was at every instant tempted to fling angrily from him, even at the risk of doing some brutal hurt.

When they reached the narrow landing—'So soon?' she said, opening her eyes. What he thought was: 'At last!' But he could not have said it, standing there pale as death with both hands pressed to his chest, which seemed to be bursting.

Their whole story was there in that climbing of the stairs, in the grey gloom of the dawn.

2

HE kept her for two days. Then she went away, leaving him with a faint sense of soft skin and fine underwear. He had learnt nothing about her beyond her name, her address, and this: 'Whenever you want me, send for me. . . . I shall always be ready.'

The tiny, elegant, perfumed card said:

FANNY LEGRAND
6 Rue de l'Arcade

He stuck it into the mirror, between an invitation to the last ball of the season at the Foreign Office and the illuminated, whimsical programme of Déchelette's entertainment, his only two smart outings in the year; and although the memory of the woman lingered about the chimneypiece for a few days, in this faint, delicate perfume, fading as the perfume did, Gaussin, a sober, hard-working young man who was thoroughly mistrustful of the lures of Paris, never felt any urge to renew that evening's dalliance.

The examination for the Ministry was to be held in November. He had only three months left to prepare for it. After that there would be three or four years' work in the Consular Office; and then he would go away, to some remote place. The thought of that exile did not trouble him; for it was a tradition with the Gaussins d'Armandy, an old Avignon family, that the eldest son should go into what was called *the service*, with the example, encouragement, and moral protection of those who had gone before. For him Paris was only the first port of call on a very long voyage that prevented him from entering into any lasting relationship either in love or in friendship.

One evening, a week or two after Déchelette's ball, as Gaussin was sitting with the lamp lighted and his books spread out on the table, just about to begin his work, there was a timid knock; and the door opened to reveal a woman in a smart, light-coloured dress. He did not recognize her until she lifted her veil.

'Here I am, you see. . . . I've come back.'

Then, catching the uneasy, embarrassed glance that he threw towards his work, she said:

'Oh, I won't disturb you! I know the way it is. . . .'

She untied her bonnet, took up a number of *Round the World*, settled herself in a chair and did not stir, apparently absorbed in her reading. But every time he raised his eyes, he met her gaze.

Indeed, he needed all his strength of mind not to take her in his arms at once, for she was very alluring, quite exquisite with her tiny head, low forehead, short nose, and lips voluptuous and kind; and the lithe fullness of her figure was revealed by a dress of wholly Parisian correctitude, which he found less alarming than the garb she had worn as a daughter of Egypt.

She left early the next morning; and she returned several times that week. She always came with the same pallor, the same chill, damp hands, and the same voice husky with feeling.

'Oh, I know I'm in your way,' she would say to him. 'I know I bore you. I ought to have more pride. . . . Just fancy! Every morning when I go away I swear I won't come back. And then it comes over me again in the evening, like madness.'

He regarded her with amusement, surprised, in his contempt for women, by this over-fond persistence. The women he had come across previously had been waitresses or skating-rink attendants, some of them young and pretty enough, but all leaving him sickened by their silly laughter, their scullery-maid's hands, and a coarseness of instinct and of expression that made him open the window after them. In his inexperienced belief, he thought all *filles de plaisir* were the same. So it astonished him to find Fanny had a sweetness and reserve that were truly womanly, with the advantage —over the good ladies of his mother's acquaintance whom he had known in the country—of having a thin veneer of accomplishment and knowledge of the world, which gave variety and interest to their conversation.

Then, too, she was musical; she would enjoy accompanying herself on the piano, in a slightly weary, unequal, but trained contralto singing a Chopin or Schumann romance, or folk-songs—Berrichon, Burgundian, or Picard airs, of which she had a whole repertory.

Gaussin had a passion for music, that art of idleness and the open air, so delighted in by the people of his own part of the country; he grew elated at the sound of it when he was at his work, and at rest was deliciously lulled by it. This was the thing about Fanny that most enchanted him. He was surprised that she did not belong to the theatre, and so discovered that she had sung at the Lyrique. 'But not for long. . . . It got on my nerves. . . .'

And indeed there was nothing of the studied, artificial theatrical manner about her, and not a trace of vanity or deceit. Only there was a certain mystery about the rest of her life; it was a mystery preserved even in their hours of passion, and her lover did not try to penetrate it, since he felt neither jealous nor curious; he left it to her to come at the hour agreed on, without even glancing at the clock, knowing nothing, as yet, of that suspense, that immense thudding of the heart that tells the instants of desire and impatience.

From time to time—the summer being very fine that year—they went out exploring all those charming spots around Paris that she knew as precisely and in detail as a map. They mingled with the crowds, in the noise and upheaval of departures from suburban railway stations, and lunched at some café on the edge of the woods or a lake, avoiding only the too popular places. One day when he suggested going to les Vaux-de-Cernay, she said:

'No, no! Not there! Too many painters go there. . . .'

And then he remembered that her antipathy towards artists had marked the very first beginning of their love. When he asked her the reason, she said:

'They're so topsy-turvy and so complicated, always talking about things that don't really exist. . . . They've done me a lot of harm.'

'But,' he protested, 'art is such a fine thing! Nothing else makes life so beautiful, so much larger. . . .'

'Don't you see, sweetheart, the really fine thing is being simple and straight like you, being twenty and in love. . . .'

Twenty! No one would have thought she was more than that, to see her quivering with life, always on tiptoe, enjoying everything, finding everything good.

One evening in the Chevreuse valley they arrived at Saint-Clair on the eve of a local festival and could not get a room. It was late; they would have had to walk three miles through the forest, by night, to get to the nearest village. In the end they were offered a folding bed, with sacking for a mattress, that happened to be free at the far end of the barn where some bricklayers were sleeping.

'Come along!' she said, laughing. 'It will remind me of the days when I was down and out.'

So she had known what it was to be down and out.

They groped their way soundlessly between the occupied beds in the big roughcast whitewashed barn, where a night-light was smoking in a dark niche on the wall. And hugging each other tightly all night long, they stifled the sound of their kisses and their laughter, hearing their companions snoring or uttering little weary moans in their sleep, the men's smocks and heavy working boots lying almost side by side with the Parisian woman's silk dress and finely made shoes.

At daybreak a cat-trap opened at the bottom of the big door, a beam of white light flickered on the sacking beds and trampled earth, and a throaty voice shouted: 'Hi there, mates!' Then the barn was left in darkness again and there began a distressful slow stirring and scrambling, a yawning and a stretching, accompanied by hacking coughs and all the sad human noises of a reawakening dormitory. One by one the men of Limoges went off heavily, in silence, never suspecting that they had been sleeping near a lovely woman.

After they had gone she got up, fumbled for her dress and slipped into it, hastily twisted up her hair, and said: 'Stay there—I'll be back in a moment.' And only a short while later she came in with an enormous armful of wild flowers all drenched in dew.

'Now let's sleep,' she said, strewing the bed with the scented flowery morning freshness that lent a sparkle to the surrounding atmosphere. And never had she seemed so lovely to him as then, coming into the barn at daybreak, laughing, her light hair floating in the breeze, and with all her frolic flowers.

Another time they were breakfasting by the lake at Ville-d'Avray. The still water was veiled in the autumn haze of early morning; the woods, already rust and gold, lay ahead. They were alone in the little restaurant garden, kissing in the intervals of eating blay. Suddenly, from a rustic arbour perched in the plane-tree at the foot of which their table stood, a loud, bantering voice called: 'I say, you people down there, when you have finished billing and cooing . . .' And the leonine face and gingery moustaches of the sculptor Caoudal peered down through an opening in the lattice of the arbour. 'I've a good mind to come down and breakfast with you. I'm as dull as an owl up here in my tree.'

Fanny did not answer, obviously embarrassed by this encounter. But Gaussin accepted fast enough, curious to see the famous artist and flattered to have him at his table.

Very dandified for all his seeming negligence of dress, in which every detail was calculated—from the white crêpe de Chine cravat to give relief to a furrowed complexion that was blotchy with carbuncles, down to the jacket fitting closely to rippling muscles and a waist still slim—Caoudal looked older, to the young man's eyes, than he had at Déchelette's ball.

But what surprised and even slightly embarrassed Gaussin was the tone of familiarity the sculptor took with his mistress. He called her Fanny and seemed on intimate terms with her. 'You know,' he said, setting out his cover on their tablecloth, 'I've been a widower for the last fortnight. Maria has gone off with Morateur. It was rather a relief to me for the first few days. But coming into the studio this morning, I felt too sluggish for words. Hopeless trying to work. . . . So I left the group to itself and came out here to have breakfast in the country. Silly idea, when you're alone. I was within inches of shedding tears into my rabbit stew.'

Then, looking at the Provençal, whose silky beard and curly hair were the colour of the Sauterne in the glasses, he said:

'What a grand thing it is to be young! No danger of this chap

here being left on his own! And the cream of it all is that it's
catching—she looks every bit as young as he does.'

'You rascal!' she exclaimed, laughing. And her laughter had the
chime of timeless seduction, the youthfulness of a woman in love,
who wants to be loved in return.

'Amazing, amazing!' Caoudal murmured, scrutinizing her as he
ate; and there was a slight twist of sadness and envy in the curl of his
mouth. 'Tell me, Fanny, you remember that breakfast here—ah
me, those are far-off days—there was Ezano, and Dejoie, the whole
crowd—and you fell into the lake. We dressed you up in man's
clothes, in the waterman's tunic. It suited you to a T.'

'Can't say I remember,' she said coldly, and without untruth, for
like all such creatures of change and random adventure she lived
only in the present moment of her love. They have no memory of
what went before and no fear of what may be yet to come.

Caoudal, on the other hand, was absorbed in the past, tossing
down the Sauterne and reeling off stories of amorous and wine-
bibbing exploits in his robust youth, of picnic expeditions, balls at
the Opera, ragging in the studio, battles and conquests. But when
he turned towards them, his eyes alight with the inward flames he
had been fanning, he saw they were hardly listening, for they were
absorbed in picking grapes from between each other's lips.

'Am I being such an utter nuisance? Yes, yes, I'm boring you to
death. Ah, confound it! It's not much fun being old.' He got up,
flinging his napkin on the table. 'Langlois, old lad, make out the bill
to me!' he called towards the restaurant.

He departed mournfully, with dragging footsteps, as though
consumed by an incurable ill. For a long time the lovers gazed after
the tall figure stooping under the golden leaves.

'Poor Caoudal! It's a fact, he is going down,' Fanny murmured
in a tone of mild commiseration. And when Gaussin waxed in-
dignant at the thought that this woman Maria, a mere model,
could make light of the sufferings of a Caoudal and instead of a
great artist prefer a—well, whom?—Morateur, a quite ungifted
nobody of a painter, with nothing to recommend him but his
youth, she burst out laughing, exclaiming: 'Ah, simpleton! simple-

ton!' And, taking his head in both her hands, she drew it down on her lap, breathing in the scent of his skin and sighing over his eyes, his hair, brushing him with her lips like a bunch of flowers.

That night for the first time Jean slept at his mistress's house. She had been plaguing him on this score for three months. 'But why don't you want to?' she would ask him.

'I don't know. It bothers me.'

'But I tell you I'm free, I'm alone! . . .'

And tired as they were after their expedition into the country, she dragged him off to the Rue de l'Arcade, which was not far from the station. The door to the mezzanine of an evidently correct and comfortable middle-class house was opened by a cantankerous-looking elderly maidservant in a peasant-style cap.

'Here's Machaume! Good evening, Machaume!' Fanny said, flinging her arms round the woman's neck. 'Look, I told you, this is my darling, my king! I've brought him home with me. Quick, light all the lights, make the house beautiful!'

Jean was left alone in a tiny drawing-room with low round-headed windows, curtained in the same commonplace blue silk that covered the divans and the seats of some lacquer chairs. On the walls the material was made lighter and airier by three or four landscape paintings, each with a scribbled dedication: 'For Fanny Legrand' or 'For my dear Fanny'. . . .

On the chimneypiece was a half-life-size marble of Caoudal's Sappho, of which one sees bronze copies everywhere; Gaussin remembered seeing it in his father's study ever since his earliest childhood. And by the light of the single candle placed near the pedestal, he observed the resemblance that this work of art, though more youthful and fine-drawn, bore to his mistress. The lines of the profile, that turn of the body under the drapery, that sweeping roundness of the arms locked round the knees—it was all known to him, all familiar. His eyes absorbed it in the memory of sensations still fonder.

Fanny, finding him lost in contemplation of this marble, casually remarked: 'It has quite a look of me, hasn't it? Caoudal's model was like me.' And she at once took him into her bedroom, where

Machaume was with a bad grace setting places for two at a small round table. All the wax candles were lighted, even those on the wardrobe mirror-brackets; there was a good log-fire flaring away behind the spark-guard, bright as a firstling fire, and the room looked as though a woman must be getting ready for a ball.

'I wanted supper in here,' she said, laughing. 'We shall be in bed all the faster.'

Never had Jean seen such dainty furnishings. Knowing only the Louis XVI silk damask and pale muslins of his mother's and his sisters' bedrooms, he could not have imagined such a softly padded and quilted nest as this, where the woodwork was hidden under the smoothest of satins and the bed was no more than a divan wider than the others, standing on white rugs at the far end of the room.

How delicious the caress of light and warmth, of the blue reflections streaking the bevelled plate-glass mirrors, now after their walk through the fields, the drenching they had got, and the mud of the narrow lanes at nightfall! But what prevented him from enjoying the ease of it as a country lad should was the maidservant's ill-humour and the suspicious glances she directed at him until Fanny sent her out of the room, saying: 'Leave us alone, Machaume. We'll look after ourselves.' And as the woman slammed the door after her, Fanny added: 'Take no notice of her, she's cross with me for loving you so very much. She says I'm throwing myself away. These country people are so grasping! But her cooking is much nicer than she is. Come now, try this hare pie.'

She cut the pastry, uncorked the champagne, and forgot to help herself, watching him eat. Each time she moved her arms she shook the sleeves of the soft white woollen Algerian *gandoura* that she always wore at home. So she reminded him of their first meeting at Déchelette's; and sitting close together on the same seat, eating from the one plate, they talked of that night.

'Oh yes,' she said, 'the moment I saw you come in I wanted to have you for myself. If I'd been able to, I would have taken you away that very moment so that the others shouldn't get you. And what did you think about me when you saw me first?'

At first he had been afraid of her; then he had felt full of confidence and completely at ease with her. 'By the way,' he added, 'I've never asked you—why were you put out? I mean about those two lines of La Gournerie's?'

She frowned just as she had at the ball, then tossed her head. 'It's too silly! Don't let's talk about it.' And winding her arms round him, she said: 'The fact is I was a bit frightened, too. I was trying to escape, trying to collect myself. But I couldn't. I shall never be able to.'

'Oh—never!'

'You'll see.'

He was content to reply with the sceptical smile of his years, without giving a thought to the passionate, almost threatening tone in which her 'You'll see' had been flung at him. The pressure of the linked arms was so gentle, so submissive: he firmly believed that he only had to make a gesture in order to free himself. . . .

But why should he free himself? He was so at his ease, lapped in the pillowing luxury of this room, deliciously stupefied by the faint breath on his flickering, sleep-laden eyelids that were full of fleeting visions—gold-tinted woods, and meadows, and water trickling over millstones, their love's long day in the open country. . . .

In the morning he was wakened with a start by Machaume's voice at the foot of the bed, exclaiming without the least concealment: 'He's here! He wants to see you.'

'What? He *wants*! So I can't call my house my own! So you let him in!'

Furious, she leapt out of bed and dashed from the room, half-naked, her nightdress open, calling over her shoulder: 'Don't stir, sweetheart. I'll be back in a moment.'

But he did not wait for her; he could not feel easy until he too had got up and dressed and had his feet firmly shod again.

While he was gathering his clothes together in the hermetically closed room where the night-light still burnt, casting a gleam over the untidy remains of their little supper, he heard sounds of a terrible argument muffled by the hangings in the drawing-room. There was a man's voice, at first excited, then imploring, crying out,

and finally breaking into sobs and feeble, whimpering cries, alternating with another voice that he did not recognize at once, it was
so harsh and raucous, tense with hatred; and the vile words it
uttered, audible even to him, reminded him of a factory-lasses'
brawl.

Now all this amorous ease was soiled, degraded as though by
mud splashes on the silk; and the woman was smudged, too,
lowered to the level of others whom he had been accustomed to
despise.

She came back, breathless and gasping, twisting up her loose
hair with a lovely gesture. 'How silly it is to see a man crying!' she
exclaimed. And then, seeing him up and dressed, she uttered a cry
of rage: 'You've got up! Go back to bed! At once! I wish it!' And
then suddenly appeased, clasping him in her arms as she entwined
him with her words, she murmured: 'No, no, don't go away. You
can't go like that. Besides, I'm certain you wouldn't come back
again.'

'Yes, I would. Why shouldn't I?'

'Swear you aren't vexed, swear you'll come back. Oh, I know
you!'

He solemnly promised what she wished, but he did not go back
to bed, in spite of her supplications and reiterated assurance that she
was in her own house, free to do as she wished and see whom she
wished. In the end she seemed to become resigned to letting him go
and accompanied him to the door, now with no more trace of the
raving bacchante, but very humble indeed and trying to get his
forgiveness.

A lingering, ardent last embrace kept them for a while in the hall.

'Well—when?' she asked, her eyes gazing deep into his. He was
about to answer, probably not telling the truth in his haste to be
outside, when a peal at the doorbell stopped him. Machaume came
out of her kitchen, but Fanny made a sign to her not to open the
door. And the three of them stood there, motionless, without uttering a word.

There was a stifled moan, then the rustling of a letter being slid
under the door, and the sound of footsteps slowly going down the

steps. 'Well, I told you I was free—now look at that!' She handed
her lover the letter that she had just opened, a pathetic love-letter,
an abject, sorry thing that had been scrawled in pencil at some café
table; the unfortunate writer begged for forgiveness for his wild act
of that morning, acknowledged that he had no claim on her beyond
whatever she might grant him, implored her in tones of utmost
supplication not to banish him for ever, promised to accept anything, was resigned to anything. . . . Only not to lose her, dear God!
not to lose her!

'What a thing!' she said, with a spiteful laugh; and that laugh was
what finally locked against her the heart she was trying to regain.
Jean thought her cruel. He did not yet know that a woman in love
has no shred of feeling for anyone but the man she loves, all her
vital resources of charity, kindness, pity, and devotion being absorbed in the welfare of one being and one only.

'It's wrong of you to make fun of it. It's dreadfully beautiful and
heart-rending,' he said. And in a low, earnest tone he added, holding
her hands: 'Come, tell me—why have you driven him away?'

'I don't want any more to do with him. I don't love him.'

'But still, he was your lover. He gave you the comfort you live
in, and always have lived in, which you can't do without.'

'Sweetheart,' she said in her tone of candour, 'when I didn't
know you, all this seemed all right. Now it's dreary and shameful.
Sometimes it makes me sick. Oh, I know, you're going to tell me
that you don't really mean anything, you don't really love me. But
I don't care, I'll take care of that for myself. Whether you like it or
not, I shall *make* you love me.'

He did not answer but agreed to see her the next day and escaped,
leaving a small sum for Machaume, the last remaining money in his
student purse, as payment for the pie. So far as he was concerned, it
was all over. What right had he to cause any upheaval in this
woman's life, and what could he offer her in exchange for what she
would lose through him?

He wrote to her that same day, saying all this as gently and as
sincerely as he could, but without admitting how he had felt
that their affair, that good-humoured, light caprice, had suddenly

turned into something violent and morbid, when after that night of love he heard the cheated lover's sobbing, alternating with her laughter and her fishwife's curses.

This lad who had grown up so far away from Paris, in the wild heathlands of Provence, had in his make-up something of his father's austerity and all the sensitive feelings, the flickering nervous intuitions, of his mother, whom he resembled as a portrait resembles the sitter. And there was yet another thing to protect him from the lures of a life of pleasure, namely the example of a brother of his father's, whose wildness and folly had almost ruined their family and had imperilled its good name.

Uncle Césaire! The mere sound of those two words, evoking a whole family drama, was enough to wring from Jean sacrifices much more terrible than the sacrifice of this little love-affair, to which he had never attached much importance. And yet to make the break was harder than he had imagined.

Although formally dismissed she returned again and again, not put off by his refusals to see her, nor by the locked door, the inexorable blank wall. 'I have no pride . . .' she wrote to him. She kept a watch for the times when he went out to a restaurant for his meals; she waited outside the café where he read the newspapers. And there were no tears, no scenes. If he was with other people, she was content to follow him, looking out for the moment when he would be alone.

'Do you want me to-night? No? Oh well, then, another time. . . .' And she would go away with the mild fatalistic air of the pedlar strapping his bundle up again, leaving Jean with a sense of remorse for his harshness and the humiliation of the invented excuse he would stammer at every meeting. The examination was so near . . . he had so little time . . . afterwards, later on, if she still cared to come. . . . Actually he hoped that as soon as he had passed his examination he would take a month's holiday in the South, and that she would forget him in that time.

Unfortunately, just after he had passed his examination Jean fell ill with tonsillitis brought on by the draughts in the Ministry corridors; at first neglected, it became rapidly worse. He knew nobody in Paris, apart from a few students from his own part of the country, with whom he had lost touch since his love-affair made such demands on him. Moreover, what was needed here was more than ordinary devotion, and from the first evening onward it was Fanny Legrand who took her place beside his bed; for ten days she did not leave him, nursing him without any sign of fatigue, without any fear of infection, without any distaste, deft as a hospital nurse, with tender, coaxing little ways that sometimes in the wanderings of his fever took him back to a bad illness he had had as a child and made him call her by his aunt's name, saying 'Thank you, Divonne,' when he felt Fanny's hands on his damp forehead.

'It's not Divonne, it's me. I'm looking after you.'

She saved him from being at the mercy of those who would have tended him only for money, saved him from clumsily put-out fires and tisanes prepared in the concierge's den; and Jean never ceased to marvel at how swift, deft, and ingenious her hands could be, hands he had always thought of as being all voluptuous indolence. She slept on the divan for a mere two hours each night; and it was just such a divan as is found in a Latin Quarter hotel, about as soft as the benches in a police-station.

'But my poor dear Fanny, don't you ever go home?' he asked her one day. 'I'm better now. Surely Machaume will be worrying about you.'

She burst out laughing. Machaume, indeed! She had long gone with the winds, and the whole house with her! It had all been sold, the furniture, the hangings, the very bedding. All she was left with was the dress she had on and a few bits of fine underwear that her maid had saved. If he sent her away now, she would be on the streets.

3

'I THINK I've got it this time. In the Rue d'Amsterdam, opposite the station. Three rooms and a big balcony. If you like we'll go and see it when you come back from the office. It's a long way up, five storeys. But you'll carry me! That was lovely—remember?'

And in delight at the thought of it she buried her head in his arms, rubbing and snuggling, searching for her old place, her own place.

Living as they did, the two of them, in the shabby hotel room, in the thick of the Latin Quarter atmosphere—women in hair-nets and clogs dawdling about on the staircase, the papered plywood walls through which they could hear their neighbours moving about, and the promiscuity of keys, candles, shoes outside the door —the whole thing became intolerable. Not to her, indeed; for any cranny in the roof or cellar, even the gutter, would have done her well enough for a nesting-place as long as she could be with Jean. But his delicacy was offended by certain contacts that he had hardly given a thought to so long as he was a man on his own. These one-night sojourns embarrassed him, for they dishonoured his own love; it made him feel something of the depression and disgust that he got from standing before the monkey-cage in the Jardin des Plantes, where the creatures went through grimacing versions of the movements and expressions of human love. And he had had enough of the restaurant on the Boulevard Saint-Michel, where he had to go twice a day for his meals, eating in a large room full of university and Beaux-Arts students and painters and architects, who, though they had no acquaintance with him, had got to know his face in the year he had been going there.

Pushing the door open, he blushed to see all those eyes turned towards Fanny and came in with that aggressive awkwardness of very young men escorting a woman. Besides, he was afraid of running into one of his superiors from the Ministry or someone from home. And then, too, there was the question of expense.

'How dear it is!' she said every time, seizing the bill and going over it point by point. 'If we were in a place of our own, I would have kept us for three days for the same money.'

'Well, what is there to stop us?'

And so they set out on their search for an apartment.

There the snare lies. All are caught in it, even the best, the most decent of all, trapped by the impulse towards orderliness and the feeling for *a home of one's own* that have been implanted in them by their family upbringing and the warm cosiness of the circle round the fire.

The apartment in the Rue d'Amsterdam was rented at once. They decided it was charming, in spite of the fact that the rooms all opened off each other—the kitchen and the living-room overlooking a mouldy courtyard that was always full of the smell of slops and chlorine from an English tavern—the bedroom overlooking the street, which was steep and noisy, shaken, day and night, with the jolting of wagons, drays, cabs, and omnibuses, and always filled with the whistle of trains arriving and departing, all the racket of the Gare de l'Ouest opposite, with its glass roof the colour of dirty water. The advantage of it was in having trains at their doorstep and Saint-Cloud, Ville-d'Avray, and Saint-Germain, all those green places along the banks of the Seine, almost under their balcony. For they possessed a broad, comfortable balcony that still had, surviving from the munificent days of some past tenants, a zinc shelter painted to look like a striped awning, dripping and melancholy when the winter rain was pattering on the roof, but ideal for dining in the fresh air in summer-time, as though in a mountain chalet.

They set about getting furniture. Jean had told his family that he meant to set up in an apartment of his own, and his Aunt Divonne, who was more or less the manager of the family's affairs, had sent him the money he needed; and her letter also heralded the arrival of a wardrobe, a chest-of-drawers, and a big cane-bottomed armchair, removed from the *windy room* for the benefit of the young man in Paris.

In his mind's eye he saw that room at the far end of a passage at

Castelet, always unoccupied, the shutters closed and barred on the inside, the door bolted; it was exposed to the full assault of the *mistral*, which made it rattle like a room in a lighthouse. There they dumped old junk, everything that each generation of inmates relegated to the past as new belongings were acquired.

Ah, if Divonne had known for what strange siestas the cane-bottomed armchair would be used and what surah silk petticoats and lace-trimmed pantalets would fill the Empire chest-of-drawers! But Gaussin's qualms of conscience on this score were soon over-whelmed by the countless small delights of setting up house.

It was so amusing to come home after the office, at the fall of dusk, and then go off shopping, arm in arm with her, walking down one of the less smart streets to choose furniture for the dining-room—the sideboard, table, and six chairs—or the flowered cretonne curtains for the windows and the bed. He was ready to take anything, with closed eyes; but Fanny was alert for two, trying the chairs, sliding the table-leaves in and out, and proving herself an experienced bargainer.

She knew a place, for instance, where a complete set of kitchen utensils suitable for a small household could be bought at wholesale price, four iron saucepans and a fifth enamel one for their morning chocolate. Not copper, of course, because it took so much cleaning. Six metal covers, a soup-ladle, and two dozen plates of strong cheerful-looking English earthenware were paid for, wrapped and packed up like a doll's dinner-service. As for sheets, towels, table-linen, and so on, she knew a merchant, the agent for a large factory in Roubaix, who could be paid so much a month; and she was always on the look-out for sales, hunting for liquidations and all that jetsam of financial wreckage that Paris is constantly throwing up in the foam on its shores. In the Boulevard de Clichy she found a magnificent bargain of a bed, almost new, and wide enough to sleep Bluebeard's seven wives all in a row.

He too would try his hand at getting bargains on his way home from the office; but he was no good at it, being incapable of saying no, incapable of leaving a shop with empty hands. Going into a dealer's to buy a second-hand cruet that she had pointed out to him and finding that it had been sold already, he brought home a drawing-room chandelier that was no use to them because they had no drawing-room.

'We'll put it on the veranda,' Fanny said to console him.

The bliss it was measuring things up and discussing where to put each piece of furniture! . . . The shrieks, the wild outbursts of laughter, the arms flung wide in despair whenever they realized that in spite of all their precautions and the very complete list of indispensable purchases, there was always something else that they had forgotten.

The sugar-grater, for instance. They were actually going to set up house without a sugar-grater!

Then, when everything was bought and arranged, the curtains hung, and a wick put in the new lamp, how wonderful that first evening was when they moved in. How meticulously they reviewed all three rooms before they went to bed, and how gay she was, holding the candle high, as he locked their door. 'Give it another turn! Another! Lock it tight! Let's be as snug as we can, in our own home!'

And so a new and entrancing life began. When his work was done he hurried home, impatient to be there in slippers at their fireside. And slopping along through the dark, muddy streets, he imagined their room with the lamp lighted and the fire burning, cheerful with his old country-house furniture that Fanny had at first regarded as lumber to be got rid of and that then turned out to be the loveliest old things; particularly the wardrobe, a gem of a Louis XVI piece, with its painted panels representing Provençal festivals, shepherds in flowered jackets dancing to the tabor and the timbrel. The presence of these old-fashioned things, familiar to his eyes since childhood, reminded him of his home and hallowed his new dwelling, the comforts of which he was thoroughly appreciating.

The moment he rang the bell Fanny came, neat, dainty, and 'ship-shape', as she said. Her black woollen dress was quite plain but of a good cut, for she had the simplicity of a woman who knows how to dress; her sleeves would be rolled up, and she would have a

C—S.

big white apron round her, for she did all the cooking and made do with a charwoman for the rough work that would have chapped or hurt her hands.

She was very good at these things. She knew a great many recipes and could make Northern and Southern dishes as varied as her repertory of popular songs; and when dinner was over and the white apron was hung up on the other side of the closed kitchen door, she would sing for him in that contralto voice of hers that was softly mellow and so full of passion.

Down below in the street the traffic rumbled along through torrents of cold rain. The drops bounced on the zinc of the veranda; and Gaussin, lying back in his armchair, with his feet to the fire, gazed across at the railway station windows, at the clerks hunched up, writing away in the white glare of the big lamps.

He was thoroughly comfortable; he let himself be lulled. And was he in love? No, but he was grateful for being enveloped in this love, this unvarying affectionate care for him. How, he wondered, had he been able to do without this happiness for so long, in the fear —which he could not take seriously now—of being caught in a spell, somehow ensnared? Was his life not much cleaner now than when he used to go from one woman to another, endangering his health?

There was no danger of trouble later on. In three years, when it was time for him to go away, the break would take place quite smoothly, quite of its own accord. Fanny knew all about it; they would talk of it together, as of death, as of some remote but inevitable fatality. The only other fear was the great distress to his family of knowing that he was not living alone, and the anger of his father, a man both strict and hasty.

But how could they know? Jean saw nobody in Paris. His father, 'the consul', as they called him there, was kept on the spot the whole year round, looking after the very considerable estate that he farmed and fighting his eternal warfare with the vine. His mother was an invalid, unable to take a single step or make any movement without help, and left it to Divonne to manage the house and look after Jean's little twin sisters, Marthe and Marie, whose unexpected birth had permanently robbed her of her strength and activity. As for Uncle Césaire, Divonne's husband, he was just a big baby whom they did not let travel about on his own.

Fanny knew the whole family now. When he received a letter from Castelet, with some lines at the end in the twins' big round childish writing, she would read it over his shoulder and fall in with his sentimental mood. Of her life he knew nothing and did not ask. He had the gallant, unconscious egotism of youth, and no jealousy, no uneasiness. Full of his own life, he let it brim over, thinking aloud, letting it all pour out, while she said nothing at all.

So the days and weeks passed by in happy tranquillity, momentarily disturbed by a circumstance that stirred them both deeply, though in different ways. She thought she was pregnant, and told him of it with such joy that he could not but share it. But the fact of the matter was that it frightened him. A child of his own, at his age! What was he to do with it? Should he acknowledge it? And what a tie it would be between this woman and himself! What a complication of the future!

Suddenly he felt the chain, heavy, cold, and binding. At night he slept no more than she did; and side by side in their great bed they lay musing, open-eyed, thousands of miles apart.

Fortunately this false alarm was not repeated, and they resumed their peaceful, exquisitely private way of life. When winter came to an end and the real sun returned at last, their dwelling became lovelier than ever, now that they could use the balcony and the tent. In the evenings they dined there under a sky tinged green, streaked with the needle-thin skimming flight of the swallows.

The street sent up hot puffs of air and all the noises from the neighbouring houses; but up here they got the least breath of fresh air there was and forgot the hours, their knees locked together, blind to the whole world. Jean remembered similar nights on the banks of the Rhône and dreamt of far-flung consulates in very hot countries and of the decks of ships about to put out to sea, where the breeze would blow with the same long sigh as that shaking the curtain of the tent. And when the tremor of lips he could not see caressed his lips with the murmured question: 'Do you love me?' he always came back from a long way off to answer: 'Oh yes! I love you.' That is what comes of taking them so young: they have too many things going on in their heads.

On the same balcony, separated from them by an iron trellis wreathed with flowering creepers, there was another couple billing and cooing: Monsieur and Madame Hettéma, who were married and very fat, and whose noisy kisses sounded like someone being slapped. Marvellously matched as to age and taste, and alike too in their ponderous ways, how touching they were, these lovers no longer in their first youth, leaning on the balustrade and softly singing a duet together, one of those old-world sentimental romances:

'But I hear him in the darkness sighing—
How beautiful the dream—ah, let me sleep!'

Fanny liked them and wished she could know them. Sometimes indeed Madame Hettéma and she looked at each other through the blackened iron of the trellis, with the smile of women who are in love and happy; but the men, as usual, maintained more reserve, and they did not speak to each other.

Jean was on his way back from the Quai d'Orsay one afternoon when he heard someone call him at the corner of the Rue Royale. It was a splendid day, and there was a hot brilliance in which Paris lay like a rose about to shed its petals, at this turn of the boulevard, which has not its equal anywhere in the world, at sundown at the time of walking in the Bois.

'Sit yourself down, handsome youth! Drink with me! It does my old eyes good to look at you!'

He was seized by two great arms, the arms of someone sitting under a café awning, where three rows of tables spread out over the pavement. He did not resist, flattered to hear all around him the eager whisperings of foreigners and provincials, people in striped blazers and bowler hats, all whispering the name: 'Caoudal!'

Next to the sculptor, whose absinthe went so well with his military bearing and the decoration in his buttonhole, was the engineer Déchelette. He had arrived the day before, the same as ever, sunburnt and sallow, his prominent cheek-bones emphasizing his kindly little eyes, his nostrils avidly sniffing up the scent of Paris. The moment the young man was seated, Caoudal waved his hand at him with comical fury:

'What a beautiful young animal it is! To think I was once that age and had curly locks the like of his! Ah, youth, youth!'

'Still at it?' Déchelette said, smiling in recognition of his friend's old hobby-horse.

'Dear boy, don't make fun of me. All I've got, all I am, the medals, the decorations, the Institute, the whole boiling—I'd give it all for that hair and that sunny colouring. . . .' Then, turning to Gaussin with his characteristic abruptness, he asked: 'And what have you done with Sappho? Nobody ever sets eyes on her now.'

Jean stared at him blankly, not understanding.

'Oh, so you're not keeping up with her any more?' And then, seeing him quite bewildered, Caoudal added impatiently: 'Sappho, you know—Fanny Legrand—Ville-d'Avray!'

'Oh, that's over long ago.'

What made him say that? Some feeling of shame and uneasiness, at hearing the name of Sappho given to his mistress, the embarrassment of speaking of her with other men, and perhaps too the desire to learn things that would not have been said in his presence otherwise.

'Sappho, eh? So she's still trundling around?' Déchelette asked absently, lost in the intoxication of seeing the Madeleine steps again, the flower-market and the long shaft of the boulevards between two rows of green leaves.

'But don't you remember she was at your place that time last year! She was marvellous in her Egyptian tunic! And that autumn morning when I found her having breakfast with this splendid fellow here, at Langlois's—you'd have thought she was just a blushing bride!'

'How old is she, actually? We've known her—let me see——'

Caoudal gazed up into the air, trying to remember. 'Let me see, how old *is* she? Well, if she was seventeen in '53 when she posed for my figure—and this is '73. Work it out for yourselves.' Suddenly his eyes lit up. 'Ah, if you had seen her twenty years ago! Lithe and slim, with a mouth like a bow, a forehead like marble—arms and shoulders still a shade thin—but that did well enough for Sappho, all burnt up like that! And what a woman! What a mistress! How much gusto there was in that body of hers, how much fire one could strike out of that flint, that harp without a single note missing! The whole sweep of the lyre, as La Gournerie said.'

Very pale, Jean asked: 'And was *he* her lover too?'

'La Gournerie? I should just think so! It was pretty bad for me. Four whole years we lived together as man and wife, four years I cherished and watched over her, wore myself out trying to cope with all her whims—singing-masters, music-masters, riding-masters—more than I can remember now. And when I had polished her up until she glittered, like a gem, remote from the gutter where I had picked her up one night outside the Bal Ragache, that simpering rhymester came and took her from me in my own house, at my table where he sat as a friend every Sunday!'

He puffed, as though to blow away the bitterness of that old love still quivering in his voice; and then he went on more calmly:

'Anyway, the cad's trick he played me did him no good. The three years they lived together were hell. The poet with the coaxing ways turned out to be mean, spiteful, and crotchety. You ought to have seen the fights they used to have! When you called on them, you'd find her with a bandage over one eye and him with his face scored with nail-scratches. But the best of it all was when he wanted to drop her. She hung on like a leech, following him about, banging at his door, sleeping on the mat outside, waiting for him to come out. One night in the depths of winter she spent five hours in the street outside Farcy's where the whole crowd had gone up. Pitiful! But the elegiac poet remained implacable, till the day came when he got the police going—to be rid of her. Oh, a nice chap! And to put the finishing touch to it, by way of thanks to that fine girl who had given him the best of her youth, her mind, and her body, he poured out a volume of loathsome, slimy poems against her, all curses and lamentations, the *Book of Love*, the best of all his books. . . .'

Gaussin sat quite still, listening, hunched up, sipping through a long straw the iced drink on the table in front of him. Surely this must be poison that he had been given, poison that was now freezing his heart and entrails.

He was shivering even in the blaze of evening sunlight, and as though through some lurid glare he saw shadows going to and fro, saw a watercart stopped in front of the Madeleine and the inter-weaving of carriages driving over the soft earth as silently as though on cotton-wool. There was not a sound in all Paris, nothing but what was being said at this table here. Now Déchelette was talking; now it was he who was pouring out the poison:

'What a frightful thing these breaks are. . . .' And his quiet, mocking voice had a note of mild and infinite pity. 'People live together for years, they sleep pressed up against each other, a mingling of dreams, a mingling of sweat. They tell each other everything, give each other everything. They take on each other's habits, each other's ways of looking at things, ways of talking, even aspects of appearance. In every sense of the word, they belong to each other from top to toe. And then suddenly they leave each other, they tear apart. How do they do it? How do they bring themselves to it? I could never do it. Oh yes, I might be deceived, outraged, smirched with mud and gibes, and the woman would only have to weep and say: "Don't go away", and I would stay. That's why when I take one, it's only for the night. No to-morrow, as old France's saying used to be. Or if so, then marriage. That settles it, and it's more decent.'

'No to-morrow! No to-morrow! It's all very well for you to talk as you do. There are women one can't keep for only one night. She's one, for instance.'

'I didn't give her a minute's grace,' Déchelette said with a placid smile that the poor lover shuddered to behold.

'Then it means you weren't her type. Otherwise . . . The sort of woman she is—when she loves, she holds on. She has a taste for domesticity. Not that she has ever had much luck when she sets up house. She took up with Dejoie, the novelist, and he died. She went on to Ezano, and he got married. After that came the handsome

Flamant, the engraver, who used to be a model once—for she's always had a hankering after talent or good looks. And you know about that appalling affair.'

'What affair?' Gaussin asked in a choking voice. And he went on sucking at his straw, listening to the lovers' story that had set all Paris agog several years earlier.

The engraver was poor and he was mad for this woman; he was afraid of being dropped, so in order to keep her in the luxury she was accustomed to, he forged bank-notes. He was discovered almost at once, he and his mistress were locked up, and he got ten years' penal servitude, while she, having been acquitted, got off with six months in the reformatory at Saint-Lazare.

Caoudal recalled to Déchelette, who had followed the case, how pretty she had been in her little prison bonnet. And game, too—no whining—loyal to her man right to the end! And the way she had spoken up to that old sheep of a judge, and the kiss she had blown to Flamant away over the gendarmes' three-cornered hats, calling out in a voice that would have wrung tears from a stone: 'Never mind, sweetheart! Good times will come again and we'll still love each other.' All the same, it had slightly put her off domesticity, poor girl.

'After that she got into the smart world and took lovers by the month or week, but never artists. Oh, she's quite frightened of artists! I've a pretty good idea that I was the only one she continued to see. At long intervals she would come to the studio and have a cigarette with me. Then months passed without my hearing a word of her, till one day I found her having breakfast with this fine lad here, eating grapes from between his lips. I said to myself: "There's my Sappho in the toils again!"'

Jean could not bear to hear any more. He felt as though he were dying of all the poison he had drunk down. After the chill of a few minutes ago came a burning heat, tightening his chest and mounting to his head, which was drumming feverishly, almost bursting, like a stove stoked up to a white heat. He crossed the road, stumbling against the wheels of passing carriages. Coachmen shouted. Whom were they yelling at, the fools?

Passing by the Madeleine market, he was troubled by the scent of heliotrope, his mistress's favourite perfume. He quickened his steps to escape it, and raging, racked with fury, he thought aloud: 'My mistress! Ah, a fine trollop! Sappho, Sappho! To think I've lived for a year with—with that!' He repeated the name furiously, re-membering that he had seen it in the social-gossip papers, jumbled up with other feminine nicknames belonging to that grotesque Almanach de Gotha of the *demi-monde*: Sappho, Cora, Caro, Phryne, Diane de Poitiers, the Siren. . . .

And with the six letters of her abominable name all this woman's life streamed past his eyes, as though pouring from a gutter. Caoudal's studio, the brawls at La Gournerie's, the sentry-go out-side low haunts at night, the vigils on the poet's door-mat. . . . Then the handsome engraver, the forgeries, the assizes . . . and the little prison bonnet that suited her so well, and the kiss thrown to her lover the forger: 'Never mind, sweetheart. . . .' Sweetheart! The same little word, the same endearment she used for him. . . . The shame of it! Ah, but he meant to clear up the whole filthy business once and for all!

And he was pursued by the scent of the heliotrope, in twilight that was the same wan mauve as the tiny flower.

Suddenly he realized that he was still pacing up and down the market as on a ship's deck. He went on his way, reached the Rue d'Amsterdam in no time, determined to drive the woman out of his apartment, to put her out on the landing without any explanations, spitting the insult of her name after her. At the door he hesitated, reflected, walked on a few steps. She would scream and sob and fill the whole house with her gutter language, just as she had done that time in the Rue de l'Arcade.

Or should he write? Yes, that was the thing. It would be better to write, to settle up with her in a few brief, savage words. He went into an English tavern, empty and desolate under the newly lit gas, and sat down at a wet, sticky table near the only other customer, a gaunt-eyed woman of the streets devouring smoked salmon, with-out anything to drink. He ordered a pint of ale, left it untouched, and began a letter. But his head seethed with all he had to say, all the words tried to come pouring out at once, and the clotted, decomposing ink would only write them out at its own speed.

He tore up two or three beginnings and in the end was going away without having written the letter, when he heard a low voice ask timidly, between the noisy gulpings of ravenous eating: 'If you're not going to drink it—do you mind?' He nodded. The wretched woman grabbed the pint mug and drank the ale down with dreadful gulps that showed what a state she was in, with just enough in her pocket to buy herself some food, but not enough to afford a glass of beer to go with it. He was seized with a feeling of pity that soothed him, suddenly making him realize what misery might beset a woman's life; he began to judge more humanely, considering his misfortune in the light of reason.

After all, she had not lied to him; and if he knew nothing about her life, it was because he had never taken the slightest interest in it. What was he blaming her for? Her time at Saint-Lazare? But after all, she had been acquitted, she had practically been carried shoulder high in triumph at the end of the trial. So what then? Other men before him? But he had known that, surely? Why should he resent it more because her former lovers' names were famous and he might meet them, speak to them, look at their pictures in dealers' windows? Could he accuse her of having done more wrong in preferring them to others?

And somewhere in the depths of his being there arose an evil pride, something he could not admit even to himself, at sharing her with those great artists, telling himself that they too had found her beautiful. At his age nobody is ever quite sure of himself; nobody really knows where he stands. It is Woman that one loves, or the idea of love; what one lacks is the eye of experience; and the young lover showing you a portrait of his mistress is waiting for a look, a sign of approval, to reassure him. Now Sappho's face seemed magnified and as though illumined, since he knew that La Gournerie had sung of it and Caoudal had immortalized it in marble and bronze.

But all at once rage swept over him again, and he got up and walked away from the bench where he had been sitting, lost in his thoughts, here on an outlying boulevard, surrounded by children's yells and the gossip of workmen's wives, in the powdery June dusk; and he walked on again, angrily talking aloud. . . . Oh, very nice, the Sappho bronze! A bronze you could buy in any shop, a figure you could see anywhere, as threadbare as a hurdy-gurdy tune or the proverbial Sappho, the name that had come drifting down the centuries, picking up all the mud of infamous legend, until all its primal grace was lost, just as a goddess's name had become the name of a disease. Ah, dear God, how sickening it all was!

So he went on and on, by turns quiet or furious, in a whirl of contradictory thoughts and feelings. The boulevard was growing darker, deserted now. A faint, sharp, dismal smell hung in the hot air; and he recognized the gate of the big cemetery where he had come the year before, one of a large gathering of young men present at the unveiling of a bust by Caoudal on the grave of Dejoie, the Latin Quarter novelist, the author of *Cenderinette*. Dejoie! Caoudal! What a strange sound those names had acquired for him now, in the last two hours! and how sombre and false the affair seemed, the student with his mistress and his little home—now that he knew the depressing facts behind it, now that he had heard Déchelette's dreadful analysis of these wayside marriages.

All this darkness, blacker yet in the neighbourhood of death, was horrifying. He retraced his steps, brushing against the fluttering shirt-sleeves of prowling forms, silent as the wings of night, and against sombre skirts of other forms in doorways to dens with murky windows. And those windows were like large, flaring pictures in a magic lantern, showing couples passing to and fro, in each other's arms. . . . What time was it? He felt bruised and exhausted, like a recruit at the end of his first route march; all that was left of his now muffled anguish was a weight in his legs, the bowed weariness of his shoulders. Oh, to lie down in bed, to sleep! . . . And then, on waking, he would speak to the woman coolly and without anger, saying: 'Look—I know who and what you are. It is neither your fault nor mine. But we can't go on living together. Let us part.' And in order to escape being pursued by her, he would go and see his mother and sisters, he would go and hug them and, in the wind blowing over the Rhône, in the free, revivifying *mistral*, he would shake off the defilement and dismay of this bad dream.

Weary of waiting, she had gone to bed and had fallen asleep in the full glare of the lamp, a book open on the sheet beside her. His coming in did not waken her; and standing by the bed he gazed at her curiously, as at a woman he had not seen before, as at a stranger he had found there.

Ah, she was beautiful, how beautiful! Her arms, breast, and shoulders were sheer amber, firm, without mark or stain. But on the reddened eyelids—perhaps it had been the novel she was reading, perhaps anxiety and suspense, waiting for him—on the features relaxed in sleep, no longer tense with the fiercely eager desire of the woman wanting to be loved—what weariness, what a confession! Here it all was, plain for anyone to see: her age, her history, her wild outbursts, her whims, her passionate liaisons, and Saint-Lazare, and the blows and tears and terrors. Here it all was, in the purplish bruises left by lust and sleeplessness, and the small twist of distaste making the lower lip droop, worn and tired as the rim of a well where the whole village comes to drink, and the beginnings of a puffiness that was already stretching the skin for the wrinkles of old age.

There was something grand, even dreadful, in this betrayal that sleep was, and the deathly silence enfolding it all: a battlefield by night, with all the horror that was revealed and the further horrors only guessed at from vague movements in the darkness.

And all at once the poor boy was shaken by a great, choking need to wash it all away in tears.

⋙ 4 ⋘

THEY were finishing dinner, sitting by the open window, and outside the long skimming of the swallows hailed the gradual withdrawal of the light. Jean was not speaking, but he was on the point of speaking—and once again of the atrocious thing that haunted him, the thing he had been torturing Fanny with ever since his encounter with Caoudal. Seeing his lowered eyes and the artificially casual air he assumed in order to ask yet more questions, she guessed his intention and forestalled him:

'Look, I know what you're going to say. Please, please save us both from having to go through it all. It's only exhausting. You see, all that is quite dead and done with, I don't love anyone but you, there's no one in the world but you.'

'If it were as dead and done with as you say . . . all that past . . .' He stopped and looked deep into her beautiful grey eyes that held a perpetual flicker and ripple as of reflections on water. 'If it were, you wouldn't keep things that remind you of it—yes, I mean the things on the top shelf in the wardrobe.'

The grey became velvety and dark with shadows. 'So you know.'

She was going to have to throw away all that jumble of letters, portraits, the lustrous archives of so many loves, records saved from so many wrecks. . . .

'Anyway, you'll believe me afterwards?'

And meeting with an incredulous smile that dared her to it, she ran to get down the lacquer box with the chased ironwork that she kept among the dainty piles of her underclothing, a box that had been fascinating her lover for some days past.

'Burn it all, tear it all up. Do what you like with it.'

But he was in no hurry to turn the little key. He was looking at the cherry-trees with pink mother-of-pearl cherries and the storks in full flight, encrusted on the lid. Then suddenly he snapped it open. All shapes of envelopes, all kinds of handwriting, tinted gilt-headed paper, old yellowed notes cracked at the folds, pencil-scrawls on leaves torn from notebooks, visiting-cards, all jostled together in the disarray to be found in a drawer where hands often fumble and search. And now he dipped his own trembling hands into it.

'Give them over to me. I'll burn them in front of your eyes.'

She spoke feverishly, crouching in front of the fireplace, a lighted candle on the floor beside her.

'Give them to me!'

'No,' he objected. 'Wait.' And then, in a lower voice, as though ashamed to say it, he added: 'I'd like to read some. . . .'

'Why? It'll only make you feel worse than ever.'

She was thinking only of the pain to him, and not of the in-delicacy of surrendering up the secrets of passion shared, the words murmured into the pillow by all those men who had loved her; and coming closer, still on her knees, she read together with him, glancing at him out of the corner of her eye.

There were ten pages of long, feline handwriting, signed La Gournerie, 1861. The poet had been dispatched to Algeria to write the official poetic record of the Emperor's and Empress's journey, and he gave his mistress a dazzling description of the festivities.

Algiers was swarming with people, overflowing—a fairy-like Baghdad of the Thousand-and-one Nights. All Africa had come hurrying there, come crowding round the city and beating at its gates almost with the violence of a simoon. There were caravans of negroes and of camels laden with gum, and pointed tents made of hides, and an odour of human musk pervading the whole men-agerie that bivouacked there beside the sea, that danced round big fires at night and fell back each morning before the arrival of tropical chieftains resembling the Magi in their Oriental pomp, with discordant music, reedy flutes, little hoarse drums, the *goum* gathered round the Prophet's three-coloured standard; and behind, led by negroes, came the horses destined as gifts for the Emperor, caparisoned in silk and silver, setting little bells tinkling and tassels swaying at every step. . . .

The poet's genius made it all seem alive and real; the words glittered on the page, like the unset stones that jewellers hold up against paper. Truly she might well be proud, this woman in whose lap such riches had been cast. She must have been loved indeed, since in spite of the fascination of these festivities the poet thought only of her and was heartsick at missing her.

'Oh, last night I was with you on the big divan in the Rue de l'Arcade. You were naked, you were crazy, you were crying out in ecstasy under my caresses—and I woke up with a start, rolled in a rug on my balcony, with a sky of stars above me. The muezzin's call rang out from a neighbouring minaret, going up like a clear, luminous rocket, more like a cry of rapture than of prayer. And yet it was you I heard still, wakening from my dream.'

What malicious force then drove him to go on with his reading, in spite of the ghastly jealousy that whitened his lips and made his hands clench and unclench? Gently, coaxingly, Fanny tried to take the letter from him; but he read on to the end, and after that another, and then another, letting them fall one by one, with the detachment of contempt and indifference, without glancing at the flame that shot up the chimney, fed on the great poet's lyrical and impassioned outpourings. And sometimes, in the overbrimming of this love, now worked to fresh heights by the African heat, the lover's lyricism was marred by some crass obscenity that would have shocked and scandalized the world of reading ladies who admired the *Book of Love*, which was of a spiritual quality as refined and immaculate as the silver peak of the Jungfrau.

What rendings the heart is subject to! It was above all these passages besmirching the pages that made Jean pause, unaware of the nervous twitchings that crossed his face each time. He even brought himself to utter a shrill laugh over this postscript to a brilliant description of a festival at Aïssouas: 'I have just re-read this letter. Some of it is really not at all bad. Keep it for me, I might want to make use of it.'

'One of the thrifty sort of gentry,' he commented, passing on to another sheet of paper with the same handwriting. Here, in the chill tones of a man of business, La Gournerie demanded the return of a collection of Arab songs and a pair of rice-straw babooshes. It was the declaration of their love's bankruptcy. Ah, La Gournerie had been able to break away, he had had the strength!

And without pause Jean went on draining this marsh, from which there rose such hot, unsavoury fumes. At nightfall he set the candle on the table and went through a series of very short notes, illegibly scribbled as though by swollen fingers holding a bodkin and constantly digging holes in the paper and tearing it, violent with desire or anger. Here were the beginnings of a liaison with Caoudal, trysts, suppers, picnics, then quarrels, imploring reconciliations, outcries, vile, coarse expressions of abuse that a labourer might have uttered, interspersed with sudden little jokes, droll phrases, sobbing reproaches, all the great artist's weakness laid bare by that break, that desertion.

The fire took that too, licking upwards with big red tongues of flame, in which the flesh, blood, and tears of a man of genius shrivelled up and turned to smoke. But what did Fanny care, she who existed only for the young lover she was watching? His high fever scorched her even through her clothes. He had just found a pen-and-ink drawing signed Gavarni, with this dedication: 'For my dear Fanny Legrand, one rainy day in an inn at Dampierre.' It was a sensitive, thoughtful head, sorrowful, with sunken eyes, with a touch of something bitter and ravaged.

'Who is it?'

'André Dejoie. I kept it because of the signature.'

His 'Keep it, it's yours,' was so constrained, so unhappy, that she took the drawing, tore it and flung it in the fire, while he plunged deep into the novelist's correspondence, a grievous series of letters dated from winter resorts by the sea and watering-places where the writer had been sent for his health. The letters revealed him in despair over his physical and mental breakdown, racking his brains for an idea, so far from Paris; and mingled with his requests for medicines and prescriptions and his financial and professional anxieties, the dispatch of proofs and bills renewed, there was always the same cry of desire and adoration, the cry for Sappho's lovely body, forbidden him by his physicians.

With the utter frankness of his helpless rage, Jean muttered:

'What on earth was the matter with them all, going after you like that?'

To his mind that was the only meaning of these despairing letters, confessing the ruin of those illustrious lives so much envied by young men and dreamt of by romantic women. . . . Yes, what on earth was the matter with them all? What had she done to bewitch them so? He was undergoing the appalling agonies of a man who is gagged and bound and sees the woman he loves violated in front of him; and yet he could not make up his mind to shut his eyes and simply empty the whole box on to the fire.

Now came the turn of the engraver, poor and unknown, with no fame beyond that of the *Police Gazette*, who owed his place in this reliquary only to the great love that she had had for him. They were dishonouring, these letters dated from Mazas, and as silly, awkward, and sentimental as a trooper's letters to his lass. But through the hackneyed, novelettish style there could be felt a ring of sincerity in the passion, a respect for the woman as a woman, and a forgetfulness of himself that distinguished the convict from all the others: as when he asked Fanny's forgiveness for the crime of having loved her too much, or when in the clerk's office at the Palais de Justice, straight after his sentence, he wrote of his joy in knowing his mistress was acquitted and free. He did not complain at all; with her, and thanks to her, he had had two years of happiness so abundant and deep that the memory of it would be enough to fill his life and alleviate the horror of his fate; and he ended by asking her to do something for him:

'You know I have a child in the country, the mother has been dead a long time. He lives with an old relation, and the place is so off the beaten track that nobody will ever hear about what has happened to me. I sent them the money I had left and said I was going a long way away, on a journey, and I am counting on you, my good sweet Nini, to get news of the poor little lad from time to time and tell me how he is getting on.'

As evidence of Fanny's having done what he asked there followed a letter of thanks, and then another, quite recent, dated from only

D—S.

six months ago: 'Oh, you are good to have come. How beautiful you were, how good you smelt, and there I was in my prison shirt, so ashamed of it.' Jean broke off and asked furiously: 'So you still see him?'

'Now and then, from pity.'

'Even since we've been together?'

'Yes, once, only once, in the visitors' room—that's the only place where you can see them.'

'Ah, you're so kind-hearted.'

The idea that in spite of their liaison she still visited the forger exasperated him more than anything else. He was too proud to say so. But another packet of letters, the last, tied up with blue ribbon, with small, delicate, sloping handwriting, obviously a woman's, unleashed all his anger.

'I change my costume after the chariot-race—come to my dressing-room then,' he read.

'No, no! Don't read that!'

She flung herself on him, tore the letters out of his hands, and flung the whole bundle into the fire, without his at first understanding, even while he saw her kneeling, crimson in the light of the flames and with the shame of her avowal:

'I was young, it was Caoudal—the great crazy creature! I used to do whatever he wanted.'

Only then did he understand. He grew very pale.

'Ah, yes.... Sappho... the whole sweep of the lyre....' And kicking her away from him, as though she were some loathsome animal, he said: 'Let me alone, don't touch me. You make my gorge rise.'

Her scream was lost in a terrific roar as of thunder, quite near and very long-drawn, at the same time as a livid flash lit up the room. The fire! She jumped to her feet in terror, mechanically seized the water-carafe that was still on the table and emptied it over the pile of papers that had sent up flames high enough to set light to the soot left there from last winter. She emptied all the water-jugs, big and small; and then, seeing she was powerless and the sparks were spurting out into the middle of the room, she ran out on to the balcony, crying: 'Fire! Fire!'

The Hettémas were the first to come, followed by the caretaker and then the police.

There were cries of: 'Pull down the back! Go up on the roof! Water! Water! No, a blanket!'

As though stunned, they watched their dwelling being invaded and defiled. And then, when the alarm was over and the fire out, when the black swarm down in the street, under the gaslight, had scattered again, and the neighbours' minds had been put at rest and they had gone back to their own apartments, the two lovers stood in the midst of this devastation of water, soot, and mud, of furniture overturned and drenched, and felt utterly sickened, rotten, lacking the energy either to resume their quarrel or to clean up the room they stood in. Something ominous and sordid had entered into their life; and they forgot their former repugnance and went to spend the night at an hotel.

Fanny's sacrifice was not to be of any avail. Burnt and vanished though the letters were, whole sentences remained in the lover's memory, haunting him, sending the angry blood rushing into his face, like certain passages in vile books. And his mistress's former lovers were almost all famous men. The dead had their immortality; and the living—their portraits and names turned up everywhere, people would talk of them in front of him, and every time it happened he felt embarrassed and dismayed, as though a family tie had been grievously broken.

This trouble sharpened his wits and his eyes. Soon he was able to perceive the traces of the first influences Fanny had been subject to, and the words, thoughts, and habits she had picked up in those days. That way of pushing out her thumb, as though to mould or knead the thing of which she was talking, with a 'You see, it's like this,' came from the sculptor. From Dejoie she had picked up a fad for clipping the ends off her words, and it was from him too that she had the folk-songs, for he had published a collection famous throughout France; from La Gournerie she had the disdainful, high-handed way of talking and the harsh judgment of modern literature.

She had assimilated it all, superimposing disparate things on each other by a process of stratification similar to that which makes it possible to tell the age of the earth and the number of its revolutions from its various geological layers. She was perhaps, in fact, not as intelligent as she had seemed to him at first. But the problem was far from being one of intelligence: had she been the most stupid woman alive, vulgar and even ten years older than she was, she would still have held him by the force of her past, by the vile jealousy that gnawed at him, with its indignations and resentments that he no longer hid from her and that came flashing out against one or the other of those men at the slightest provocation.

Dejoie's novels no longer sold; the whole collection could be picked up on the quays for twenty-five centimes a volume. And that old fool, Caoudal, falling in love and making a fool of himself at his age! 'You know he hasn't any teeth left. I was watching him that time at breakfast, at Ville-d'Avray. He eats with his front teeth, like a goat.' And his talent was played out too. What a bungled thing that Bacchante of his had been, at the last Salon! 'It didn't hold together.' It was an expression he had from her and she had got it from the sculptor: 'It didn't hold together.' When he began setting about one of his rivals of past days in this fashion, Fanny would echo all he said in order to please him. Anyone listening would have heard this young lad who knew nothing about art or life or anything else and this shallow little mopsy, with her smattering of wit picked up from those famous artists, both sitting in judgment on them all and solemnly condemning them.

But Gaussin's special enemy was Flamant, the engraver. All he knew about this man was that he was very handsome and as fair as himself, that he was called 'sweetheart,' that he was secretly visited, and that when he attacked him like the others, calling him 'Love's convict lost' or 'The handsome hermit,' Fanny turned her head away without speaking. Soon he accused her of still having a soft spot for the rogue, and she had to state her case, gently enough, but quite firmly too.

'You know quite well I don't love him any more, Jean, because I love you. I don't go there any more, I don't answer his letters. But you'll never make me say any harm of the man who loved me to madness, to the point of crime.' At this note of frankness, which was one of the best things about her, Jean did not protest, but he was still tormented by jealous hatred and racked by uneasiness so that he would sometimes go back to the Rue d'Amsterdam in the middle of the day, to take her unawares. 'Supposing she's gone to see him!'

He always found her there, perfectly stay-at-home, as reclusive in their little apartment as any Oriental woman, or perhaps at the piano, giving a singing lesson to their fat neighbour, Madame Hettéma. Since the evening of the fire they had struck up an acquaintance with these worthy, placid, full-blooded people who liked to live in a perpetual draught, with all the doors and windows wide open.

The husband, a draughtsman at the Artillery Museum, used to bring work home with him; and every evening during the week, and all Sunday, he could be seen bowed over his wide trestle table, sweating, puffing, his jacket off, occasionally shaking out his shirt-sleeves to get some air circulating through them, and only his eyes peeping out of his bushy whiskers. His fat wife would sit beside him in her camisole, also almost on the point of swooning, though she never did anything. Now and then they refreshed themselves by striking up one of their favourite duets.

A close friendship soon developed between the two households.

About ten o'clock in the morning Hettéma's deep voice would be heard shouting outside the door: 'You ready, Gaussin?' And as their offices were both in the same direction, they went off together. Hettéma was thoroughly dull, clumsy, and commonplace; he was several degrees lower on the social scale than his young companion; and he talked little, spluttering as though he had as thick a beard in his mouth as on his cheeks. But Jean could not help feeling that he was a decent sort; and, in his state of mental and emotional stress, he had need of such a contact. He valued it most of all for Fanny's sake, for she lived in a solitude populated with memories and regrets even more dangerous, perhaps, than the relationships that she had renounced of her own free will; with Madame Hettéma—who had no thought for anything but her husband and the dainty little dish she would surprise him with for dinner or the new ballad she would sing to him at dessert—she found a friendship that was decent and healthy.

However, when the acquaintance became closer, reaching the stage when invitations were exchanged, he felt scruples. These people doubtless believed they were married, but his conscience would not allow any false pretence; and he told Fanny she must explain to Madame Hettéma, so that there should be no misunderstanding. She listened to him and then burst out laughing. Poor baby! There was nobody like him for simplicity! 'They never for a moment thought we were married! And what do they care, anyway! If you knew where he'd picked his wife up! Whatever I've done, I'm a saint compared with her. He only married her so as to have her all to himself, and you can see he doesn't trouble much about her past.'

He could not get over it. So she was a veteran—this comfortable soul with the clear eyes, the gurgling childish laugh, the smooth-skinned face, and the drawling provincial speech, this woman for whom no song could be sentimental enough nor any words noble enough! And the husband—so placid, so secure in the cheerful contentment of his love! Gaussin saw him walking along beside him, his pipe between his teeth, uttering little puffs of bliss, while he himself was always a prey to thought and eaten up by helpless rage.

'You'll get over it, sweetheart,' Fanny would say gently, at those times when lovers tell each other everything. And she would soothe him, tender and delightful as on the first day, but with a trace of something like abandonment, something that Jean could not define.

It was there in her freer bearing and way of expressing herself, in her consciousness of power, her queer, sudden, unasked-for confidences about her past life, her bygone debauches and mad acts of curiosity. She no longer refrained from smoking but twirled a cigarette between her fingers, putting it down everywhere on the furniture—the eternal cigarette that quietly drugs all such women's days. And in their discussions she would utter the most cynical theories about life, the infamy of men, and the sluttishness of women. Then even her eyes would change, darkening as though lying deep under stagnant water, lit only by flashes of libertine laughter.

And the intimacy of their sensual love was changing too. At first she had had reserves, out of respect for her youthful lover's innocence and illusions; but she no longer felt any need for restraint after seeing the effect that the sudden revelation of her sordid past had on him, the swampy fever that she had lit up in his blood. And the perverse caresses that she had so long suppressed, all the raving words she had clenched her teeth against, she now let loose, letting herself go, yielding herself to the nature of her being—now utterly the courtesan, amorous, adept, living up to the dreadful fame that had earned her the name Sappho.

What was the use of being chaste or reserved? Men were all alike, maddened by vice and corruption, and this boy was the same as the rest. Luring them on with what they wanted was always the best way of keeping them. And all she knew, all the depravities of lust that others had implanted in her, Jean learnt from her in his turn, to pass them on to others. So the poison spreads, running through the world, a consuming fire in body and soul like those torches the Latin poet tells of, passed on from hand to hand by runners in the stadium.

5

HANGING in their room, next to a fine portrait of Fanny by James Tissot, one piece of jetsam from the days of her former brilliance, there was a Provençal landscape in black and white, crudely caught in the sunlight by a country photographer.

There was a rocky hillside with vines clambering up it, shored up with stonework, and on top, behind ranks of cypresses as protection against the north wind, nestling against a little grove of pines and shiny-leaved glittering myrtles, there was the big white house, half farmhouse, half château, with its wide flight of steps up to the veranda, its Italian roof, escutcheoned doors, and russet walls characteristic of the Provençal villa, and there were the perches for the peacocks and cribs for the flocks and the black openings of the lean-to sheds, with a gleam of ploughs and harrows. The ruins of ancient ramparts, and a huge tower standing out across a cloudless sky, crowned it all, and in the distance were some rooftops and the romanesque belfry of Châteauneuf-des-Papes. There the family of Gaussin d'Armandy had lived since the beginning of time.

Castelet, with its gardens and farmlands, rich in the vineyards that were as famous as those of La Nerte or the Hermitage, was handed down from father to son, jointly held by all the children but always worked by the younger son, according to the family tradition that sent the elder into the consular service. Unfortunately nature often crosses such plans; and if ever there was any human being incapable of managing an estate, or of managing anything at all, it was Césaire Gaussin, on whom this heavy responsibility fell when he was twenty-four years of age.

A libertine, a wencher and gambler known to all the places of ill-fame in the district, Césaire, or rather the ne'er-do-well, the scapegrace, The Rip, as he had been called in his youth, was an extreme example of a contradiction that occurs at long intervals in even the most austere families, as it were as a safety-valve.

After some years of his feckless negligence, idiotic extravagance, and disastrous card-playing in the Avignon and Orange clubs, the vineyards were mortgaged, the reserve cellars exhausted, and the crops to come sold in advance; and then one day, on the eve of a final seizure, The Rip forged his brother's signature, writing out three drafts on the consulate at Shanghai, convinced that before they fell due he would find the money to call them in; but they reached the elder brother at the appointed time, together with a frantic letter confessing to bankruptcy and forgery. The consul hastened to Châteauneuf, straightened out the desperate situation with the aid of his savings and his wife's dowry, and seeing The Rip's incapacity, although *the service* was just beginning to hold out brilliant prospects, he gave it up and settled down as an ordinary wine-grower.

This brother was a real Gaussin, traditional to the point of obsession, violent under his calm, like those extinct volcanoes that still have a look of menace, suggesting that they may erupt at any moment; he was a hard worker, too, with a gift for farming. Thanks to him, Castelet prospered and was enlarged by the addition of all the land down to the Rhône; and then, as luck always comes in series, little Jean came on to the scene, among the myrtles of the domain. All this time The Rip used to wander vaguely about the house, crushed by the weight of his offence, hardly daring to lift his eyes to his brother, whose contemptuous silence overwhelmed him; he could not breathe freely anywhere but out in the fields, shooting or fishing, wearing out his misery by doing futile jobs like picking up snails, whittling superb walking-sticks out of myrtle or reeds, and lunching quite alone in the open air on skewered warblers that he roasted over a fire of olive-twigs, out on the heath. Coming in at evening to dine at his brother's table, he did not utter a word, in spite of indulgent smiles from his sister-in-law, who was sorry for the poor wretch and supplied him with pocket-money; this she did unknown to her husband, who was inexorable with regard to The Rip, less on account of his past follies than on account of all those he might still commit. And surely enough, not long after that first great folly, Gaussin the elder suffered another blow to his pride.

Three times a week a pretty girl came to Castelet to do a day's sewing. This was Divonne Abrieu, a fisherman's daughter, born in the osier-grounds on the edge of the Rhône. And a true water-lily she was, supple and long-stemmed. In her three-sided bonnet close-fitting to her little head, with the ribbons thrown back to let the admiring eye rest on the curve of the throat, slightly sunburnt like the face, and the delicate snowy softness of the neck and shoulders, she made one think of some donna of those courts of love that reigned in former times round Châteauneuf, at Courthezon and Vacqueiras, in those old donjons, the ruins now crumbling on the hills.

This historical reminiscence did not enter into Césaire's love, simple soul that he was, as devoid of ideals as of book-learning. But he was one of those short men who are attracted by tall women, and he was a captive from the very first day. Oh, The Rip well knew the way to carry on these rustic flirtations: a country-dance on the green on Sunday, a present of some game, then at the first encounter in the fields the swift storming and carrying of the position, lying among the lavender and the hay. But it turned out that Divonne did not dance, that she brought the game back to the kitchen, and that being as strong as one of the poplars by the river-bank, white and pliant as they were, she sent the seducer flying ten paces off. From then on she kept him at a distance with the point of the scissors that hung from a steel key-ring on her belt, and drove him mad with love, till he talked of marrying her and confided in his sister-in-law. Madame Gaussin had known Divonne Abrieu since her childhood and knew her for a right-minded, scrupulous girl; so she thought to herself that this misalliance might be The Rip's salvation. But the consul's pride revolted at the idea of a Gaussin d'Armandy marrying a peasant girl. 'If Césaire does this thing, I shall not see him again.' And he kept his word.

Once he was married Césaire left Castelet, going to live with his wife's parents down by the edge of the Rhône on a small allowance that his brother made him, which was brought him every month by his indulgent sister-in-law. Little Jean would accompany his mother on these visits and was enchanted with the Abrieus' cottage, which was a kind of smoky rotunda, shaken by all the winds that blew, and held up in the middle by a single beam like a mast.

Through the open door one could see the little jetty where the nets were drying, with the bright, pearly silver of fish-scales glittering and flickering in them, and two or three big boats rising and falling with the waves, their mooring-ropes creaking, and the bright, broad, shining lovely river, all a-ripple in the wind that brushed it back against its wispy, pale green islets. And while he was still a little boy, Jean grew to have a longing for far travels, and for the sea that he had never seen.

Uncle Césaire's exile lasted two or three years and might never have come to an end had it not been for a family event: the birth of the twins, Marthe and Marie. As a result of this double birth the mother fell ill, and Césaire and his wife were given permission to come and see her. The two brothers' reconciliation followed, an irrational, purely instinctive act, a surrender to the omnipotence of blood-kinship. After that the whole family lived at Castelet, and as the poor mother was immobilized by an incurable anaemia, soon complicated by arthritis, Divonne found herself responsible for looking after the household, providing food for the babies and the numerous servants and labourers, going twice a week to see Jean at his school in Avignon, and of course being called on to do things for the invalid at every other moment.

Being a woman of strong mind, with a natural talent for organizing, she made up for a lack of education by sheer intelligence, peasant shrewdness, and odds and ends of knowledge picked up from the now tamed and disciplined Rip. The consul entrusted her with all the household finances, which was a heavy burden, with expenses increasing and income falling off from year to year as phylloxera gnawed away at the roots of the vine. The whole plain was stricken by this disease, but the enclosed vineyards had still escaped; the consul's only thought was research and experiment to save the vineyards.

Divonne Abrieu, who remained faithful to her caps and her seamstress's scissors-ring, and who kept so modestly to her place as steward, housekeeper, and companion, saved the household from want in those years of crisis, saw to it that the sick woman was always supplied with the same expensive medicaments and little luxuries, that her wards were properly brought up under their mother's eye, and that Jean's fees were promptly paid, first at the Lycée, then at Aix, where he read law, and finally at Paris, where he went on to take his degree.

By what miracles of orderliness and vigilance she managed it, nobody knew, any more than she did herself. But every time that Jean thought of Castelet, every time he raised his eyes to the photograph with the pale gleams, washed out by so much light, the first face called to mind, the first name uttered, was that of Divonne, the great-hearted, simple countrywoman whose presence he could feel everywhere in the squire's house, which she kept together by sheer force of will. Yet for some days now, since he had known what sort of woman his mistress was, he had not uttered this revered name in her presence, or that of his mother and the rest of his family; even to look at the photograph had become embarrassing, it now seemed so out of place, so lost, there on the wall above Sappho's bed.

One day when he came home to dinner he was surprised to see three covers laid instead of two, and still more surprised to find Fanny playing cards with a little man whom he did not at first recognize. But, turning round, the little man showed him the bright eyes of a mad goat, the large overbearing nose in the devil-may-care sunburnt face, the bald head and Henri IV beard of Uncle Césaire. At his nephew's exclamation, he said, without putting his cards down:

'I'm not bored, you see! I'm having a game of bezique with my niece.'

His niece!

And this after Jean had taken such care to keep his liaison a secret from everybody! He was upset by this familiarity, as also by the comments Césaire made in a low voice while Fanny was getting the dinner: 'Congratulations, my boy—what eyes! what arms! a very nice little piece!' It was worse still when they sat down at table and The Rip began to talk, without the slightest reserve, about Castelet business and what had brought him to Paris.

The excuse for the journey was a sum of money to be collected—
eight thousand francs that he had lent to his friend Courbebaisse in
the old days and had never expected to see again. A notary's letter
had come, informing him of Courbebaisse's death—'Lord bless
my soul!'—and the imminent repayment of his eight thousand
francs. But the real reason for his coming, since after all the money
could have been sent, 'the real reason is your mother's health, I'm
sorry to say, dear boy. . . . She's been losing strength for some
time now and there are times when she wanders a bit in her
mind, she forgets things, she even forgets the little girls' names.
The other evening your father came out of his bedroom and she
asked Divonne who the kind gentleman was who came to see
her so often. Nobody's noticed it yet but your aunt, and she only
spoke about it to me to get me to come and consult Bouchereau
about the poor woman's condition. He treated her in the old
days.'

'Have you ever before had any insanity in your family?' Fanny
sagely and solemnly asked, with her La Gournerie expression.

'Never,' The Rip said, adding, with a sly smile that crinkled his
face right up to his eyebrows, that he had been a little cracked in his
youth, 'but my sort of craziness went down quite well with the
ladies and there was no call to have me shut up.'

Gazing at them, Jean felt quite sickened. There was not only the
grief he felt at this sad news, but the oppressive uneasiness of hearing
this woman talking of his mother and her infirmities at the critical
age she had reached, talking about it all with the freedom of
language and experienced air of a matron, her elbows on the tablecloth, rolling a cigarette. And the other, gossipy and tactless as he
was, let himself run on, blurting out the family's most intimate
secrets.

Ah, the vineyards! It was all up with the vineyards! Not even the
enclosure would last long; half the vines were already eaten up, and
the rest were only saved by a miracle, by treating each bunch of
grapes, each single grape, like sick children, with medicaments that
cost a lot of money. The worst of it was that the consul had set his
heart on continually planting new vines, which were then also

attacked by the worm, instead of growing olives and caper-trees on all that good earth now being wasted, covered with rusty, blotchy vine-branches.

Fortunately he, Césaire, had a few acres down by the Rhône, which he treated by immersion, a wonderful discovery only of use on low-lying ground. He had already had one good vintage to encourage him, a not too fiery little wine, 'pond-water,' as the consul disdainfully called it. But The Rip was obstinate too, and he was going to use Courbebaisse's eight thousand francs to buy La Piboulette.

'You know, my boy, the first island in the Rhône, a bit below the Abrieus'.... But this is quite between ourselves. It wouldn't do for anyone at Castelet to suspect anything yet.'

'Not even Divonne, uncle?' Fanny asked, smiling.

At the sound of his wife's name, The Rip's eyes grew moist.

'Ah, Divonne!' he said. 'I never do anything without her. And she believes in my idea, what's more. She'll be so glad to see her poor old Césaire restoring the Castelet fortunes, after having begun the ruin of them.'

Jean started. Was he going to confess it all, was he going to tell the whole deplorable story of the forgery? But Césaire was absorbed in his affectionate thoughts of Divonne and began to talk about her and the happiness that she gave him. And how beautiful she was too, 'what magnificent raking lines . . .!'

'Here you are, niece, being a woman you ought to have an eye for such things.'

He held out a portrait photograph that he had taken out of his wallet, one that he always carried about with him.

From the filial tone that Jean used in speaking of his aunt and from the motherly advice she sent him, in big, rather shaky writing, Fanny had imagined her like one of the kerchiefed village women of Seine-et-Oise. She was startled to see this lovely, delicate-featured face framed in the narrow white coif, and the elegant, supple figure of a woman of thirty-five.

'Yes, indeed, very beautiful,' she said in a strange tone of voice and tightened her lips.

'And what raking lines, eh!' Uncle Césaire said, who was fond of this phrase.

Then they went out on to the balcony. After the hot day—the veranda zinc was still burning to the touch—a stray cloud was sending down a small light shower, just enough to freshen the air, tinkling gaily on the roofs and splashing the pavements. Paris seemed to smile in this sudden rain, and all the crowds, the carriages, the roar of it all rising through the air, went to the countryman's head, which was empty and flighty as a little bell, and rolled about inside it, wakening memories of his youth and a three months' stay with his friend Courbebaisse some thirty years ago.

What goings-on, my children! What rip-roarings! And how they had gone into the Prado one night at carnival time, Courbebaisse in the tight trousers and plumed helmet of a Chicard, and his mistress, la Mornas, as a ballad-seller, a disguise that brought her luck, for she became celebrated as a café-concert singer. He himself, Uncle Césaire, had a little piece in tow nicknamed Dandruff. . . . And growing merrier every minute, he laughed from ear to ear, hummed dance tunes, took his niece by the waist and twirled her round. At midnight, when he left them to go back to the Hôtel Cujas, the only hotel he knew in Paris, he sang at the top of his voice going down the stairs, blew kisses up to his niece, who was holding the lamp to light him down, and called to Jean:

'I say, you know—keep an eye on her!'

As soon as he was gone, Fanny, on whose brow there was still a furrow of thought, went swiftly into her dressing-room and began to talk, in an almost casual tone, through the open door, while Jean was getting ready for bed. 'I must say she is very good-looking, your aunt. It doesn't surprise me now that you talked about her such a lot. You must have made her unfaithful to that poor Rip— and with his looks, no wonder!'

He protested with an outburst of indignation. Divonne—who had been a second mother to him, who had washed him and dressed him when he was a little boy! She had saved his life when he was ill. Never could he have felt any temptation to such infamy!

'Oh, go on with you!' the woman's strident voice began again, through a mouthful of pins. 'You won't make me believe that, with those eyes, and the raking lines that fool kept on talking about! When his Divonne had a handsome fair-haired boy like you, with a baby skin like yours, living under the same roof with her, she couldn't never feel a twinge! Take it from me, on the banks of the Rhône, or anywhere else, we're all the same.'

She said it with conviction, believing her whole sex to be given to wanton whim, all-yielding at the first desire. He protested, but he was troubled all the same, searching through his memory, wondering if ever any light innocent kiss or touch could have warned him of possible danger; and although he found nothing, the candour of his affection was spoilt, the pure cameo streaked by a nail-scratch.

'Here, look! Here's the sort of cap they wear in your part of the country.'

Over her high-piled, beautiful, braided hair, she had pinned a white fichu that was a fair imitation of the three-cornered *catalane*, the cap the girls wore at Châteauneuf. And standing there before him, her muslin nightdress falling in milky folds, her eyes glowing, she asked him:

'Do I look like Divonne?'

Oh no, not in the least. She was like nobody but herself in that little cap. It was only a reminder of that other cap, the one she had worn at Saint-Lazare, which had suited her so well, they said, as she blew a farewell kiss across the crowded court to her convict lover: 'Never mind, sweetheart, good times will come again. . . .'

And the thought of it made him feel so wretched that as soon as his mistress was in bed he put the light out quickly, not wanting to see her any more.

Early the next morning his uncle came blustering in, swinging his cane, shouting: 'Hello there, my babes!' in the frisky, protective tone Courbebaisse used to adopt when he came to rouse him from Dandruff's arms. He seemed even more excitable than the day before; doubtless it was the Hôtel Cujas and, even more, the eight thousand francs folded away in his wallet. It was the money for La

Piboulette, oh yes, sure enough, but he supposed he had the right to slip a few louis out of it to take his niece out for a picnic!

'How about Bouchereau?' asked his nephew, who could not stay away from his office for two days in succession. It was arranged that they would breakfast in the Champs-Élysées and that the two men would go on to see the great doctor afterwards.

It was not what The Rip had imagined—a grand-style arrival at Saint-Cloud, the carriage piled high with champagne. But it was a delightful meal, all the same, out on the restaurant terrace shaded by acacias and Japanese sumach, with the fol-de-rol-lol of a re-hearsal floating through the leaves from the café-concert next door. Césaire was very talkative and very gallant, airing all his charms to dazzle the Parisienne. He was always catching the waiter's eye; he complimented the chef on his sauce meunière; and Fanny laughed with a silly, forced merriment and all the foolishness appropriate to a *cabinet particulier*, which dismayed Gaussin at least as much as did the intimacy growing up between uncle and niece, quite beyond his control.

One would have thought they were friends of twenty years' standing. Growing sentimental with wine, The Rip talked about Castelet, Divonne, and his dear boy Jean. He was glad to know the boy was with her, a sensible woman who would see he did nothing foolish. And talking of the young man's rather gloomy temperament, he gave her advice about how to handle him, patting her on the arm and speaking to her as to a young bride, his speech thick, his eyes glazed and full of tears.

He sobered down at Bouchereau's. They were kept waiting for two hours on the first floor of the house in the Place Vendôme, in those enormous, high-ceilinged chilly drawing-rooms full of people waiting, in silence, in agonies of suspense. It was an inferno of anxiety that they went through, passing through one circle after another, going from one drawing-room to the next, until they reached the renowned specialist's consulting-room.

Bouchereau, whose memory was amazing, remembered Madame Gaussin distinctly. He had been called in to a consultation at Castelet ten years previously, at the beginning of her illness. He

got them to describe the various phases of the illness, read through
the old prescriptions, and at once reassured the two men on the
score of the cerebral disturbances that had occurred recently; he
attributed them to the use of certain drugs. While he sat motionless,
his bushy eyebrows drawn together over his sharp, searching little
eyes, writing a long letter to his colleague at Avignon, the uncle
and the nephew held their breath and listened to the squeaking of
the pen, that one tiny sound that for them blotted out all the hum of
the great brilliant city. And suddenly they felt the power a doctor
has in these modern times, the last priest, source of supreme faith
and invincible superstition . . .

As they left, Césaire, sobered up and quite serious, said to his
nephew:

'I'm going back to the hotel to strap my bag up. This Paris air is
bad for me, you know, laddie. If I stayed here, I would only do
something silly. I'll take the seven o'clock train this evening. You'll
make my excuses to my niece, eh, won't you?'

Jean was careful not to discourage him; he was nervous about
his uncle's feather-brained childishness. And waking up the next
morning he was just congratulating himself that his uncle was back
again with Divonne, under lock and key, so to speak, when there
he suddenly was, all creased and crumpled, the very picture of
distraction.

'Good God, uncle, what has happened to you?'

Uncle Césaire collapsed into an armchair, unable to speak or
move. Then gradually reviving, he confessed that he had met someone he had known in the days of Courbebaisse, and there had been
an all-too-lavish dinner, and the eight thousand francs had all been
lost overnight in a gambling-hell. Not a brass farthing left!
Nothing! How was he to go back and tell Divonne? And he had
been going to buy La Piboulette! Suddenly he was overwhelmed
by a sort of frenzy and, pressing his hands over his eyes and stopping
his ears with his thumbs, frantically howling and sobbing, he reviled
himself with Provençal intensity and flourished his remorse before
them in a general confession covering his whole life. He was the
shame and sorrow of his family! People like him in families like his

were something there should be a law against! They should be hounded down like wolves! Where would he have been without his brother's generosity? At hard labour with robbers and forgers!

'Uncle, oh, uncle!' Jean said very unhappily, trying to stop him.

But Césaire chose to be blind and deaf, wallowing in public confession of his crime, telling the whole story down to the smallest details, while Fanny gazed at him in mingled pity and admiration. At least the fellow had some go in him! He was the sort of hot-head that appealed to her; and, stirred to the depths of her good-nature, all the golden-hearted whore, she tried to think of a way of helping him. But what? Who? She had not seen anyone for a year, and Jean had no social contacts. Suddenly a name leapt into her mind: Déchelette! He must be in Paris at this very moment, and he was such a good fellow.

'But I hardly know him,' Jean said.

'I'll go myself.'

'What? You would . . .'

'Why not?'

Their eyes met. Each understood the other. So Déchelette had been her lover too, a one-night lover she scarcely remembered. But he did not forget a single one of them; they were all listed in order in his mind, like the saints in the calendar.

'If you have anything against it . . .' she began, rather awkwardly.

But at that moment Césaire, who had stopped howling to listen in great suspense during this brief discussion, cast on them such a look of supplication that Jean gave way, clenched his teeth and agreed. . . .

How long that hour seemed to both of them, racked by thoughts that they would not admit to each other, leaning on the balcony railing, watching out for the woman's return.

'This chap Déchelette—does he live far from here?'

'Oh no, Rue de Rome—just round the corner,' Jean answered furiously, also thinking that it was taking Fanny a long time to come back. He tried to calm himself by quoting the engineer's motto: 'No to-morrow,' and the contemptuous manner in which he had heard him talk of Sappho as of a worn-out light-of-love belonging to the past; but his lover's pride rebelled at the thought, and he caught himself hoping that Déchelette would find her still beautiful and desirable. Ah, why must this crack-brained old Uncle Césaire come along and reopen all his wounds like this?

At last they saw Fanny's short cloak turning the corner of the street. She came in, radiant.

'There! I've got the money.'

With the eight thousand francs spread out before him, Uncle Césaire wept for joy and spoke of making out a receipt, fixing the interest and the date of repayment.

'There's no need for that, uncle. I didn't mention your name. The money was lent to me and so it's me you owe it to, and for as long as you like.'

'Services of this kind, my dear,' Césaire replied, rapturous with gratitude, 'are repaid with undying friendship.' And at the station, where Jean took him to make sure of his departure this time, he repeated with tears in his eyes: 'What a woman! What a treasure! You must see that you make her happy.'

Jean was seriously put out by this incident, which made him realize that the heavy chain that bound him was being riveted tighter and tighter, and two things that his natural delicacy of feeling had always kept separate and distinct—his family and his liaison —were in danger of becoming mixed up with each other. There was Césaire keeping Jean's mistress informed of the progress he was making in his vineyards and sending her news of all that was going on at Castelet; and Fanny would criticize the consul's obstinacy in the matter of the vines, talking about his mother's health and infuriating Jean with misplaced solicitude and advice. She never made any reference to the service rendered, nor to The Rip's bygone adventure, that blot on the d'Armandy escutcheon that Jean's uncle had revealed to her. Only once did she turn it to account against him, and then in the following circumstances.

They were going home after the theatre and, as it was raining, got into a cab at a boulevard cab-stand. The vehicle was one of

those old rattle-traps that only come out on the streets after midnight; it took a long time to get started, for the man was asleep and
the horse was shaking its nose-bag. While they were sitting inside,
sheltering, an old cabbie engaged in fixing a new lash to his whip
calmly came up to the window, his cord between his teeth, and,
breathing out wine-fumes, said hoarsely to Fanny:

'Evening! How're you getting on?'

'Oh, so it's you?' She was quick to control a little shudder, saying
to her lover in a low voice: 'My father!'

So this was her father! This cabman in the long mud-splashed
topcoat, remnant of some old livery, from which most of the metal
buttons were missing. . . . The gaslight from the lamp on the pavement showed a bloated, purplish, alcoholic face, in which Gaussin
thought he could see a coarse resemblance to Fanny's regular profile, with all its sensuality, and her large voluptuous eyes. Without
paying any attention to the man with his daughter, and as if he had
not seen him at all, old Legrand gave her the news from home. 'The
old woman's been at Necker this last fortnight. She's pretty bad.
Why don't you go and see her one of these Thursdays? It would set
her up a bit. Lucky for me, my carcass is tough enough. Good cord
makes a good whip, that's what it is. Business isn't what it used to
be, though. If you're wanting a good coachman the job would just
suit me. Oh, you don't? Well, it can't be helped. See you again one
of these days.'

They shook hands limply, and the cab drove off.

'Well, what do you think of that?' Fanny murmured. And at
once she began to tell him all about her family, a thing she had
always avoided before—'it was so beastly, so vile'—but now
they knew each other better, now there was no need to hide
anything.

She had been born at Moulin-aux-Anglais, on the outskirts of
Paris, of this father, an ex-dragoon, then driving coaches between
Paris and Châtillon, and a barmaid at an inn—a child of chance,
conceived between two turns at the bar.

She had never known her mother, who died in child-birth. But
the roadhouse people, who were a decent couple, forced the father

to acknowledge his little girl and pay for a nurse for her. He did not dare to refuse, for he was deeply in debt to the house; and when Fanny was four years old he used to take her out on his coach like a little dog, perched away up on top, underneath the hood, thoroughly enjoying bowling along the roads, seeing the light of the lamps streaking away on each side and the horses' backs steaming and heaving, and falling asleep in the darkness, with the cold wind blowing, to the sound of the little bells jingling.

But father Legrand was soon tired of striking paternal attitudes, for however little it cost, still the brat's food and clothes had to be paid for. Then too she was an obstacle to his marrying a market-gardener's widow whose melon frames had caught his eye as he drove past the field with the trimly planted cabbages. It was then that she got a very definite feeling that her father meant to ruin her; his drunkard's obsession was that he must at all costs get rid of this child. And if the widow herself, the excellent Machaume, had not taken the little girl under her protection . . .

'Oh, but of course, you've met her,' Fanny said. 'Machaume!'

'What! The maid I saw at your house?'

'She was my stepmother. She was very good to me when I was small. I took her to get her away from that rascal of a husband of hers, for when he had eaten her out of house and home he took to beating her and made her wait on a slut he was living with. Oh, poor Machaume, she knows the price there is to pay for a handsome husband! Well, when she had left me in spite of all I could say to her, she rushed back to take up with him again, and there she is now in hospital. How the old scoundrel lets himself go to pieces without her! Wasn't he dirty! What an old tramp he looked! He hasn't a thing but his whip—did you see how straight he carried it? Even when he's rolling drunk he carries it like a candle in front of him and keeps it in his room at night. It's always been the only decent thing about him. Good cord makes a good whip—that's what he always says.'

She talked quite unconstrainedly, as though of a stranger, without either disgust or shame. It appalled Jean to hear her. What a father! What a mother! What a contrast to the consul's austere countenance and Madame Gaussin's angelic smile! And suddenly realizing all that her lover's silence meant, all his revulsion from the social mud bespattering him as he sat beside her, Fanny said in a philosophic tone: 'After all, there's a bit of something like it in every family and it isn't a person's own fault. I've got Legrand for a father. You've got your Uncle Césaire.'

6

'My dearest boy, I am writing to you still trembling from the dreadful distress we have just been in. Our twins vanished. . . . They disappeared from Castelet for a whole day and a night and the morning of the next day!

'It was breakfast-time on Sunday when we noticed that the little girls were nowhere to be seen. I had made them neat and pretty for eight o'clock mass, and the consul was taking them to church. Then I thought no more about it, being kept with your mother, who was more nervous than usual, as though she had a premonition of the misfortune hovering about us. You know she has always been rather like that since her illness, foreseeing what is to come. And the less she can move, the more goes on in her head.

'Fortunately your mother was in her room, and you can imagine us all in the dining-room, waiting for the little girls. We called to them everywhere in the grounds, and the shepherd blew on the big horn that he calls the sheep home with, and then Césaire went out in one direction and I in another, and Rousseline and Tardive too, and there we all were chasing about Castelet, saying every time we met: "Well?" "Not a thing." In the end we didn't dare to go on asking. With thumping hearts we went to the wells, we looked down from the high windows in the barn. What a day! And I had to keep running up to your mother all the time, smiling quite calmly, explaining why the little girls weren't there by saying I had sent them to spend Sunday with their aunt at Villamuris. She seemed to believe it. But late in the evening, when I was sitting with her and glancing out of the window at the lights moving this way and that across the fields and on the Rhône, in search of the children, I heard her quietly crying in bed. And when I asked her what the matter was, she said: "I'm crying about something that's being kept from me, but I've guessed, all the same." She said it in that little childish voice she has got again now from being so ill. And we didn't say any more about it, but from that moment we shared the same trouble, in our solitude up there.

'In the end—for I don't want to spin out this wretched story, my dearest boy—on Monday morning our little girls were brought back to us by workmen your uncle employs on the island. They had found them on a heap of vine-twigs, pale with cold and hunger after a night in the open air, out there on the water. And this is what they told us in the innocence of their little hearts. For a long time they had been haunted by the idea of doing what their patron saints had done, for they had read the story of Saint Martha and Saint Mary, and wanted to go away in a boat without sails or oars or provisions of any kind, to spread the Gospel on the first shore where the winds of heaven would blow them. So after mass on Sunday they untied one of the fishing-boats and knelt down in the bottom like the holy women, and the current swept them out and they drifted gently along till they ran aground among the rushes of La Piboulette, in spite of the heavy water running at this season, and the wind blowing and the eddies too. Yes, God Himself kept them safe and it is He who brought them back to us, the darlings! their Sunday pinafores a little crushed and some of the gold spoilt on their prayer-books. We hadn't the heart to scold them, only kissed them and hugged them hard. But afterwards we were all quite ill from the fright we had had.

'The one who was most stricken was your mother. Before we told her anything about it, she felt—she told us how she felt death passing over Castelet. And though she is usually so quiet and so cheerful, now there is some sadness about her that nothing will cure, in spite of how your father and I and everyone cares for her and cherishes her. . . . And what I really want to say to you, Jean dear, is this—it's you more than anything that she longs for and worries about. She doesn't dare to admit it in front of your father, who wants you to be left to get on with your work, but you didn't come after your exam as you promised. Give us a surprise and come for Christmas. Make our invalid smile her dear smile again. If you knew how sorry one is, when parents are gone, that one didn't give them more time . . .'

Standing by the window where slothful wintry daylight was filtering through the fog, as Jean read the letter he could feel the

wild free fragrance, the loving memories of another world, all
affection and sunshine.

'What is it? Let me see.'

Fanny had been wakened by the yellow light let in by the drawing of the curtain and, puffy from sleep, was reaching out mechanically for the packet of Maryland always kept on the bedside-table.
He hesitated, knowing how mad with jealousy she became at the
mere sound of Divonne's name. But how was he to conceal the
nature of the letter, when she recognized it by its shape?

At first she was sweetly touched by the little girls' escapade, and
sat there, arms and breast bare, propped up against the pillows with
her dark hair loose about her, reading and rolling herself a cigarette.
But the end whipped her into fury. She crumpled the letter up and
hurled it across the room, crying: 'I don't care *that* for all this talk
about saints! It's all just a story to make you go away! She wants
her handsome nephew, the ——'

He tried to stop her, but he was not quick enough to prevent her
flinging out the obscene word and then a string of others. She had
never before let herself be so carried away in his presence, never
been so foul-mouthed in her over-brimming filthy rage, like a
sewer-pipe bursting and letting all its mire and muck go pouring
out. Here was the language of her past, the language of whores and
of the underworld, her throat pulsing with it, her lips swollen and
trembling.

Oh, it didn't take much to see what they were all after! Césaire
had talked and now the family had put their heads together to
break things up and get him back to the country, with Divonne's
raking lines as a bait.

'I may as well tell you, if you go, I shall write to her simpleton of
a husband! I'm warning you! Oh, I tell you . . . !'

As she spoke, she hunched herself up on the bed in a convulsion
of hatred, her face white and twisted, her features larger, like an
angry animal on the point of springing.

Gaussin remembered having seen her like that in the Rue de
l'Arcade. But now it was turned against him—this shrieking hatred
that made him want to throw himself on her and beat her. For in

those sensual loves where there is no trace of any regard or respect for the person loved, brutality is always breaking out, in moments of anger as of lust. He was afraid of what he might do, and hurried out to his office; and as he walked through the streets he felt his wrath rising against the life he had made for himself. This would teach him to get into the clutches of a woman like that! What infamy! What horrible beastliness! The things she had said about his sisters, his mother, everybody! What! so he had not even the right to go and see his family? Oh, what a prison had he shut himself up in! And the whole story of their relationship rose before his inner eye; he remembered the Egyptian woman's beautiful bare arms twined round his neck that night after the ball, and realized how tyrannically, how hard they held fast, cutting him off from his friends and his family. Now he had made up his mind. That very evening, come what might, he was setting out for Castelet.

When he had settled some business and obtained leave of absence from his office, he went home early, expecting a terrible scene. He was ready for anything, even a final break. But the very subdued greeting that Fanny met him with, and her swollen eyes and tear-stained cheeks, made him almost unable to do anything decisive.

'I'm going away this evening,' he said, stiffening himself up.

'You're quite right, sweetheart. Go and see your mother. And the main thing—' she came up close to him, coaxingly, 'forget I was cross. I love you too much, it makes me go mad.'

All the rest of the day, packing his trunk for him with all sorts of affectionate fuss, as gentle as in their early days together, she kept her penitent air, perhaps in the hope of making him change his mind. But she did not once say: 'Stay with me.' And when the last moment came, when everything was done and all hope gone, she clung to him, nestled up to him, tried to impregnate him with some essence of her being, her presence, that would be there all through his journey and his absence. And, kissing him good-bye, she only murmured: 'Tell me, Jean, you aren't cross with me, are you?'

Oh, in the morning, the joy of waking in the little room he had had as a child, his heart still warm from so much hugging and his family's delight at his arrival! And there, in just the same place on the mosquito-net over his narrow bed, was the same bar of light that he had looked for in his dreams. And there were the peacocks screaming from their perches, there was the squeak of the well-pulley, the pattering of the sheep being hurried by. And when he had flung the shutters crashing back against the walls, there was that wonderful hot light falling in sheets, as though through an opened sluice, and the lovely sloping outline of the vines, cypresses, and olives, and the glittering pine-wood, sinking away towards the Rhône, under a deep, pure sky without a trace of haze even at this early hour: a green sky that the *mistral* had swept all night, the *mistral* even now blowing strongly and cheerfully through the immense valley.

Jean compared this awakening with those in Paris under a sky as murky as his passion, and he felt happy and free. He went down-stairs. The white sunshiny house was still asleep, all its shutters closed like eyes; and he was glad of an interval of solitude to pull himself together, in this convalescence of the spirit that he could feel was now beginning.

He walked out on to the terrace and then turned into a path leading uphill through the park—they called it the park—a wood of pines and myrtles scattered at random on Castelet's rough flank, run through with uneven paths all slippery with dry needles. His dog Miracle, grown old and lame, had come out of his kennel and followed in silence, keeping to heel. They had taken this morning walk together so often!

At the entrance to the vineyards, fenced in with tall cypresses that bowed their pointed tops, the dog hesitated; he knew that the ground here, with the thick layer of sand that was the latest remedy the consul was trying against phylloxera, would be hard going for his old paws, just as were the shored-up steps of the terrace. How-ever, the joy of following his master drew him on; and at every obstacle he uttered little frightened whimpers, stopping and fum-bling, like a crab on a rock. Jean did not look at him, being pre-occupied with the new Alicante slips that his father had talked about for a long time the night before. The stems seemed to be doing well on the smooth, shining sand. So the poor man was going to be rewarded for his dogged efforts and the Castelet vineyards would live again when those of La Nerte and the Hermitage and all the great wine-lands of the South were dead!

All at once a little white coif bobbed up in front of him. It was Divonne, the first member of the household to get up. She had a pruning-knife in her hand and something else that she threw away, and her usually creamy cheeks flushed bright red. 'Oh, is it you, Jean? You gave me a start. I thought it was your father.' Then she recovered herself and kissed him. 'Did you sleep well?'

'Very well, aunt. But why were you afraid it might be father coming along?'

'Because . . .' She picked up the vine-root that she had just torn up and said: 'The consul told you that he's sure of succeeding this time, didn't he? Well, tch! there the creature is.'

Jean looked at a tiny yellowish moss encrusted in the wood; it was the almost imperceptible mould that had gradually ruined whole provinces, inch by inch. What irony on nature's part, this splendid morning under the life-giving sun and this infinitely small destroyer that could not be destroyed!

'This is the beginning. In three months the whole vineyard will be eaten up and your father will begin all over again, because it's a point of pride. There will be new slips planted, new remedies—and then one day . . .' A despairing gesture completed and underlined what she meant.

'Oh. So it's as bad as that?'

'Well, you know what the consul is like. He never says anything, he gives me the housekeeping money just as he has always done. But I can see he's worried. He goes off to Avignon and Orange, trying to raise money.'

'And how about Césaire? How are his immersions going?' the young man asked, horrified.

Thanks be to God, all was well in that quarter. They had had fifty hogshead of light wine from the last vintage, and it would be double that this year. In consideration of this success the consul had made over to his brother all the vineyards down on the low ground, which had previously lain fallow, all set out in lines of dead wood like a country cemetery; and now they had had them all under water for the last three months.

And proud of what her husband, her Rip, was achieving, from where they were standing on the hill she pointed out to Jean the big ponds padded round with lime, like brine-pits.

'That plantation will give us a yield in two years from now. It will take the same time for La Piboulette, as well as the Ile de Lamotte, which your uncle bought without telling anyone. Then we shall be rich. But it means holding out till then, and each of us must do what he can and make some sacrifice.'

She talked of sacrifice cheerfully, in the tone of a woman who no longer thinks anything of it, and with such easy briskness that Jean, into whose mind a sudden thought flashed, replied in the same tone:

'The sacrifices will be made, Divonne.'

The same day he wrote to tell Fanny that his parents could not go on making him his allowance, that he would have nothing but his salary and that in these circumstances it would be impossible for them to go on living together. It meant the break came sooner than he had thought, three or four years before his expected departure abroad; but he was relying on her to realize how serious the reasons were and to have pity on him in his distress and help in the painful execution of a duty.

Was it really a sacrifice? On the contrary, was he not glad to finish with a life that he felt was odious and unsavoury, all the more so since he had found his way back to nature and his family and all this simple, frank affection? His letter was written without a struggle, without any pain; and once that was done, he would find his defence against her answer, which he expected would be furious, full of threats and ravings, in the honest, loyal affection of these generous-hearted people to whom he belonged: there was the example of his father, upright and proud as a man could be, the little twin saints with their shining smiles, and these wide and tranquil horizons with the sheer mountain light and mountain air, this over-arching sky, this swiftly flowing, sweeping river. For as he looked back on his passion, and all the small sordid elements of which it was made up, it seemed to him as though he were recovering from a dangerous fever, a fever such as one may get from the miasma hovering over swampy ground.

Five or six days passed in the silence following the delivery of a great blow. Morning and evening Jean went to the post and came back empty-handed, singularly perturbed. What was she doing? What had she decided? And whatever it was, why did she not answer? He could think of nothing else. And at night, when all Castelet was sleeping to the lullaby murmur of the wind blowing through the long passages, Césaire and he would sit in his little bedroom and have long talks about it.

'She's quite capable of turning up here!' Uncle Césaire would say. And his anxiety was increased by the fact that he had put two notes of hand into the envelope with Jean's final letter: one was at six months, one at a year, in settlement of his debt, with interest. How was he to meet these bills? How could he explain to Divonne? He shuddered at the mere thought of it; and his nephew's heart ached for him as he stood up, his long nose drooping more sadly than ever, and knocked out his pipe at the end of their discussion and said: 'Oh well, good night. Anyway, it's a very good thing you've done what you have.'

At last the long-awaited answer came. At the very first lines: 'My own dear man, I didn't write to you sooner because I wanted to show you not only in words how utterly I do understand and love you . . .' Jean stopped, startled as a man who hears a symphony instead of the beating of drums he has been expecting. He turned quickly to the last page, where he read: '. . . always until death your dog that loves you, that you can beat, that leaps to caress you. . . .'

So then she had not received his letter! But reading it through line by line, with tears in his eyes, he saw that it was indeed an answer and that it told him Fanny had long been expecting this bad news; she had been expecting that difficulties at Castelet would bring about the inevitable separation. She had instantly set out in search of work, in order not to remain a burden to him, and she had found a situation as manageress of a very rich woman's boarding-

house in the Avenue du Bois-de-Boulogne. A hundred francs a
month, free board and lodging, and her Sundays free. . . .

'You see, my own man—a whole day every week for our love.
For you do still want us to be together, don't you? You will reward
me for the great effort I am making, it's the first time in my life
that I have done any work, and I am taking on day and night
slavery, with humiliations that you can't imagine—it will be very
hard for me, with my wild love of independence. But it gives me a
feeling of extraordinary contentment to be able to suffer for love of
you. I owe you so much. You have made me realize so many good
and decent things that nobody else ever talked to me about! Ah, if
only we had met each other sooner! But you hadn't even learnt to
walk when I was already lying in men's arms. Not one of them all
will ever be able to boast that he inspired me with such determination to keep him for just a little, little bit longer. . . . Now come
back whenever you want to. The apartment is free. I have cleared
all my things out. That was the hardest thing of all, turning out the
drawers, turning out memories. You won't find anything but my
portrait, and that won't cost you anything, only the kind looks that
I beg for it. Oh, sweetheart, sweetheart! And so, if you will only
keep my Sunday and my own special place on your shoulder—my
place, you know . . .'

And then came endearments and coaxing words, the smooth, sensual
lickings of a mother cat washing her kitten, and words of passion that
made him rub his face against the glossy paper as though the caress
could reach out of the page and touch him, human, alive, and warm.

'Doesn't she say anything about my bills?' Uncle Césaire asked
timidly.

'She has sent them back. She says you're to repay her when you
are rich.'

His uncle gave a sigh of relief, his forehead wrinkled up with
pleasure, and pompously complacent he said in his strong Provençal accent:

'Ah, let me tell you, my boy—that woman is a saint.'

Then, passing on to another order of ideas, with that will-o'-the-wisp agility of his, that failure of logic and memory that was one of the oddities of his character: 'And what a temperament, my dear lad! All on fire! It makes my throat dry to think of, the way it did when Courbebaisse used to read me the letters he got from la Mornas. . . .'

Once again Jean had to hear all about Uncle Césaire's first visit to Paris, and the Hôtel Cujas, and Dandruff. But he was not listening. He sat at the open window with his elbows on the sill, looking out into the still night bathed in moonlight so bright that the cocks woke up and hailed it as the dawn.

So after all it was true: there *was* that redemption by love that the poets talked of. He felt an upsurge of pride at the thought that all those great and famous men whom Fanny had loved before him, far from regenerating her, had only depraved her more, and yet here was he, perhaps about to pull her out of the mire for ever by the mere force of his own decency.

He was grateful to her for having found this compromise, this way of loosening the bond between them; and she would get into new habits, though it would be very difficult for her to get used to working, indolent as she was by nature. And the next day he wrote to her—in a paternal manner, an old man talking, encouraging her to reform, expressing concern about the type of boarding-house that she was managing, and the sort of people who came there; for he was mistrustful of her indulgence and the ease with which she gave way, saying: 'What can you expect? Things are like that. . . .'

Fanny wrote to him by every post, docile as a little girl, giving him a picture of her boarding-house, which was a thoroughgoing family hotel occupied by foreigners. On the first floor were Peruvians, father, mother, children, and numerous servants; on the second, Russians and a rich Dutchman, a coral merchant. The rooms on the third floor were occupied by two ring-masters from the Hippodrome—Englishmen, very smart, very correct in every way—and the most interesting little ménage, Fräulein Minna Vogel, a zither-player from Stuttgart, with her brother Leo, a poor tubercular boy who had had to give up the Conservatoire, where he was studying the clarinet; his elder sister had come to nurse him,

F—S.

and they had no resources but the takings from a few concerts, which paid for their rooms and their food.

'It's all as touching and as respectable as anyone could imagine, as you see, my darling own man. As for me, I pass for a widow and receive all sorts of little attentions. Certainly I would not allow it to be otherwise; your wife must be respected. When I say "your wife," please understand the way I mean it. I know that you will go away some day and I shall lose you, but afterwards there will never be anyone else. I shall be yours for ever, keeping the feeling of your touch, your love, and the good instincts you have wakened in me. . . . It's funny, isn't it—Sappho turning virtuous! Yes, I shall be virtuous when you are no longer there. But for you I shall stay the way you have loved me, wild and burning. . . . I love you madly. . . .'

All at once Jean felt a great wave of weariness and depression sweep over him. These homecomings of the prodigal son, with all the rejoicings of arrival, the fatted calf, the feastings, the outpourings of emotion, are always spoilt by haunting recollections of the nomad life, regret for the bitter husks and days with only the grunting swine to herd. A disenchantment comes over things and persons; suddenly they look bleak and faded. The winter mornings in Provence no longer had the same clean cheerfulness, nor was there any delight in hunting the beautiful red-brown otters along the steep river-banks, nor in taking out old Abrieu's flat-bottomed boat, to shoot the wild duck. It seemed to Jean that the wind was keen and the water rough, and it was always the same when he walked through the flooded vineyards with his uncle there at his side, explaining his system of sluices and conduits.

The village that in the first few days he looked at as he had known it on his joyful scamperings about the countryside as a little lad, with its tumble-down cottages, some of them abandoned, now had the look of death and desolation that the villages often have in Italy; and when he went to the post, at every tottering doorway that he passed he had to run the gauntlet of the old men's endless mumbling stories—old men twisted like trees under a prevailing wind, their

arms wrapped in bits of knitted stockings—and the old women
with chins like yellow boxwood, with their tight-fitting caps, their
little eyes shiny, twinkling like lizards flickering on ancient walls.

There were always the same lamentations about the dying vines,
the decay of the madder, the blight in the mulberries, the seven
plagues of Egypt laying waste the lovely land of Provence. And to
avoid them he would sometimes go home through steep lanes running along the old walls of the château of the Popes—deserted lanes
overgrown with bushes and those tall herbs that Saint Roch used
for curing skin-disease, weeds in their right place here where the
Middle Ages still seemed to linger, in the shadow of the enormous
castellated ruin standing up against the sky.

Then he would meet Father Malassagne returning after saying
mass, coming down the lane with swift, ravening strides, his neck-
band awry and the skirts of his soutane held high in both hands
because of the brambles and burrs. The priest would stop and in-
veigh against the peasants' lack of religion and the monstrous
attitude taken by the municipal council, casting his malediction on
the fields, and on the beasts, and on men, villains who no longer
came to church, who buried their dead without sacraments and
treated their sick by magnetism or spiritism, to save paying the
doctor and the priest.

'Yes, spiritism, my dear sir! That's what the people have sunk to
in our part of the country! And then do you wonder if the vines
become diseased!'

Jean, who had Fanny's letter open in his pocket, almost in flames,
would have to listen, an absent look in his eyes; and as soon as he
could tear himself away from the priest's harangue he would hurry
back to Castelet to shelter in a cranny in the rocks, what the
Provençals call a skulking-place, out of the wind that was blowing
all about him, in the hot sunlight reflected from the sides of the rock.

He always chose the remotest and wildest place among black-
berry-briars and red oaks, and there he burrowed out a place for
himself, to read his letter. And little by little, from the faint scent
that it gave off, from the velvety feeling of the words and the
scenes evoked, he would become aware of a sensual intoxication

quickening his pulse, hallucinating him until his surroundings seemed to disappear like a meaningless backcloth on a stage—the river, the clusters of little islands, the villages nestling in the hollow of the Alpilles, the whole curve of the immense valley where the wild wind blew in squalls, puffing the sun-shot dust along in clouds. He was back in their bedroom, looking out on the grey-roofed railway station, a prey to the wild love-making, the raging desires that held them fast, clutching and clinging to each other with the desperation of people drowning. . . .

Suddenly he heard footsteps coming along the path and a burst of light laughter. 'There he is!' Here came his sisters, their little bare legs brushing against the lavender, and old Miracle trotting ahead, wagging his tail triumphantly, very proud of having tracked his master down. But Jean kicked him away and spurned the children's bashful suggestions that they should play hide-and-seek or run races. Yet he was fond of these little girls who adored their big brother from afar; he had become a child again for their sake from the moment he arrived, and delighted in the contrast between the two pretty little things born at the same time and yet so unlike each other. One was tall and dark, frizzy-haired, dreamy, and self-willed; it was she who had had the idea of setting out in the boat, in a state of exaltation after listening to Father Malassagne. She was the little Mary of Egypt who had borne off her fair-haired sister Marthe, the shy and yielding one who took after her mother and brother.

But how hideously it embarrassed him, with those memories just freshly stirred in his mind, to have these children innocently snuggling up against him, rubbing their cheeks in the coquettish perfume that his mistress's letter left on him. 'No, leave me alone,' he said. 'I have some work to do.' And he was going to shut himself up in his own room, when he heard his father calling to him:

'There you are, Jean. Just listen to this.'

Each post brought new cause for dejection. Melancholy by nature, in his years in the East the consul had become accustomed to long spells of grave silence, interrupted by sudden outbursts of reminiscence—'When I was consul at Hong Kong'—like fireworks going up in a blaze. While Jean was listening to his father reading and commenting on the morning newspaper, he would gaze up at the mantelpiece and Caoudal's Sappho there, her arms linked round her knees, her lyre beside her—*the whole sweep of the lyre*—a bronze bought twenty years ago at a time when Castelet was being beautified. And the factory-made bronze that sickened him in so many shop windows in Paris, here in his isolation stirred his love into flame again, making him want to kiss those shoulders, unlink those cold, polished arms, and make her say: 'Sappho for you, and for you alone!'

The seductive image of her loomed before him whenever he went out; it walked with him, it echoed in the sound of his footsteps on the wide, lofty staircase. It was to the rhythm of Sappho's name that the pendulum of the old grandfather clock swung to and fro, her name that the wind whispered in the big, stone-paved chilly passages of this summer dwelling, her name that he found in all the books he opened in this country-house library, old worn volumes with red edges and binding out of which crumbs fell, crumbs he had dropped there as a child, nibbling cake. And her obsessive memory pursued him even into his mother's bedroom where Divonne was doing the sick woman's hair, drawing the beautiful white tresses back from a face that was still rosy and peaceful in expression in spite of the unceasing pain that racked all parts of her body.

'Ah, here is our Jean,' his mother would say.

But with her neck bare, her little coif, her sleeves turned up to do these things that only she could do for the invalid, his aunt reminded him of other awakenings, other mornings, called to his mind yet once again how his mistress used to spring out of bed in a cloud of smoke from her first cigarette. He hated himself for having such thoughts, in this room of all places. And yet what could he do to shake them off?

'He is not the boy he used to be, sister,' Madame Gaussin said sadly. 'What can be the matter?' And the two of them thought about it a great deal. Divonne racked her simple brains and would have liked to question him; but he seemed to be avoiding her, apparently did not want to be alone with her.

Once she watched where he was going and surprised him in his skulking-place, in the fever of his letters and his bad dreams. He got up, a sombre look in his eyes. But she held him back and sat down beside him on the hot stone, saying: 'Don't you love me any more? Am I not your Divonne any more? Your Divonne you used to talk to about all your troubles?'

'Oh yes, yes, you are,' he stammered, troubled by her affectionate air. He turned his eyes away so that she should not see something reflected there, something he had just read, passionate appeals, an abandoned outcry, all the nostalgic longing of distant love.

'What's the matter? Why are you sad?' Divonne murmured, her voice and her hands full of the little petting ways that people have with children. He was almost her own little boy; for her he was still only ten years old, at the age when children are just beginning to find their feet in the adult world.

Set on fire by what he had been reading, he became over-excited by the disturbing charm of this lovely body so close to his, this cool mouth still more brightly reddened by the breeze that tossed her hair and sent light curls of it dancing over her forehead in what was now the Paris fashion. And all Sappho's doctrines—'All women are the same—there's only one idea in their heads when they're with a man'—made him see something provocative in the country-woman's happy smile and the hand laid on his arm, to keep him there to answer her affectionate questions.

Suddenly he felt an evil temptation rising like vertigo, and the effort that he made to resist it shook him with a convulsive shudder. Divonne was startled to see him turn so pale, and his teeth chatter-ing. 'Oh, poor darling—he's in a fever!' In her unthinking tender-ness for him she untied the big scarf she had knotted round her shoulders to put it round his neck. But she was suddenly seized, wrapped in his arms, and felt the burning touch of mad kisses on the nape of her neck, her shoulders, all this sparkling flesh that had suddenly been laid bare to the sun. She had no time to cry out or defend herself, perhaps not even time to understand what was really happening.

'Oh, I'm crazy, crazy!' he exclaimed and rushed away, was already far away on the heath, where the stones clattered dismally under his running feet.

At lunch that day Jean announced that he was going back to Paris that same evening, having been recalled to his office. 'Going? Already? But you said . . . But you've only just come!' And there were cries and supplications. Yet he could not stay with them now, since Sappho's disquieting, corrupting influence had come between him and their affection for him. Besides, had he not made the biggest sacrifice he could make for them, by ceasing to live with her? The final break would be made a while later; and then he would come back to throw his arms round all these dear good people and love them without uneasiness or shame.

It was late in the night and everyone was asleep, all the lights out, when Césaire came back from seeing his nephew on to the train at Avignon. Having given his horse its oats and scrutinized the sky— that glance at the weather-signs, that upward look of all men who live by the land—he was about to go indoors, when he saw a white figure on a seat on the terrace.

'Is that you, Divonne?' he asked.

'Yes. I've been waiting for you.'

She was very busy all day long, without a moment to spare for her adored Rip, and so at night they would meet like this to talk things over and take a stroll round the garden. It may have been the brief scene between Jean and herself, a scene that she had thought over and come to understand even better than she liked; or it may have been her distress at seeing the poor mother silently weeping all day long. Her voice was strained and there was an unusual suggestion of stress about her, she who was usually the quiet personification of duty. 'Do you know anything about it? Do you know why he left us so suddenly?' She did not believe his story about being recalled to the office, and suspected that there was some bad influence drawing the boy away from his family. How many dangers there were, how many random ways of going to one's doom in that dreadful city, Paris!

Césaire, who was incapable of keeping anything from her, admitted that there was indeed a woman in Jean's life; but, he said, she was a good soul who would not dream of taking him away from those who loved him. He spoke of her devotion, and the moving letters she wrote; he particularly praised her courageous determination to work—a thing that to the countrywoman seemed only natural—'After all, people do have to work for their living.'

'Not that sort of woman,' Césaire said.

'So it was a hussy Jean was living with! And you *went* there!'

'I give you my word, Divonne, since she has known him there hasn't been a chaster and more decent woman anywhere. Love has rehabilitated her.'

But that was too long a word for Divonne; she did not understand that sort of talk. For her Jean's mistress was relegated to the category of outcasts whom she called 'bad women', and the thought that her Jean was such a creature's victim roused her wrath. If the consul were to suspect such a thing!

Césaire did his best to calm her down, screwing up his jolly face into a network of wrinkles, as he tried to convince her that no young man of that age could do without a woman.

'Well then, why doesn't he get married?' she said with heart-rending simplicity.

'The long and the short of it is, they're not living together any more. It's always the same.'

'Listen, Césaire,' she said gravely. 'You know what people say in these parts: "Misfortune stays longer than he who brings it." If it's really the way you tell me, if Jean has dragged this woman out of the mud, perhaps he has got thoroughly splashed for his pains. Perhaps he really has made her a better and more decent woman. But how do we know whether the badness that was in her may not have entered right into our boy's heart!'

They walked back towards the terrace. Darkness lay peaceful and cloudless over all the silent valley where nothing seemed awake, only the gliding moonlight, the fast-flowing river, the silvery, glassy ponds. They breathed deeply of this great calm, remote from all the world in the tranquillity of a dreamless sleep. Then suddenly they heard the train coming up the hill beside the Rhône, puffing and rumbling along with full steam up.

'Oh, that place, Paris!' Divonne said, shaking her fist in the direction of the enemy that all country people curse. 'Paris! To think what we give to it, and what it gives us back!'

7

IT was four o'clock on a chill, misty afternoon, gloomy even here in the broad Champs-Élysées where the carriages went hurrying along, the sound of the wheels muffled as though wrapped in cottonwool. Coming up to the little garden with the trellis gate open, Jean could only just manage to read the high gilded letters over the mezzanine of a house with a quiet look of wealth and ease: FURNISHED APARTMENTS, FAMILY BOARDING-HOUSE. There was a brougham drawn up at the pavement outside.

Pushing open the office door, Jean saw her at once—saw the woman he was looking for, sitting at the window to get what light there was, leafing through a big account-book, and opposite her another woman, tall and smartly dressed, with a handkerchief in her hands and a little money-bag beside her.

'What can I do for you, sir?' Fanny said, then recognized him, stood up with a startled look and walked past the other woman, murmuring: 'It's my boy.' The other woman looked Gaussin up and down with the splendid coolness of long experience and said loudly, quite without embarrassment: 'Kiss each other, my dears. I'm not looking at you.' Then she sat down in Fanny's place and went on checking the figures.

They took each other's hands and whispered silly little scraps of sentences, like: 'Well, how are you?' 'Not too bad, thanks.' 'So you started out last night?' But the change in their voices gave the words their real meaning. And sitting down on the divan, they gradually recovered themselves and Fanny asked in a low voice: 'Don't you recognize my employer? Don't you remember? You saw her at Déchelette's ball, as a Spanish bride. Slightly faded bride, I must say.'

'Oh, it's——'

'Rosario Sanchès, de Potter's woman.'

Rosario, or Rosa, as her real name was—a name scrawled on the mirrors of late-night eating-houses, always with the addition of some obscenity—had been a circus-rider at the Hippodrome, renowned throughout the 'fast' world as utterly cynical and shame-less and inclined to use her foul tongue and her horsewhip in a way much sought after by men of the ring, whom she handled as she did her horses.

A Spaniard from Oran, she had been handsome rather than pretty and still in certain lights could make effective use of her dark-circled black eyes and eyebrows that met in the middle; but here, even in this artificial light, she looked her full fifty years, her face flat and hard, the skin pimpled and yellow as the lemons of her native country. She had been a close friend of Fanny Legrand's for many years, chaperoning her in her amorous affairs; and the mere sound of her name was enough to horrify Gaussin.

Realizing what the trembling of his arm meant, Fanny tried to make excuses. To whom could she turn to find work? She had really been in difficulties. Besides, Rosa was living in retirement now; she was very well-off, very well-off indeed, and lived either at her hotel in the Avenue de Villiers or in her villa at Enghien, where she received a few old friends but only one lover, always the same man, the composer.

'De Potter?' Jean asked. 'I thought he was married.'

'Yes, he's married and has children, and they say his wife's pretty, too. But that hasn't stopped him from going back to his old sweetheart. And you should just hear how she speaks to him! The way she treats him! Oh, he's got it badly, poor fellow.' She was clutching his hand with affectionate reproach. At that moment the other woman broke off her reading and turned her attention to her bag, which was leaping about by itself at the end of its silk cord:

'Now you just be quiet! Do you hear me?' Then in a tone of command, to her manageress: 'Here, give me a bit of sugar for Bichito.'

Fanny got up and brought the sugar-lump, which she held close to the opening of the bag, murmuring all sorts of endearments and cajoleries. 'Just look at the little pet,' she said to her lover, showing him a kind of large, misshapen, horny lizard, tufted and notched, with a hooded head, its body a mass of shivering, gelatinous flesh, embedded in cotton-wool. It was a chameleon that Rosa had been sent from Algeria. She kept it alive through the Parisian winter by wrapping it up warmly and taking constant care of it. She loved it as she had never loved any man; and from Fanny's sycophantic fawning Jean guessed what place the dreadful creature occupied in the house.

The woman shut the book and prepared to leave. 'Not too bad for a second fortnight. Better watch the candles, though.'

She ran a proprietorial eye over the little room, all neat and tidy with its plush-upholstered furniture, blew some dust off the yucca on the side-table, and pointed out a hole in the gimp cross-curtains. This done she cast a knowing glance at the lovers and said: 'Now, my pets, no fooling about, you know. This is a respectable establishment,' and went out to get into the carriage waiting outside the door for her, to take her afternoon drive in the Bois.

'Isn't it a bore?' Fanny said. 'I get either her or her mother on top of me here twice a week. Her mother's even worse, and *mean*! You see how much I must love you to last out in a dump like this. But here you are now! I've still got you! I was so frightened. . . .' And she put her arms round him as they stood there and held him for a long time, hard, her lips pressed to his, the shudder of the kiss assuring her that he was still all hers. But there were people coming and going in the passage outside and they had to be careful. When the lamp had been brought in she sat down in her usual place with some needlework, with him sitting at her side like a visitor.

'Have I changed, eh? Do you think it's still me?'

She smiled, showing him how awkwardly she held her crochet-hook, like a little girl. She had always detested needlework, occupying herself with a book, or her piano, or her cigarette, or turning up her sleeves to make some little dish for him—that was all she would do with herself. But what was she to do here? She could not dream of touching the piano in the sitting-room, being obliged to stay in the office all day. What about novels, then? But she herself knew far more about life than was in any of the stories that novels could tell her. In place of the forbidden cigarette, she took up this lace-work, which kept her fingers busy and left her free to think; and so she had come to realize why women liked the kind of fine work that she had always so much despised.

And while she was catching at her thread, still clumsily enough, bending over it with the concentration of inexperience, Jean watched her and thought how restful she looked in her simple dress with the little straight collar, her hair smoothly swept up over the classical roundness of her head, and her whole air so right, so sensible. Outside in the streets, against the background of wealth and luxury, an endless procession of dashing courtesans went past, perched high in their phaetons, coming back into Paris and its noisy boulevards. And Fanny did not seem to feel any regret for that glittering, triumphant vice that she could have had her share in and had disdained for his sake. So long as he agreed to see her from time to time she would be content with her life of servitude and even find it had its amusing side.

All the inmates of the boarding-house were very fond of her. The women, all foreigners without a shred of taste, consulted her as to what clothes they should buy; every morning she gave singing-lessons to the eldest of the Peruvian girls; she advised the men about the books to read and the plays to see, and they all treated her with the greatest of respect and attention, particularly the Dutchman on the second floor. 'He sits down there where you are and gazes at me till I say: "Kuyper, you're getting on my nerves." Then he says: "Goot" and off he goes. He gave me this little coral brooch. It's not worth more than a franc, you know. I just took it to keep him quiet.'

A waiter came in carrying a laid tray, which he put down on the edge of the side-table, pushing the potted plant to one side. 'This is where I have my meals by myself, an hour before the table d'hôte.' She pointed to two dishes on the long and varied menu, for the manageress was only entitled to two courses and soup. 'Rosario can't help being stingy, you know. Anyway, I'd rather have my meals like this. I don't have to talk to anyone and I read your letters over again. That's company for me.'

She broke off to get a tablecloth and napkins. She was constantly being disturbed, with orders to be given, a cupboard to be opened, a complaint to be dealt with. Jean realized that he would be in her way if he stayed longer. Then her dinner was brought, and the little soup tureen with the soup for one looked so paltry, steaming there on the table, that they both thought regretfully of how they used to sit down to their meals together at home.

'Till Sunday—Sunday!' she murmured, almost whispering, as she sent him away. And as they could not kiss because of the servants and the boarders coming downstairs, she took his hand and laid it against her breast, pressing it there as though in this way she would be able to keep the touch of it in her heart.

All that evening and all that night he thought of her, grieved by her humiliating servitude to that trollop and her fat lizard. He was perturbed at the thought of the Dutchman too, and could hardly live until Sunday. In reality this partial rupture that was supposed to smooth the way for the ending of their liaison was more like the snipping with the pruning-knife that makes a tired tree revive. They wrote to each other almost every day, the sort of fond notes that impatient lovers are always scribbling; or sometimes when he left the Ministry he would go and sit with her in her office and they would chat quietly as she bent her head over her needlework.

To the other inmates of the boarding-house she referred to him as 'a relation of mine' and under cover of this vague description he sometimes came and spent the evening in the sitting-room, feeling as though he were a thousand miles away from Paris. He got to know the Peruvian family with the innumerable daughters, all frightfully attired in shrieking colours and dotted round the sitting-room, for all the world like macaws on their perches. He heard Fräulein Minna Vogel's zither, which was wreathed in ribbons like a maypole, and saw her sick brother, almost voiceless now, rapturously nodding his head in time to the music as he fingered an imaginary clarinet, for he was forbidden to play a real one. He had a game of whist with Fanny's Dutchman, a big, bald, heavy, dismal-looking lump of a man who had sailed the seven seas, and who, when he was asked something about Australia, where he had recently spent some months, rolled up his eyes and said: 'You know what cost at Melbourne the potatoes?' The only thing that had made an impression on him was this solitary fact: how dear potatoes were in every country where he went.

Fanny was the life and soul of these gatherings, chatting, singing, and generally playing the well-informed Parisian woman of the world; and whatever traces of Bohemianism, the manners of the artist's studio, still clung to her, it was not apparent to these foreigners, or it struck them as the *real thing*. She dazzled them with talk of the famous people she had known in the world of art and literature, telling the Russian lady, who had a passion for Dejoie's works, about the novelist's method of writing, the number of cups of coffee he would drink in a night, and the exact ridiculous figure that the publishers of *Cenderinette* had paid for the masterpiece that made their fortune. And his mistress's social success made Gaussin so proud that he forgot to be jealous and would gladly have borne witness to the truth of all she said, had anyone doubted it.

While he was admiring her in this peaceful sitting-room lit by shaded lamps, watching her pouring out tea or accompanying the songs the girls sang and playing the big sister to them, there was a special secret delight in imagining her quite differently, as she was when she came to him on Sunday morning, drenched and shivering, and, without even going near to the fire flaming away in her honour, undressing as fast as she could and slipping into the big bed, next to him. What embracings there were then, what long raptures, their vengeance for a whole week's constraints and the separation that kept their desire alive, the essence of their love!

The hours would pass away, one fading into the next; they did not get out of bed till evening. There was nothing else that could tempt them: no pleasure, nobody they wanted to see, not even the Hettémas, who had decided to go and live in the country for the sake of economy. With their little luncheon all ready on the bed-side-table, they would lie there lost to the world, listening to the murmur of the Sunday crowds slopping through the streets of Paris, and the whistling of the trains, the rumble of cabs filled to bursting; and the rain drumming in big drops on the zinc of the balcony roof, and the hasty beating of their hearts, marked their remoteness from the rest of life, without a notion of the time, till dusk.

Then the gas would be lighted opposite and send its wan beam across the ceiling; then they would have to get up, for Fanny had to be back by seven o'clock. In the half-light of the bedroom all her weariness and sick disgust came over her again, weighing more heavily, more cruelly now as she put on her little boots, still wet from her walk there in the morning, and her petticoat and her manageress's dress, the black uniform worn by all poor women.

And what made her heart swell with bitterness was the sight of the dear accustomed things around her, the furniture, the little dressing-table that belonged to happier days. She tore herself away, saying: 'Come on!' And so that they should be together as long as possible, Jean saw her back to the hotel; they would walk up the Champs-Élysées together, slowly, with linked arms, very close, the double row of street-lamps leading away to the Arc-de-Triomphe at the top, lonely in the darkness, and two or three stars twinkling in a patch of sky, like a background in a diorama. At the corner of the Rue Pergolèse, only a few steps from the boarding-house, she raised her veil for one last kiss and so left him—suddenly bewildered and lost, dreading his room, to which he returned as late as possible, cursing his poverty, almost bearing a grudge against his people at Castelet because of the sacrifice he had made for them.

For two or three months they dragged on in this way, gradually coming to feel that such an existence was absolutely unendurable; for Jean had had to cut down his visits to the boarding-house on account of some talk among the servants, and Fanny was more and more exasperated by the miserliness of the Sanchès mother and daughter. She had secret thoughts of going back to a little apartment together, and she could feel that her lover was at the end of his tether too; but she wanted him to be the first to speak.

One Sunday in April Fanny arrived more smartly dressed than usual, wearing a hat and a spring dress that was simple enough—for she had little money to spend—but cut to show off the graceful lines of her body.

'Get up quickly, we're going to have lunch in the country.'
'In the country!'
'Yes, at Enghien, at Rosa's. She's invited us both.' At first he said
no, but she insisted: Rosa would never forgive a refusal. 'You might
come for my sake. I do enough, I should think.'

The place was by the lake at Enghien and looked out on a vast
lawn sweeping down to a little boat-house where some rowing-
boats and punts were moored, swaying lightly on the water. The
house itself was a large chalet, marvellously decorated and furnished,
with mirrors let into the ceilings and walls to reflect the sparkle of
the water and the superb young hornbeams growing in the park,
already a-quiver with the first hurried touches of green, and the
flowering lilac. There were servants in immaculate livery; there
were walks where not a twig lay on the ground; it was a credit to
Rosario's and old Pilar's joint vigilance.

The rest of the party was at table when they arrived, for they had
been misdirected and had wasted time going all round the lake,
along little paths between high garden walls. Jean was completely
put out of countenance by the chilly welcome given them by the
mistress of the house, who was furious at having been kept waiting,
and by the extraordinary appearance of the hags, looking like the
Fatal Sisters themselves, to whom Rosa introduced him, her voice
hoarse as a drayman's. They were three *élégantes*, as the most expensive cocottes referred to themselves: three ancient whores who
had been among the most brilliant figures of the Second Empire,
with names as famous as any great poet's or any victorious general's
—Wilkie Cob, Sombreuse, and Clara Desfous.

The *élégantes* were smart enough even now, certainly, got up to
the nines in the latest fashion, in pale summery colours, all exquisite
lace and ribbons from their little collars down to their little boots.
Only how withered, how raddled and frizzed! There Sombreuse
sat with blank, lashless eyes, her lower lip hanging, and fumbled
about with plate, fork, or glass. La Desfous was a vast blotchy-
looking woman with a hot-water bottle at her feet and her poor
gnarled rheumatic fingers spread out on the tablecloth to show off
her glittering rings, which were as difficult to get on and off as the

G—S.

rings of a Chinese puzzle. Cob was very slim, but her youthful figure only made her lean fleshless face seem more horrible than ever; with her mop of yellow tow-like hair she looked like a sick clown. Ruined and desperate, she had gone to try a last fling at Monte Carlo and had come back without a penny, frantic with love for a handsome croupier who had not wanted to have anything to do with her. Rosa had taken her in and fed her and was making a great boast of it.

All these women knew Fanny, whom they greeted with a patron-izingly friendly: 'Well, how are things, dear?' The fact was that in her dress made of stuff costing three francs a yard and with no jewel but Kuyper's red brooch, she looked like a raw recruit among these ghastly old women who had long ago won their stripes on the field of amorous adventure and who looked more spectral than ever framed in this luxurious setting, the light reflected from lake and sky, and the air coming in through the dining-room windows, gusty with scents of spring.

There was also old Mother Pilar, 'the monkey,' as she called herself, talking her broken French interlarded with Spanish. Indeed she looked a thorough macacus, with her loose, rough skin and an expression of ferocious spite on her face, always grimacing, her hair cut short like a man's and grey over her ears. Her old black satin dress was topped with a big blue collar like a master mariner's.

'And last but not least, Monsieur Bichito,' Rosa said after intro-ducing all her guests, and showed Gaussin a bundle of pink cotton-wool on the tablecloth, with the chameleon shivering in it.

'Well, and what about me, eh? Am I not to be introduced?' came an exclamation in tones of forced joviality from a big man with a grizzled moustache, very correctly, even rather formally dressed, in his light-coloured jacket and high stiff collar.

'That's true. What about Tatave?' the women cried, laughing.

The mistress of the house dropped his name casually.

Tatave was none other than de Potter, the eminent composer, celebrated for his *Claudia* and *Savonarola*. Jean, who had only caught a glimpse of him at Déchelette's, was astonished to see how far from genial the great man looked, his face like a hard, regular-featured wooden mask, his faded eyes showing signs of the crazed, incurable passion that had made him cling to this trollop for years, making him leave his wife and children in order to be a hanger-on in this house that he had bought with part of the considerable fortune he had made in the theatre, this house in which he was treated worse than a servant. It was startling to see the annoyed air Rosa assumed the moment he began to tell a story, and the contemptuous tone in which she ordered him to be quiet. And Pilar never failed to outdo her daughter by adding firmly:

'Shutta your trap, my lad.'

Jean was sitting next to this old woman; and the old chops smacking, and the grunting, as of an animal at its feed, and the inquisitorial glances shot at his plate, were torture to him, already embarrassed enough by the condescending manner in which Rosa treated Fanny, teasing her about the musical evenings at the hotel and the gullibility of those silly fools of foreigners who took the manageress for a society woman fallen on evil days. The one-time circus queen, now unhealthily fat and puffy, with uncut stones worth ten thousand francs dangling in each ear, seemed to envy her friend the renewal of youth and beauty that she drew from this young and handsome lover. And, far from being put out, Fanny kept them all amused, making fun of the inmates of the boarding-house—the Peruvian who had turned up the whites of his eyes as he confessed that he was dying to know *a really important cocotte*, and the silent, walrus-like snuffling attentions paid her by the Dutch-man, who would lean over her chair from behind, gustily breathing into her ear: 'Guess how much cost in Batavia the potatoes?'

But Gaussin hardly laughed at all. Nor did Pilar, who was busy keeping an eye on her daughter's silver or reaching out abruptly, grabbing at a fly on her plate or on her neighbour's sleeve, and presenting it to the chameleon with a muttered gibberish of endearments: 'Eaty up, *mi alma*, eaty up, *mi corazon*,' while the hideous little animal lay flopped on the tablecloth, withered, wrinkled, and shapeless as la Desfous's fingers.

Sometimes, when all the flies were routed, she would notice one on the dresser or on the glass of the door and get up and go and seize it triumphantly. This often repeated performance irritated her daughter, who was obviously in a very nervous condition that morning. She exclaimed:

'Don't keep getting up every other minute! It makes me tired.'

In exactly the same voice, only two degrees stronger as to foreign accent, the mother replied: 'You are all eating, *bos otros*, so why should not he eat, the little one?'

'Leave the table or keep quiet. You get on our nerves.'

The old woman bridled up, and then the two of them began to swear at each other with all the resources that devout Spaniards have, mingling references to the devil and hell with the invective of the gutter:

'*Hija del demonio!*'

'*Cuerno de Satanas!*'

'*Puta!*'

'*Mi madre!*'

Jean gazed at them in horror, while the other guests, who were used to such family scenes, calmly went on eating. Only de Potter intervened out of regard for the stranger:

'I say, look, don't quarrel!'

But Rosa spun round on him furiously. 'What are you butting in for, eh? That's a nice way to behave! Can't I talk if I like? You go home to your wife if that's what things have come to! I've had enough of you staring at me like a dying duck in a thunderstorm, and seeing your bald head all over the place. Go on back to your goose of a wife! It's high time.'

De Potter smiled, rather pale, and murmured under his moustache: 'Fancy having to live with that!'

'It's just about all you're worth!' she yelled, leaning right over the table towards him. 'You know the door's open—clear out—out you go!'

'Look here, Rosa,' he pleaded, a pathetic look in his lack-lustre eyes. And Mother Pilar, who had begun to eat again, said 'Shutta your trap, my lad!' with such comical stolidity that everyone burst out laughing, even Rosa, even de Potter, who kissed his mistress although she was still grumbling and then, to complete his restoration to her good graces, caught a fly and, holding it by the wings, delicately presented it to Bichito.

So this was de Potter, the renowned composer, the pride of French music! How was it this woman held him? What spells had she woven, coarsened and aged with debauchery as she was, with that mother abetting her in infamy and showing what she would be like in another twenty years' time, a distorted reflection as in a witch-ball?

Coffee was served beside the lake, in a little shell-work grotto draped inside with pale silk that held flickering gleams, as though shot with the rippling of the nearby water—one of those exquisite dovecots that originated in eighteenth-century romances, with a mirror in the ceiling, reflecting the poses of the ancient Fates. They had spread out their skirts on the wide divan and lolled there in a post-prandial swoon, while Rosa, her cheeks bright under the rouge, stretched her arms out behind her, pressing up against her lover, the composer, and murmuring:

'Oh, my dear Tatave! My darling Tatave!'

But this amorous warmth evaporated with the warmth of the Chartreuse; and, one of the women having been struck by the idea of going out in a boat, she sent de Potter off to make preparations.

'The boat, mind! Not the punt!'

'Supposing I told Désiré——'

'Désiré's having his meal.'

'The fact is, the boat's full of water. It'll have to be baled out, and it's quite a job.'

'Jean'll go with you, de Potter,' Fanny said, seeing that another scene was on the way.

Sitting on seats opposite each other in the boat, their knees wide apart, they got on with the baling-out at a brisk pace, neither talking nor glancing at each other, as though hypnotized by the rhythm of the water spirting out of the two scoops. They were in the shade of a big catalpa that cast its scented coolness over them, standing out against the lake waters all a-twinkle with sunshine.

'Have you been living with Fanny for long?' the composer asked suddenly, pausing in his labour.

'Two years,' Gaussin replied, rather surprised.

'Only two years! Then what you've seen to-day may be of some use to you. Look at me now—it's twenty years that I've been living with Rosa, twenty years since I came back from Italy after my three Prix de Rome years there, and went to the Hippodrome one night and saw her standing up in her little chariot, just turning the corner of the track, coming straight at me, her whip in the air, her helmet wreathed in serpents and her gilded coat of mail locked round her, reaching halfway down her thighs. Oh, if anyone could have told me . . .'

Bending down and going on with his scooping, he began to tell the story of how his family had at first made fun of the affair; then, as it became more serious, what efforts they had made, how they had begged and pleaded, what sacrifices they were ready to make to put an end to it. Two or three times she had left him, having been bought off, but he had always gone after her. 'Let us try travelling,' his mother said. So he travelled, came back and took up with the woman again. Then he let himself be married off: a good-looking girl, a rich dowry, and the prospect of membership of the Institute among the wedding presents. . . . And three months later he left his new home to go back to the old affair. 'Oh, young man, young man! . . .'

He told the story of his life in a hard, dull voice, not a muscle quivering in his mask-like face, rigid as the starched collar that held his head so straight. And boats sailed by, crowded with students and girls, overflowing with song, young laughter, and ecstasy. How many of those unsuspecting beings would have done well to pause and take their share of his terrible lesson!

Meanwhile in the grotto the old *élégantes* were trying to make Fanny Legrand see reason, preaching to her as though it had been agreed that they would all do their best to bring about the end of this affair. 'Nice boy, of course—but not a penny. Where will it get her?'

'But you see, the thing is—I love him!'

Rosa shrugged her shoulders. 'Let her alone. She'll go and make a mess of her Dutchman just the way I've seen her mess up all the good things she was on to. I must say, after that affair with Flamant she did try to have some sense, but now she's crazier than ever.'

'*Ay, vellaca!*' Mother Pilar muttered.

The Englishwoman with the clown's head intervened to say with the horrible accent that had for so long made her a success:

'It's all very well being in love with love, pet. Love's a very nice thing, of course. But you've got to love money too. Now take me, if I were still rich, would my croupier go and say I'm ugly—what do you think?' She gave a start of rage and raised her voice shrilly: 'Oh, it's terrible, though! Terrible, the way it is with things! First you're famous and popular and known to everyone, like a monument, like a boulevard—so famous that there wouldn't be one single wretched cabbie who wouldn't know the way if you just said: Wilkie Cob! And I had princes at my feet too, and kings, and if I spat on the floor, they said it was pretty to look at! And now there's that rotten blackguard who wouldn't have anything to do with me because he said I was ugly, and I hadn't even the money to get him for a single night!'

And beside herself at the thought that anyone should find her ugly, she whipped her dress open, crying:

'My face, yes, all right, I grant you that. But what about my breast, my shoulders? It's white, isn't it? It's firm, isn't it?'

Unashamed, she revealed her bewitching flesh, still miraculously youthful after thirty years in the fires of debauchery, while the head poised above it was shrivelled and macabre down to the neck-line.

'Ladies! The boat's ready!' de Potter called.

And hooking her dress up again over all that was left of her youth, the Englishwoman muttered in comical despair:

'But after all I can't walk about the streets stark naked!'

In this setting, like a picture by Lancret, where the dainty whiteness of the villas sparkled out among the fresh greenery, and terraces and lawns framed the little lake all flaked with sunlight, what an embarkation it was—what an aged and limping Cythera it was, the blind Sombreuse, and the old clown, and Desfous the paralytic, leaving in their wake, as they floated over the water, the musk-like perfume of their powder and their rouge. . . .

Jean took the oars and rowed, with bent back, ashamed and wretched at the thought that people seeing him might think he played some vile part in this gloomy allegorical boat. Fortunately, for the refreshment of his heart and eyes, he had Fanny Legrand sitting opposite him, in the stern, beside the tiller that de Potter held—Fanny whose smile had never seemed so young, doubtless by contrast.

'Sing us something, dear,' la Desfous asked, made sentimental by the spring air.

In her deep, expressive voice Fanny began the barcarolle from *Claudia*, and, stirred by this reminiscence of his first great success, the composer joined in, humming the pattern woven by the orchestra, that rippling that went over and under the melody like sunlight on dancing water. At this hour, and in this setting, it was delightful. From a neighbouring terrace someone shouted: 'Bravo!' And the Provençal, keeping time with the oars, thirsted for the music's beauty on his mistress's lips and felt a longing to put his mouth to that upswelling spring and drink of it in the sun, his head flung back, for ever.

Suddenly Rosa could no longer endure the marriage of these two voices and interrupted the cantilena with an infuriated outburst: 'Hi, you with your concert! Haven't you had enough of warbling away at each other? You needn't think it's any fun for us listening to your old dirge. That's enough of it now. Anyway, it's late, it's time for Fanny to go back to the dump.' And with an enraged wave of her arm towards the nearest landing-stage, she said to her lover: 'Put ashore there. It'll be nearer to the station for them.'

It was a brutal enough dismissal; but the former circus queen had made her acquaintances used to her manners, and nobody dared protest. Once the couple was put on shore, after a few cold conventional words to the young man and some orders hissed at Fanny, the boat glided away again, its cargo all an outcry of wrangling voices that ended in an insulting burst of laughter borne back across the still surface of the water.

'Do you hear, do you hear!' Fanny said, white with rage. 'She's laughing at us! At us!'

And all her humiliations, all her rancour rising up at this last insult, she poured it all out to him on their way to the station, admitting even those things that she had always kept from him. Rosa was bent on getting her away from him, bent on providing opportunities for her to be unfaithful. 'You should have heard all the things she said to make me have that Dutchman! Only just now they all made a set at me about it. I love you too much, you see, and that's a nuisance to her with her vices, for she's got them all, the worst you can think of, the most monstrous things. And because I won't do it any more . . .'

She broke off, seeing how pale he was, his lips trembling as they had that evening when he had stirred up the dunghill of the letters.

'Oh, you needn't be frightened,' she said. 'Your love has cured me of all those dreadful things. I'm absolutely sick of her and her beastly chameleon—they're both disgusting.'

'I don't wish you to stay there any longer,' he said, maddened by morbid jealousy. 'There's too much foulness mixed up in the bread you earn. You shall come back to me. We'll manage somehow.'

She had been waiting for this cry, had for a long time been trying to bring him to it. And yet she resisted, objecting that they would be hard put to it, living together on his salary of three hundred francs, and that they might have to separate once again. 'And it upset me so dreadfully, leaving our poor house!'

There were seats here and there under the acacias along the edge of the road, where high in the telegraph-wires the swallows poised. To talk the better, they sat down, both deeply moved, their arms linked.

'Three hundred francs a month,' Jean said. 'But how do the Hettémas manage? They've only got two hundred and fifty.'

'They live in the country all the year round, out at Chaville.'

'Well, we'll do the same. I don't care for Paris.'

'Truly? You really would? Oh, sweetheart, sweetheart!'

A crowd of people was coming along the road, a galloping of donkeys bearing away the remnants of a wedding-party. They could not kiss now, and sat quite still, pressed close up against each other, dreaming of happiness renewed in the long summer evenings that would have that sylvan sweetness, that mild calm now and then enlivened by distant rifle-shots or hurdy-gurdy music from some scene of rustic rejoicings.

8

THEY moved to Chaville, between the low-lying country and the hills, on that old forest road called the Woodman's Walk, and settled down in a former hunting-box on the very edge of the woods. There were three rooms hardly bigger than those in Paris, and all the same furniture, the rush-bottomed armchair, the painted wardrobe, and, to adorn the frightful green wallpaper in their bedroom, nothing but Fanny's portrait, for the photograph of Castelet had been smashed in its frame during the move and was now fading up in the loft, among the rafters.

They hardly spoke of poor old Castelet any more since uncle and niece had broken off their correspondence.

'A slippery customer, I must say,' she would remark, remembering The Rip's readiness to assist the first break. Only the little girls kept their brother supplied with news; Divonne had stopped writing. Perhaps she still bore some resentment against her nephew; or perhaps she guessed that the bad woman had come back to tear open and comment on her simple, motherly letters written in big, round, peasant handwriting.

There were times when they could almost have believed themselves still in the Rue d'Amsterdam, when they woke up to hear the singing of the Hettémas, now once more their neighbours, and the whistling of the trains continually passing up or down the line on the other side of the road, glimpsed through the branches of trees in a large park. But instead of the wan glass roof of the Gare de l'Ouest, with the uncurtained windows where the clerks could be seen hunched over their desks, and the rumbling roar from the steep street, they had all the wide, green silence to enjoy, the open space beyond their little orchard with other gardens beyond, little houses among clumps of trees, all sliding away down to the bottom of the hill.

Before he left in the morning Jean breakfasted in their little dining-room, the window open on to the wide paved road, which had patches of grass showing up here and there and was bordered by hedges of white hawthorn with its sweet, sad perfume. That was the way he went on his ten minutes' walk to the station, along the edge of the teeming, rustling park; and when he came home at night the murmur of it all was growing still, the shadows creeping from the coppice over the moss of the green road, now crimsoned in the sunset, and the cuckoos calling from every quarter of the woods, mingled with the trilling of nightingales among the ivy.

But once they had settled down and his astonishment at the quietness of things around him had passed off, he once more began to feel the torments of barren, questing jealousy. His mistress's quarrel with Rosa and the departure from the boarding-house had brought about a dreadfully suggestive laying of all cards on the table, reviving all his suspicions, his most disturbing anxieties; and when he went to town he would look out of the train at their one-storeyed house, one floor with a round dormer-window above, and try to pierce the walls with his gaze. 'Who knows?' he would think to himself. And the thought haunted him even in his office, among the papers and red-tape.

Coming home in the evening, he would make her give him a detailed account of how she had spent her day, and of everything that had gone through her mind, no matter how uninteresting it generally was, and would startle her with a 'What are you thinking about? Quick!' always fearing that she might be regretting something or someone belonging to that dreadful past, to which she always confessed with the same imperturbable frankness.

Only while they were not seeing each other except on Sundays, hungering for each other, he had had no time for these moral inquisitions that were as outrageous as they were minute. But now that they were together again, in the continuity of their joint life, they tormented each other even in their embraces, in the intensest moments of their love-making, stirred by a muffled anger and the aching awareness of something gone irreparably wrong: he always exhausted himself in trying to give this woman, hardened in all the ways of love, some surge of experience she had never known before, and she ready to sacrifice herself in any way to give him a delight that had not already been the lot of ten others, and not succeeding, and weeping with helpless rage.

Then a time came when they inwardly relaxed; perhaps it was from sensual satiety in the cool enveloping atmosphere of nature, or perhaps nothing more than having the Hettémas near them. For of all the households camping out there on the outskirts of Paris, perhaps there was never one that so much enjoyed the little liberties of country life, the joy of going about dressed in their oldest clothes, in straw hats, madame uncorseted and monsieur in rope-soled sandals—getting up from meals to take the crusts out to the ducks and the scraps to the rabbits, and then weeding, raking, grafting, watering. . . .

Oh, the watering of the garden! . . .

The Hettémas set about it the moment he came home and changed out of his office suit into a coat like Robinson Crusoe's. They went back to it after dinner; and long after night had fallen, in the darkness of the little garden, from which there came the cold clean smell of wet soil, one could hear the squeaking of the pump, the clattering and banging of the big watering-cans, and great panting sighs wandering from one flower-bed to another, accompanied by a trickling sound, as though it were the sweat from the toilers' foreheads that trickled out of the roses of their watering-cans, and then from time to time a cry of triumph:

'I've given these greedy peas thirty-two lots!'

'I've given the balsam fourteen!'

They were people who were not content merely to be happy, but liked to roll their happiness on the tongue and taste it, until it was enough to make one's mouth water: especially the husband, with his irresistible way of talking about the delights of a cosy winter just for two.

'This is all very well now, but wait till you see what it's like in December! You come home all splashed and muddy, fed up with all the worries there are in Paris. You come home to a good fire and the lamp lit, the soup steaming sweetly and underneath the table a pair of clogs stuffed with straw. Ah, let me tell you, when you've tucked into a plateful of cabbage and sausages and a chunk of

Gruyère that's been kept fresh in a cloth, and pour yourself out on top of that a pint of something that hasn't been through the excise, how good it is to pull your armchair up to the fire, light your pipe and drink your coffee laced with a little brandy for the sweetness of it and have a little snooze there, the two of you, one on each side of the fire, while the rain drips and freezes outside on the window-panes. . . . Just a tiny little snooze, just long enough for digestion to get well under way. After that you do a bit of drawing while the wife clears the table and potters round, turns down the quilt and puts the warming-pan in the bed. . . . And when she's got into bed and warmed it up, you bundle in too, and your whole body begins to toast, it's just as if you'd got right down into one of your own clogs with the straw in it.'

He became almost eloquent in praise of the corporeal joys—this great hairy, heavy-jawed man who was generally so diffident that he could hardly speak at all without blushing and stammering.

This exaggerated timidity, so comical a contrast to his gigantic breadth and that black beard of his, had been the making of his marriage and his quiet life. At twenty-five, when he had been bursting with health and vigour, Hettéma had known nothing of love or of women, when one day after a club dinner at Nevers his companions dragged him off to a disorderly house, too drunk to know what he was doing, and forced him to make his choice. He left the place shocked and stunned, then went back, picked the same girl out again, paid her debts, carried her off and, terrified at the notion that someone might take her from him and that he would then have to begin all over again with a fresh conquest, he ended up by marrying her.

'All legally married, my dear,' Fanny would say, with a triumphant laugh that it shocked Jean to hear. 'And of all the legal marriages I've known, it's by far the most honest and decent one.'

She made the assertion in all the sincerity of her ignorance; for doubtless the legally respectable households that she had been able to see inside deserved no other judgment. All her notions about life were as wrong and as sincere as this one.

There was something soothing in having the Hettémas near; for they were always even-tempered, as well as being ready to do little favours that did not put them out overmuch, and with a horror of scenes—the sort of quarrels in which they might become involved —and in general of anything that might upset good digestion. The wife tried to initiate Fanny into the keeping of hens and rabbits and the healthy delights of watering the garden: but in vain.

Gaussin's mistress, who had come from the back-streets of Paris by way of Bohemian life, had no particular love of the country except in fits and starts, as a place for picnics, where one could romp and shout and go off with one's lover and get lost. She hated all exertion; she hated work. And the six months she had spent as manageress of the boarding-house had exhausted her energy for a long time to come, so that she sank quietly into a vague torpor, an intoxicated sense of well-being, dreamy in the open air, with hardly strength enough to dress herself or do her hair, even to open her piano.

The housework being left entirely to a country girl, when evening came and she summed up her day to tell Jean all about it, she could not find a trace of anything beyond a call from Olympe Hettéma, a bit of gossip over the fence, and cigarettes, the heaps of cigarettes that left a trail of ash and stubs on the marble hearth. Six o'clock already! There was scarcely time to slip into a dress and pin a flower on her breast before she went along the green road to meet him.

But with the coming of the autumn mists and rain, and darkness falling early, she had more than one pretext for not going out; and he would often come home to find her still wearing one of those big loose white woollen *gandouras* that she put on in the morning, and her hair tucked up just as it had been when he went out. He thought she looked charming like this, the nape of her neck still girlish, her skin smooth and tempting, a pulsing in the untrammelled flesh. Yet the decline in standards shocked him and frightened him, like a danger looming up.

He had indeed exerted himself tremendously to make some slight increase to their resources without having to apply to Castelet, and spent whole evenings over plans, reproductions of pieces of artillery, caissons, and new models of rifles that he drew for Hettéma; but suddenly he felt himself attacked by the dissolving influence of country life and solitude, an influence to which even the strongest and most active surrender and to which he was specially susceptible, the enervating seeds of it having been implanted in him by a childhood spent in the remote depths of the country.

And to this came their stout neighbours' wallowing in material things, which was communicated to them in the perpetual goings and comings from house to house, together with something of the Hettémas' moral abasement and monstrous appetite, until Gaussin and his mistress themselves reached the stage of solemnly discussing problems of meals and when to go to bed. Césaire sent them a hogshead of his pond-water wine, whereupon they spent a whole Sunday running it off into bottles, the door of their little cellar wide open to the year's last sunshine and a blue sky adrift with clouds pink as the heather in the woods. It would not be long now till the time came for clogs stuffed with warm straw, and the little after-dinner nap, one on each side of the log fire. Fortunately something happened to distract them.

One evening he found her in a state of profound excitement. Olympe had just told her the story of a poor child who had been brought up by a grandmother in the Morvan district: the father and mother, timber-merchants in Paris, had stopped writing and had not sent any money for months. Now the grandmother had suddenly died and some barge-people had brought the little boy along, up the Yonne canal, to hand him over to his parents; but there was nobody to be found. The timber-yard was shut, the mother had gone off with a lover, the drunken father had gone bankrupt and disappeared. There was a respectable legal marriage for you! And there was the poor little creature, six years old, such a love, with nothing to eat, and no clothes, all alone in the world.

She was moved to the point of tears, but then suddenly asked:

'How about taking him? What do you say?'

'Madness!'

'Why?' And coming very close, wheedling, she began: 'You know how I've always wanted to have a child of yours. We could bring him up like our own, we could make something of him. After a time these children that are picked up like that—you get as fond of them in time as if they were your own. . . .'

And she pleaded the interest that it would provide for her, alone all day, growing dull and stupid, always mulling over the same wretched, hateful thoughts. A child was a safeguard. Then, seeing that he was frightened by the expense, she said: 'And of course it would hardly cost anything at all! Just think—he's only six! We'll make his clothes out of your cast-offs. Olympe knows all about it and she swears we wouldn't even notice it.'

'Why doesn't she take him then?' Jean asked, with the ill-humour of a man who feels himself defeated by his own weakness. Nevertheless he still put up some resistance, making use of the decisive argument: 'And how about when I'm gone?' He rarely spoke of the time when he would go away, in order not to depress Fanny, but he thought of it often enough and used it as a way of reassuring himself in the face of the dangers this ménage implied and the gloomy confidences of de Potter. 'What a complication a child would be! What a burden for you in the future!'

Fanny's eyes became veiled. 'That's where you're wrong, sweetheart. It would be someone to talk to about you, a consolation, and a responsibility too. It would give me the strength to work, it would give me something to live for.'

He considered for a minute, seeing her all alone in the empty house.

'Where is the child?'

'At Bas-Meudon, with a barge-man who's taken him home for a few days. After that it'll be the workhouse.'

'Very well, go and get him, if it means so much to you.'

She flung her arms round his neck. And all that evening she was childishly happy, and played the piano, and sang, enraptured, exuberant, quite transfigured.

The next morning in the train Jean mentioned the matter to fat Hettéma, who seemed to know all about it, though wishing not to

H—S.

be involved in any way. Hunched up in his corner of the carriage, behind his outspread newspaper, he stammered into his beard:

'Yes, I know—it's the ladies—none of my business.' And peering over the top of the paper for an instant, he said: 'Your wife seems to be very romantic.'

Romantic or not, she was at her wits' end that evening, kneeling down with a plate of soup in one hand, trying to tame the little boy from Morvan. The child was standing with his back to the wall, hiding his face, his head all a shock of fair hair, and stubbornly refusing to talk or eat or even look at her, only saying over and over again in a loud, monotonous, choked voice:

'Want Ménine. Want Ménine.'

'Ménine's his grandmother, I suppose. I haven't been able to get another thing out of him for the last two hours.'

Jean joined in the attempt to make him eat his soup, but without success. There the two of them stayed kneeling beside him, the one holding the plate, the other the spoon, as though they were tending a sick lamb. They repeated all the encouraging and affectionate remarks they could think of, trying to talk him over.

'Let's sit down, perhaps we're frightening him. He'll eat if we stop looking at him.'

But he went on standing there, quite still, as though stupefied, keeping up his plaint like a little wild animal. 'Want Ménine,' he went on whimpering, rending their hearts, until at last he fell asleep where he stood leaning against the sideboard—so soundly asleep that they were able to undress him and put him to bed in the heavy peasant-style swing-cot they had borrowed from a neighbour, and he did not even open his eyes.

'Look how lovely he is,' Fanny said, very proud of her acquisition. And she made Gaussin admire the obstinate forehead, the thin, delicate features with their outdoor tan, and the perfection of the little body with the sturdy flanks, strong arms, and the legs of a little faun, long and springy and already touched with down. She lost herself in contemplation of this childish beauty.

'Cover him up, he'll be cold,' Jean said. The sound of his voice made her start, as though wakening her from a dream. And as she drew the blankets tenderly over him, the little boy uttered long, sobbing sighs, a deep welling up of despair even in sleep.

And in the night he began to talk in his sleep:

'*Guerlaudé mé—Ménine!*'

'What is he saying? Listen.'

He wanted to be *guerlaudé*. But what did the dialect word mean? At random Jean stretched out one arm and began to rock the heavy cradle. As he did so the child became quieter and fell asleep again, clutching in his strong little chapped hand the hand that he believed was his *Ménine's*, a fortnight dead.

It was like having a wild cat in the house, scratching, biting, and eating on his own, growling whenever anyone came near his plate. The few words that could be got out of him belonged to an out-landish dialect spoken by the Morvan woodcutters, a language that nobody would have been able to understand, had it not been that the Hettémas came from the same part of the country. Gradually, by means of care and kindliness, they managed to tame him some-what. He allowed them to change the rags in which he had been brought to them for warm, clean clothes, the mere sight of which had driven him into a frenzy of rage in the first few days—a jackal refusing to be dressed up in a lapdog's little coat. He learnt to eat at table, learnt how to use a fork and a spoon, and to answer, when he was asked his name, that in the country he had been called 'Josaph'.

As for giving him any lessons, it was far too soon even to think of that. He had been brought up in the depths of the forest, in a charcoal-burner's hut, and the murmur of nature's rustling and swarming still echoed in his hard little woodland-dweller's skull, like the sound of the sea in the spirallings of a top-shell; and there was no way of getting anything else into his head or of keeping him in the house even in the wildest of weather. In the rain, and in the snow, when the leafless trees stood coralled with rime, he would slip out, thrashing his way through the undergrowth, burrowing into the rabbit-holes with the deft cruel ways of a ferret out for blood; and when he came in, weak with hunger, mud-splashed up to his waist, tucked into his tattered fustian jacket or in the pocket of his little trousers there was always some creature either stunned or dead, bird, mole, or fieldmouse, or, failing that, beet or potatoes torn out of the ground, out in the fields.

Nothing could check his poacher's marauding instincts, which were complicated by a rustic mania for pocketing every sort of little shiny object, brass buttons, jet beads, silver paper from the wrappings round chocolate—all such things Josaph would pick up, closing his fist round them and carrying them off to hiding-places he had, like a thieving magpie. To all this plunder he gave the vague generic name of 'vittles'; and no amount of reasoning, or cuffing, would stop him from collecting his 'vittles' at the expense of everyone and everything.

Only the Hettémas had a way of dealing with the situation. Just within reach, on the table round which the little wild creature would prowl, attracted by the compasses and coloured crayons, Hettéma kept a dog-whip, which he would flick at his legs. But neither Jean nor Fanny would have made use of such threats, although the child's attitude to them was sly and mistrustful and he would not be tamed even by their fond attempts to spoil him; it was as though his *ménine* in dying had robbed him of all capacity for affection. Fanny, because she 'stank nice,' could sometimes manage to keep him on her lap for a short while, but although Jean was always very gentle, with him the child remained the little wild beast that he had been when he first came, with furtive eyes and claws ready to scratch.

This invincible and, as it seemed, instinctive repulsion on the child's part, and the curious malice in his little blue eyes with the albino lashes, and above all Fanny's sudden blind affection for the stranger who had suddenly dropped into their life, troubled Jean with a new suspicion. Perhaps the child was her own, brought up by foster-parents or by her stepmother; and when news of Machaume's death came about that same time, it seemed coincidence enough to increase his torment. Sometimes at night when he was holding the little hand that clutched so hard at his—for in the vague realms of sleep and dream the child continued to believe he was reaching out to his *ménine*—he would ask the unspoken questions that loomed up out of the trouble in his inmost heart: 'Where do you come from? Who are you?' hoping that somehow the warmth of the child, and his touch, might enable him to guess the mystery of his birth.

But his anxiety faded after he heard a remark made by old Legrand, who came to ask for help in paying for a memorial stone to his late wife. Seeing Josaph's cot, he cried out to his daughter:

'Ha, a brat! I'll bet you're pleased, aren't you? Seeing how you never could manage to pull one off.'

Jean was so happy that he paid for the memorial without asking to see the specification, and invited old Legrand to stay to lunch.

The old coachman, now working on the tramway between Paris and Versailles, was purple from much drinking and high blood-pressure, but still hale and hearty under his top-hat—now, as a sign of respect to the dead, surrounded by a broad band of crêpe that made him look absolutely like an undertaker's mute. He seemed delighted with the reception given him by his daughter's young man, and would drop in from time to time to take a bowl of soup with them. He looked quite the old buffoon with his white hair round his clean-shaven, bloated face and his majestical drunken airs; and this, together with his reverence for his whip, which he would lay down safely in some corner with all the care of a nurse laying a baby down, made a great impression on the child. The old man and he instantly became the firmest of friends. One day when they were just finishing dinner, all of them together, the Hettémas came bursting in.

'Oh, excuse me! A family gathering, I see,' the woman said, simpering. The expression struck Jean like a blow; it was humiliating as a slap in the face.

His family! This waif snoring there with his head on the table, this soft-brained old filibuster with his pipe stuck in his mouth, huskily explaining for the hundredth time that two coppers' worth of whipcord lasted him for six months and that he had not had to get a new handle for twenty years. . . . His family! What an idea! It was no more his family than this woman Fanny Legrand was his wife, this ageing, tired woman slumped forward on her elbows, in a haze of cigarette-smoke. In less than a year from now all this would vanish out of his life, grow shadowy as those casual encounters that travel brings, the acquaintances made at table in hotels.

But at other times this idea of departure—which he would summon up as an excuse for his weakness whenever he felt himself sliding, drawn down into the depths—instead of reassuring him and giving him back his peace of mind, would make him feel the many bonds that held him fast and the wrench that his going away would be: not merely one break, but ten. It would cost him something even to let go this childish hand that clung to his at night. Or even La Balue, the golden oriole twittering and singing in its cage, which was too small and always about to be changed, where it perched as bowed as the old cardinal it was named after, in his iron prison—even La Balue had taken possession of a corner of his heart and was yet another thing that it would be painful to tear out.

And yet the inevitable separation was drawing nearer; and the splendid month of June, when all nature was in its heyday, would probably be the last that they would spend together. Was that what made her nervous and excitable, or was it her abrupt ardour to undertake Josaph's education, to the great disgust of the child, who spent hours sitting over his letters without seeing them or pronouncing them, his forehead as though bolted and barred, like the gate to a farmyard. From one day to the next she became more and more given to wild outbursts and fits of tears, making endless scenes in spite of Jean's efforts to bear with her; but she was so abusive and in her anger poured out such a gutter-stream of resentment and hatred for her lover's youthfulness, his education, his family, and the gulf between his destiny and hers, which life was about to make still larger, and was so expert in touching him just on the most sensitive spots, that in the end he too would lose his temper and fling back at her.

Yet in his anger there were still reserves; there was in it the pitying awareness of a man of breeding; there were retorts that he did not make, finding them too grievous and all too easy. Whereas she let fly with a whore's abandon, without any sense of responsibility or of shame, turning everything to account, watching her victim's face with cruel delight over every wince of pain she caused, and then all at once throwing herself into his arms and imploring his forgiveness.

The Hettémas' faces were a sight to see when they were present at the outbreak of such quarrels, which almost always occurred at mealtimes, just when everyone had sat down and the lid was being lifted off the soup-tureen or the knife cutting into the roast. Across the table they would exchange a glance of comical horror. Would they get their meal, or would the joint go flying out into the garden together with the dish, the sauce, and the haricot stew?

'Only don't let's have any scenes!' they would say every time there was any question of a gathering. And they used the same expression in answer to a suggestion that they should all have lunch together in the forest—an invitation Fanny threw out one Sunday, talking over the garden wall. Oh no, there would be no quarrelling to-day, it was far too beautiful a day for that! And she ran in to dress the child and load up the hampers.

Everything was ready and they were just starting out when the postman brought a registered letter with a signature that made Jean remain behind. He caught up with the party at the edge of the woods and said in a low voice to Fanny:

'It's from Uncle. He's in the seventh heaven. Wonderful vintage, and all sold straight off. He's sent back the eight thousand francs for Déchelette, with all sorts of compliments and thanks to his niece.'

'Oh yes, his niece! Gascon style, eh! Old rascal . . .' Fanny said, with no illusions left about uncles from Provence. Then she exclaimed radiantly: 'We'll have to put the money into something.'

He gazed at her in stupefaction, having always known her as utterly scrupulous in all matters of financial probity. 'Put it into something? But it isn't yours!'

'Well, actually, I didn't tell you, but—' she blushed, and her eyes became veiled as they always did when she deviated in the slightest from the truth. This good fellow Déchelette, she said, had heard what they were doing for Josaph and had written to her saying that the money would be of use in bringing up the little boy. 'But of course if you don't like the idea of it we can give him back his eight thousand. He's in Paris.'

The Hettémas had tactfully walked on some way ahead. Now their voices rang out under the trees:

'Right or left?'

'To the right! to the right! To the Pools!' Fanny called. Then, turning back to her lover, she said: 'I say, you're not going to start eating your heart out over a silly little thing like that! Hang it all, we've been together long enough, haven't we?'

She knew this shuddering pallor of his lips, this glance shot at the little boy, questioning him from head to foot. But this time it was only a faint flicker of jealous violence. He was reaching the stage of slackening into habitual acquiescence, making concessions for the sake of peace and quiet. 'What's the use of torturing myself, trying to get to the bottom of things? If the child is hers, what could be more obvious than that she should take him in, keeping the truth from me, after all the scenes, all the inquisitions that I've put her through? Isn't it more sensible to take things as they are and have a quiet time for the few months we have left?'

And down the dipping woodland paths he went along, carrying their picnic luncheon in a heavy basket draped in white, resigned, weary, bowed like an old gardener, while the mother and child walked on ahead together, Josaph in his Sunday best, much hampered by a smart new suit in which he could not run properly, she in a light-coloured peignoir, her head and neck bare under a Japanese parasol, her waist thickened now, her gait a little shambling, and in the beautiful twists of her hair a wide streak of white that she no longer went to the trouble of concealing.

Still further ahead, some way down the hill, the Hettémas walked, squeezed together, both of them topped by gigantic straw hats like those worn by Touareg raiders, and dressed in red flannel, loaded with provisions, fishing-tackle, and shrimping-nets; and she, to lighten her husband's burdens, valiantly wore across her colossal bosom the hunting-horn without which he could not dream of taking a walk in the forest. As they walked, they sang:

'I love the sound of the dipping oars
    At evening on the water.
I love the sound of the belling stag . . .'

Olympe had an inexhaustible repertoire of such commonplace sentimentalities; and when one envisaged where she had picked them up, in what shameful half-light behind drawn shutters, and how many men she had sung them to, there seemed a quite extra-ordinary grandeur in the serenity with which her husband sang third to her. What the grenadier said at Waterloo—'There are too many of them'—must have been the basis of the man's philosophi-cal indifference.

While Jean was dreamily watching the enormous couple dis-appearing down a glen where he was about to follow them, a creaking of wheels came up the track, accompanied by flights of childish voices lifted in wild laughter. And suddenly, only a few paces from him, a cartload of little girls loomed up, all flying ribbons and floating hair, in a governess-cart drawn by a small donkey, and a young girl hardly any older than the others tugging at the bridle, pulling it along the bumpy track.

It was plain enough to see that Jean formed part of the band whose weird turn-out, and particularly that of the stout lady with the hunting-horn slung round her middle, had set the little crowd off into gales of mirth. So the girl tried to impose a moment's silence on the children. But the sight of yet another Touareg hat only let out another wave of rippling mockery, and as they passed by the man, who stepped to one side to make way for the governess-cart, a gentle smile, just a shade embarrassed, asked his forgiveness and hinted some naïve astonishment at finding the old gardener with so young and likeable a face.

He saluted her timidly, blushing without being quite sure what he was so ashamed of; and when the party halted at the top of the rise, where there was a parting of the ways, and a prattling of little voices flowered forth, reading aloud the names on the signpost, which were half-washed off by rain—Way to the Pools, Royal Huntsman's Oak, Rest Not Long, Vélizy Way—Jean turned round to look back along the green track, sun-spangled and carpeted with moss, and caught a last glimpse of the wheels turning on the velvety floor: that eddy of fair-haired child-hood, that little cartload of happiness, all summery colours, all sparkling fountain-sprays of laughter among the overhanging branches.

A sudden frantic bugle-call from Hettéma startled him out of his musing. The others had settled down by the edge of the pool and were busy unpacking the provisions; and from a long way off he could see, reflected in the sheer water, the white of the tablecloth on the cropped grass and the red flannel jackets like huntsmen's coats making a splash among the greenery.

'Do come on! You've got the lobster!' the fat man called. And then came Fanny's voice, edgy with excitement:

'It was the Bouchereau girl that held you up, I suppose?'

Jean started at the name of Bouchereau, which took him back to Castelet, to his sick mother's bedside.

'That's right,' Hettéma said, taking the hamper from him. 'The grown-up one, the one leading the donkey, she's the doctor's niece. Daughter of a brother of his. He has her to live with him. They live at Vélizy all summer. She's pretty.'

'Oh well, pretty! Brazen-faced enough, anyway,' Fanny said, cutting bread and scanning her lover's face, uneasy at the absent look in his eyes.

Madame Hettéma, very solemnly unwrapping the ham, was strongly disapproving of this way of letting young girls go wandering about the woods on their own. 'It's all very well telling me it's the English style, and she was brought up in London—it doesn't make any difference, it really isn't respectable.'

'No, but it's just the thing for a bit of fun.'

'Oh, Fanny!'

'Excuse me, I was forgetting. The gentleman believes in little innocents.'

'Well, well, how about having some lunch?' Hettéma said, beginning to be afraid of a scene. But she could not be stopped from regaling them with all she knew about upper-class young ladies. Fine stories she had heard—convents and boarding-schools—what goings-on! They left those places exhausted, all their bloom gone, sickened by the thought of men, and incapable even of bearing children. 'And that's when you get them handed over to you, you poor silly fools! A sweet innocent girl, eh! As if there were any sweet innocent girls at all! Society or not society, there aren't any girls that don't know what's what, from the day they're born. Take me, for instance—when I was twelve there wasn't anything I didn't know. And that goes for you too, doesn't it, Olympe?'

"Course,' Madame Hettéma said, shrugging her shoulders. But she was much more interested in the fate of the luncheon, now that she could hear that Gaussin's temper was going and that he was saying there were girls and girls, and in some families one could still find . . .

'Oh, yes, families!' his mistress threw back at him with a scornful air. 'Let's talk about families! Especially yours!'

'Be quiet! I forbid you——'

'Snob!'

'Hussy! I'm thankful it'll all be over soon. I won't have to put up with you for long now.'

'Go on, go on! Clear off! I shall be downright glad of it.'

They hurled abuse at each other, with the child lying there on his belly on the grass, watching them with morbid curiosity. And then the noise of their quarrel was suddenly engulfed by an appalling trumpeting that echoed back a hundredfold from the pool and the serried masses of the trees.

'Have you had enough? Do you want any more of it?' Crimson, with bursting lungs, big fat Hettéma, who had known no other way to make them be quiet, stood waiting, the mouthpiece to his lips, the great bell of the trumpet looming like a menace over them.

9

USUALLY their wrangles lasted only a short time, melting away in a scrap of music, with Fanny softening into coaxing, sentimental mood. But this time he was deeply resentful, and for several days afterwards he had the same furrow on his forehead and kept up the same sullen silence, sitting down to his drawing straight after meals and even refusing to go out with her.

It was as though all at once he had been overtaken by shame at the abject condition in which he was living, and fear of again meeting with the little governess-cart coming up the track, and that limpid young smile he was always thinking of. Then as the fading dream began to blur, like a stage-setting being taken to pieces to make way for some other fairyland scene, the apparition lost its clear outline, vanishing into the woodland distances, and Jean did not see it again. Only he was left with a shade of depression that Fanny thought she understood, and she resolved to put matters right.

'There, it's done,' she said to him in delight one day. 'I've seen Déchelette. I've given him back the money. He agrees with you that it's more correct that way. I must say I don't see why! Oh well, there it is. Later on, when I'm on my own, he'll think of the child. Are you pleased? Are you still cross with me?'

And then she told him all about her visit to the Rue de Rome, and her astonishment at finding, not the usual mad, rackety caravanserai and delirious crowds, but a quiet bourgeois house, and very strict injunctions at the door as to the sort of people to be let in. There were to be no more galas, no more masked balls; and the explanation of this change, in the words some baffled and furious parasite had chalked up on the doorway to the studio: 'Closed for the mating-season.'

'And that's the plain truth, my dear. Déchelette came back and fell straight in love with a skating-rink girl, Alice Doré. He's had her with him for a month, they've set up house together, positively set up house! A nice little thing she is, very harmless and quiet. They hardly utter a squeak between the two of them. I've promised that we'll go and see them. It'll make a change from the hunting-horn and the barcarolles. It's all the same in the long run, isn't it—the philosopher and his theories! No to-morrow, no belonging to anyone. Oh, I did fairly tease him!'

Jean allowed himself to be taken to see Déchelette, whom he had not encountered since their meeting outside the Madeleine. He would have been amazed then if anyone had told him that a day would come when he would be in and out of the house where this man lived, his mistress's cynical and disdainful former lover, and practically become his friend. From the very first visit he was astonished to feel so much at home, charmed by the gentleness of this Cossack-bearded man with the good-hearted childlike laughter and an evenness of temper that was not affected by dreadful attacks of the liver complaint that was the reason why his skin was yellow and he had dark rings round his eyes.

And how easy it was to understand the adoration he inspired in this woman called Alice Doré, this woman with the long, soft, white hands and the insignificant fair prettiness that had its special charm in the Flemish clarity of her skin, as golden as her name; and there was gold in her hair and in the irises of her eyes, gold fringing her eyelashes and sparkling in her skin, even under her fingernails.

Déchelette had picked her up on the skating-rink among all the coarseness and brutality of that trade, among the whirls of smoke that men spat out into the girls' painted faces, as they named a sum; and she had been amazed and touched by Déchelette's courteous treatment of her. She could think of herself as a woman again, after being a poor miserable beast of pleasure; and when he would have sent her away with a handful of coin after a good breakfast the next morning, in accordance with his principles, her heart was so full and she so gently, so winningly, begged: 'Keep me a little longer,' that he could not find it in him to refuse. Since then, half from a sense of human dignity, half from weariness, he kept his door shut on this random honeymoon that he was spending in the airiness and calm of his summer palace, so well designed for ease; and the two of them were living quite blissfully together, she enjoying all the little sweet attentions that she had never known, he enjoying the happiness that he could give the poor wretch and the simple-hearted gratitude she gave him back, so for the first time, and without realizing it, falling under the subtle spell of living at close quarters with a woman—that mysterious sorcery of life *à deux* in a harmony of sweetness and kind ways.

For Gaussin the studio in the Rue de Rome was a diversion from the vile and furtive environment in which he dragged along, a humble clerk with an irregular union. He enjoyed talk with this cultivated and well-read man of artistic tastes, this philosopher in the Persian robe as light and loose as his own attitude to life; he enjoyed Déchelette's stories of his travels, sketched in as few words as possible, all of it so perfectly in place here among the Oriental hangings, the gilded Buddhas and bronze dragons, all the exotic splendour of this vast room where the light fell from a high skylight —glimmering woodland light flickering between the frail spears of the bamboo, the lacy fronds of tree-ferns, and the huge leaves of the stillingia mingled with philodendrons' slim, wavering lines, water-plants always seeking moisture and gloom.

Most of all on Sundays, in that wide bay that opened on to a Paris street now deserted in the summer heat, among the shiver of leaves and the smell of fresh earth round the potted plants, it was almost as much the country and the woods as anything at Chaville, minus the Hettémas with their promiscuity and their hunting-horn. There was never anything like a party. Yet once as Gaussin and his mistress were coming in, on their way to dinner, from the doorway they heard the eager sound of several voices. Daylight was fading, drinks were served in the conservatory, and the discussion seemed lively.

'Well, my view is that five years' hard labour, his reputation gone and his career smashed up is paying dearly enough for something done when a man was mad with love and didn't know what he was doing. I'll sign your petition, Déchelette.'

'That's Caoudal,' Fanny said in a low voice, trembling.

Someone else replied in a brusque tone of refusal: 'I'm not going to sign anything, I'm not going to associate myself with that fellow in any way at all.'

'And that's La Gournerie.' Fanny pressed close to her lover, murmuring: 'We'll go away if you don't want to see them.'

'Oh, why? I don't mind at all.' Actually he did not altogether realize what it would feel like to be face to face with these men; but he did not want to run away from the ordeal, and perhaps indeed he wanted to know the precise degree of the jealousy that had made his wretched love what it was.

'Come along,' he said, and they walked into a rosy, sunset light that was shining on the bald heads and grizzled beards of Déchelette's friends, sprawled on the low divans round an Oriental coffee-table on which stood five or six glasses, a-flicker with the milky aniseed liqueur that Alice was just pouring out. The women kissed each other. 'You know everybody, don't you, Gaussin?' Déchelette asked, tilting quietly to and fro in his rocking-chair.

Ah, he knew them indeed! Two of them at least were familiar to him from the hours he had spent staring at their portraits in shop-windows, among arrays of celebrities. How they had made him suffer! What hatred he had felt for them!—the hatred of the late-comer who would gladly have leapt on them, torn the very heart out of them, when he encountered them in the street! But Fanny had been right in saying he would get over it; now their faces were for him the faces of people he had long known, almost of relations, perhaps long-lost distant uncles.

'Still as handsome as ever, isn't he?' Caoudal said, stretched out to his full gigantic length, holding a fan over his eyelids to save his eyes from the glare. 'And Fanny! Well, well!' He propped himself up on his elbow and narrowed his expert eyes. 'Face still wearing very well, but the figure—you ought to lace yourself in, you know! Ah well, if it's any comfort to you, my dear girl, La Gournerie is even fatter than you are.'

The poet pursed his thin lips disdainfully. Sitting cross-legged on a pile of cushions—since his Algerian journey he asserted that he could not bear to sit otherwise—enormous, podgy and clammy-looking, with no trace of intelligence in his appearance except for the mighty brow under a forest of white hair and the hard, slave-driving eyes, he treated Fanny with an affectation of sophisticated reserve and exaggerated politeness, as though to give Caoudal a lesson.

Two landscape-painters, with a bronzed, open-air look, completed the party. They too knew Jean's mistress, and the younger of them, shaking hands with her, said:

'Déchelette has been telling us all about the child. It's very nice of you to do what you've done, my dear.'

'Yes indeed,' Caoudal said to Gaussin. 'Very decent, adopting the child. Quite the thing.'

She seemed embarrassed by these praises. And then just at that moment someone bumped into a piece of furniture in the dark studio, and a voice asked:

'Anybody there?'

'Here's Ezano,' Déchelette said.

This was somebody Jean had never seen; but he knew what place this Bohemian, this eccentric, now married and settled down and head of a faculty at the Beaux-Arts, had had in Fanny Legrand's life, and he remembered a packet of impassioned and delightful letters. A little man came in, hollow-cheeked, withered, and jerky, shaking hands at arm's length, keeping people at a distance, from the habit of always being on the platform, always playing an official role. He seemed very surprised to see Fanny, and above all to find her still beautiful after so many years.

'Upon my word! Sappho!' he exclaimed, and a fleeting red tinged his cheeks.

The name Sappho, which brought up all the past and linked her so much more closely with her old lovers again, caused a certain embarrassment.

'And Monsieur d'Armandy, who has brought her along,' Déchelette said swiftly, to enlighten the new arrival. Ezano bowed. And the talk went on. Reassured at seeing the way her lover was taking things, and proud of him, proud of his good looks and his youth, in front of these artists here, these connoisseurs, Fanny became very gay and full of high spirits. Quite given up to her present passion, she hardly remembered her affairs with these men; and yet the years of cohabitation counted for something—all that shared life in which each always takes on something of the other's habits, the little tricks picked up from people one is with, things that survive a parting—down to that way of rolling cigarettes that she had from Ezano, and his preference for Job and Maryland.

Jean was quite unmoved at observing this little detail, which would have exasperated him in earlier days; and finding himself so calm, he felt the joy a prisoner feels when he has filed his chain through and knows he has only to make the smallest effort in order to escape.

'Ah, my poor dear Fanny,' Caoudal said, nonchalantly teasing, indicating the others, 'what a falling off! Haven't they got old, haven't they got flabby? It's only the two of us who have lasted out.'

Fanny burst out laughing. 'Oh no, I'm sorry, Colonel'—he was sometimes nicknamed so on account of his moustache—'it's not quite the same thing, though! I haven't the same years of service!'

'Caoudal's always forgetting that he's one of the old brigade,' La Gournerie said. And at a movement from the sculptor, whom he could always touch on the raw, he raised his strident voice and exclaimed: 'Gold-medallist of 1840—that dates you, old boy!'

Between these two old friends there was still something of an aggressive tone, a muffled antipathy that had never separated them but would flash out in their glances, in their slightest words, and had done so from the time twenty years ago when the poet had gone off with the sculptor's mistress. So far as they were concerned Fanny no longer counted; both of them had run through other delights, with other bitter after-tastes; but the rancour persisted, working deeper in with the passing of the years.

'Just look at the two of us and say frankly—am I the one who's so much the old brigade?' Caoudal planted himself firmly on his feet, showing himself off in the tight-fitting jacket that revealed his bulging muscles, throwing out his chest and shaking back the flaming mane of hair that had no trace of white. 'Gold-medallist of 1840—fifty-eight in three months—and what does that prove? Is it age that makes a man old? It's only at the Comédie-Française and the Conservatoire that men of sixty mumble and shuffle, with shaking heads, bent backs and their legs giving way under them,

I—S.

and liable to all sorts of little senile misfortunes. Damn it all, at sixty a man carries himself straighter than he did at thirty, because he keeps an eye on himself. And the women still run after you, so long as your heart's still young and warm and keeps the rest of your carcass in trim.'

'D'you really think so?' La Gournerie said, looking at Fanny, with a sneering laugh.

Déchelette intervened to say, with his good-natured smile: 'And yet you're always saying there's nothing like youth. You're always telling us that.'

'It's my dear little Cousinard who's made me change my mind. Cousinard's my new model—eighteen, plump, and dimpled all over, a perfect Clodion piece. And so thoroughly jolly, so splendidly common, utterly the personification of the Halles—her mother sells poultry there. She says the stupidest things, it's endearing enough to make you hug her. The other day in the studio she came across a novel of Dejoie's, looked at the title, *Thérèse*, and cast it aside again with a lovely sulky look. "If it'd been called *Poor Thérèse*," she said, "I'd have sat up all night reading it." I'm mad about her, I tell you.'

'And in a twinkling you've set up house with her. And in another six months there'll be a smash, a shedding of tears as big as your fist, the mere thought of work will make you sick, you'll get into rages fit to murder anyone you set eyes on. . . .'

Caoudal's brow clouded. 'It's a fact, nothing lasts for long. You take up with someone, you separate again. . . .'

'Well then, why take up?'

'And what about yourself? I suppose you think you've settled down for life with your Flemish lass?'

'Oh, we're different, we haven't set up—true, isn't it, Alice?'

'Definitely,' the young woman answered, her voice gentle and absent. She was standing on a chair, plucking wistaria and green leaves to decorate the table.

'There won't be any smash where we're concerned,' Déchelette went on. 'Hardly as much as a leave-taking. We've given ourselves a lease of two months together. On the last day we'll go our separate ways without sorrow and without surprise. I shall be going back to Ispahan—I've just booked my sleeper—and Alice will go back to her little flat in the Rue La Bruyère, which she's kept on meanwhile.'

'Third above the ground floor, as convenient as anyone could imagine for chucking yourself out of the window!'

As she spoke, the young woman smiled, glowing, bathed in the last rays of russet light, in her hand the great bunch of purple flowers. But the tone in which she uttered the words held a depth of seriousness, and no one answered. The wind was freshening; the houses opposite seemed to grow taller.

'Let's get round the table,' the colonel exclaimed, 'and let's talk all the nonsense we can.'

'That's it! *Gaudeamus igitur!* Let's enjoy ourselves while we're young—eh, Caoudal?' La Gournerie said with a laugh that did not ring true.

Going along to the Rue de Rome some days later, Jean found the studio shut up, the big blind drawn across the window, and the silence of desolation reigning everywhere, from the cellars to the flat roof. Déchelette had gone; the appointed time had come, the lease had run out. And he thought: 'It's a fine thing to make what one wants of life, to have mind and heart under control. Shall I ever be able to do it?'

Someone laid a hand on his shoulder, and a voice said: 'Hello, Gaussin!'

There was Déchelette, looking tired, yellower and more furrowed than usual, explaining that he was not going away for a while yet, having been kept in Paris on business. He was staying at the Grand Hotel, for the studio gave him the horrors since that appalling thing. . . .

'What do you mean?'

'Ah yes, you don't know. Alice is dead. She killed herself. Wait for me, I'm just going to look and see if there are any letters.'

He came almost straight back and, with one finger nervously snapping at the rubber bands round the rolls of newspapers, he talked blankly, like a man in his sleep, without looking at Gaussin walking at his side.

'Yes, she killed herself. Threw herself out of the window, just as she said that evening when you were there. What can one say? I didn't know, of course, I couldn't suspect. The day when I was supposed to be leaving, she said to me quite serenely: "Take me with you, Déchelette. Don't leave me alone. I won't be able to live without you." I just laughed. Can you imagine me with a woman out there, among those Kurds? Out in the desert—fever—nights camping out. . . . She said the same thing again at dinner. She said: "I won't get in your way, you'll see how good I'll be." Then she saw she was bothering me and she gave it up. After that we went to our box at the Variety. . . . It was all fixed up beforehand. She seemed quite happy, she held my hand all the time and kept saying softly: "I do feel good." As I was leaving by the night train, I drove her back to her place. But we were both rather sad, and we didn't talk. She didn't even say "thank you" for a little parcel I slipped into her pocket, enough to live on in peace for a year or two. When we got to the Rue La Bruyère she asked me to go upstairs with her. I didn't want to. "Please, please—just to the door," she said. But that was the utmost I would do, I didn't go in. My seat was booked and my trunk packed, and then I had made such a point of it—that I *was* going. I was going downstairs again, feeling rather overcome, when I heard her call something out to me, something like "I'll be there first," but I didn't know what she meant until I was down there in the street. *Oh . . .*'

He stopped, his eyes on the ground, confronting the dreadful vision that the pavement showed him now at every step: that inert, black-clad heap, groaning. . . .

'She died two hours later, without a word, without a cry, looking straight at me with those golden eyes of hers. Was she in pain? Did she recognize me? We had laid her on her bed, all dressed as she was, with a big lace mantilla covering one side of her head, to hide the wound in the skull. She was very pale, with a trace of blood on one temple. She was still lovely, the quiet thing she always was. . . . But as I leaned over her to wipe away that drop of blood, which kept on coming again, inexhaustibly, it seemed to me that her gaze took on another expression, a great anger, a terrible reproach. . . .

It was a silent curse the poor thing was casting on me. And what difference would it have made to me to stay for a while or take her with me, as she was ready for anything and never a nuisance? No, it was pride, the obstinacy of having given my word. Well, so I didn't give way, and she's dead. She died because of me, and yet I loved her. . . .'

He was working himself up, talking loudly, so that people turned round in amazement to stare at the man elbowing them aside as he made his way along the Rue d'Amsterdam. And Gaussin, passing his former apartment, noticing the balcony, the veranda, felt his thoughts turn to Fanny and their own story, and suddenly shuddered.

'I took her to Montparnasse,' Déchelette went on. 'No friends, no family. I wanted to be the only one to look after her. And since then, here I am, always thinking the same thing, and I can't make up my mind to go so long as I have this obsession, and I can't bear my house, where I spent two such happy months with her. I live out, I rush about, I try to amuse myself, I try to escape from that dead gaze staring at me accusingly, with a trickle of blood there. . . .'

And stopping, wrapped up in this remorse, with two great tears sliding down his little snub nose looking so friendly and so fond of life, he said:

'I say, you know, my dear fellow—I'm not really bad. Only—it's going a bit far, doing what I've done this time.'

Jean tried to comfort him, talking as though everything were a matter of chance, of bad luck. But Déchelette went on shaking his head and muttering between clenched teeth: 'No, no. I'll never forgive myself. I wish I could punish myself.'

This desire for expiation did not cease to haunt him. He talked about it to all his friends, among them Gaussin, whom he would come to meet after office hours.

'Oh, you ought to go away, Déchelette. Travel! Work! That'll cheer you up.' That was what Caoudal and the others would say; they were rather anxious about his fixed idea and the desperate intensity with which he kept on trying to make them say he was not bad. At last—perhaps wanting to see the studio again before leaving, or perhaps with a very swift resolution to make an end of his grief—he went back to his house one night. And in the morning the workmen coming in from the outlying districts found him lying with shattered skull on the pavement outside his door, having died the same death as the woman had, with the same anguish, the same frantic despair, the same plunge headlong to the ground.

The shuttered studio was crowded with a throng of artists, models, and actresses, all those who had danced and supped at the last festivities he had held. There was a noise of footsteps and whisperings, a murmuring as in a chapel below the short candle-flames. Through the creeping tendrils and the leaves they gazed at the body laid out in silken stuff embroidered with golden flowers, a turban hiding the hideous wound in the head—he lay stretched out to his full length, his white hands clasped in a gesture as of abandonment, of supreme relaxation, there on the low divan, over-shadowed by wistaria, where Gaussin and his mistress had first met on the night of the ball.

10

AND so people did sometimes die of these separations!... Now, when they quarrelled, Jean no longer dared to speak of going away; he no longer cried out in exasperation: 'Luckily this'll soon be over!' She would only have had to answer: 'Very well, go away— I'll kill myself, I'll do what *she* did.' And that threat, which he thought he gathered from the melancholy of her gaze and of the airs she sang, and from her dreamy moods of silence, haunted him to the point of terror.

Yet he had passed the competitive examination that concluded the consular attachés' period at the Ministry. He had passed out high up on the list and was to be sent to fill one of the first free posts, so that it was no more than a matter of weeks now, perhaps only of days.... And everything about them, at this fading season with the hours of sunshine growing less each day, was hurrying towards the winter's changes. One morning, opening the window into the first mist, Fanny exclaimed:

'Look, the swallows have gone!'

One after the other the summer villas closed their shutters. All along the road to Versailles, one after the other, went removal vans and big country wagons loaded up with parcels, sprays of greenery from potted plants on the platform, while the leaves sped away in whirls, scudding like clouds in full flight, under the low sky, and the ricks stood high in the gleaned fields. Behind the orchard, now bare, as though shrunken without its green foliage, there were the deserted bungalows and, further on, the laundry with its red-roofed drying-rooms massed high against the sad landscape, and on the other side of the house the railway-line, stripped naked, running along the edge of the grey woods, a black ribbon unfurling into the distance.

What cruelty it was to leave her all alone in this melancholy that had befallen the living world! He felt his heart already failing him; he would never bring himself to say good-bye. That was undoubtedly what she was counting on, waiting for that failure at the hour of crisis; and till then she was easy, never mentioning it, faithful to her promise not to put obstacles in the way of a departure that had been foreseen and agreed to from the beginning. One day he came home with the news:

'I've got my appointment.'

'Ah—and where is it?'

The tone in which she asked was casual, but her lips and eyes were livid, her face so convulsed that he could not bear to keep her waiting longer. 'No, no, not yet. I've given up my turn to Hédouin. That gives us another six months, anyway.'

Then came a flood of tears and laughter and mad kisses, a stammering of: 'Thank you, thank you! What a good life I shall give you now! That was it, you see, that was what made me bad—thinking about how you would go away.' Now she would be better able to prepare herself for it, gradually she would learn to resign herself. And then, in another six months, it would no longer be autumn and this hovering sense of death would have passed away.

She kept her word. There were no more outbreaks of nerves, no more quarrels; and she even went so far as to board the child out at Versailles, to avoid the stress that he caused. He did not come to them except on Sundays, and if this new régime did not at once tame his wild, rebellious nature, at least it was teaching him hypocrisy. They led a life of perfect calm; their dinners with the Hettémas passed off without storms, and the piano was opened again and their favourite pieces played and sung. But at the bottom of his heart Jean was more troubled, more perplexed than ever before, wondering where his weakness would lead him and sometimes thinking of giving up the idea of a consulate altogether and going over to office work. That would mean Paris; it would mean giving their liaison a lease of life indefinitely prolonged; but it also meant throwing over the whole dream of his boyhood. And then there was the grief to his family, the break it would certainly mean with his father, who would never forgive him for abandoning his real career, especially if he knew why.

And for whose sake? For a faded, ageing creature whom he no

longer loved: that, after all, he had realized clearly since that meeting with her former lovers. What spell then held him fast to this life with her?

As he got into the train one morning near the end of October, a girl's gaze meeting his suddenly recalled his encounter in the woods and all the radiant grace of the young creature, hardly more than a child, whose memory had haunted him for months. She was wearing the same light dress that had been so deliciously splashed with sunlight through the branches, but with a wide travelling-coat over it now; and the things she had with her in the compartment—books, a small handbag, a bunch of tall rushes and the year's last flowers—all spoke of a return to Paris, the end of a season in the country. She had recognized him, too, and there was a half-smile in her eyes like a faint rippling over the limpid waters of a well. And for a second an unuttered thought hovered between the two of them—complete understanding.

'How is your mother, Monsieur d'Armandy?' old Bouchereau suddenly asked. Jean had been too dazzled to notice him there, tucked away in his corner, his pale face bent forward over a newspaper.

Jean gave him what news there was, very touched that his family and he himself should have been remembered, and still more deeply stirred when the girl asked after the two little twins who had written her uncle such a very nice letter, thanking him for the care he had taken of their mother. So she knew them! That filled him with joy; then, as he was, it seemed, in an extraordinarily emotional state that morning, he at once fell sad at hearing that they were going back to Paris, as Bouchereau had to begin his term's lectures at the School of Medicine. He would have no more opportunity of seeing her. . . . And the fields gliding away past the windows, brightly shining only a moment earlier, now seemed gloomy and the light that of an eclipse.

The engine gave a long shriek; they were almost there. He bowed and lost sight of them; but on the way out of the station they met again, and in the tumult of the crowd Bouchereau told him that after the next Thursday they would be at home in the Place Vendôme and if he felt inclined to drink tea with them . . . She took her uncle's arm, and it seemed to Jean that it was she who invited him, without saying a word.

After having several times decided that he would go to see Bouchereau, and then that he would not—for what was the use of causing futile regrets?—one day he announced at home that there was soon to be a great reception at the Ministry, to which he would have to go. Fanny got out his evening clothes and had his white ties freshly ironed for him; and then suddenly when Thursday evening came he had not the slightest desire to go out. His mistress argued that he must go through with it, as a social duty, and reproached herself with having taken up too much of his attention and selfishly kept him to herself; and she made him change his mind and then helped him to get ready, playfully, tenderly giving another touch to the set of his tie and the wave in his hair, laughing because her fingers smelt of the cigarette that she took up and put down again on the mantelpiece every minute: his dancing-partners would make a face over it, she said. And seeing her so very gay and very kind, he felt remorse for having lied to her, and would rather have stayed with her at their own fireside, if she had not forced him to go. 'I want you to go—you must,' she said, gently pushing him out into the darkness of the road.

It was late when he came home. She was asleep, and the lamp-light falling on this weary slumber reminded him of a similar home-coming, three years ago—so long ago already!—after the terrible revelations that had just been made to him. What a coward he had been then! How had he contrived to turn things so that what should have snapped his chain had only riveted it on more firmly? He felt a wave of nausea, of physical loathing. The room, the bed, the woman all inspired him with equal horror. He picked up the lamp and carried it, softly, into the next room. He wanted so much to be alone, to think about what had happened to him—oh nothing, almost nothing at all. . . .

He was in love.

In some words that we use quite commonly there is a secret spring to make them suddenly open up, right to the bottom, and so reveal the rare, real meaning that they have; then the word folds up again, resumes its everyday form and goes rolling on, insignificantly, worn by habitual and mechanical use. 'Love' is one of these words. Those who have once seen it light up in its full glow will understand the delicious anguish that Jean had been living in for the last hour, without at first realizing what it really was that had happened to him.

There in that corner of the Place Vendôme drawing-room where they sat and talked together for so long, he had felt nothing more than a gentle, enveloping charm, a great sense of being at ease and at home.

It was only when he was out in the street, with the door once more closed behind him, that he was overcome by a feeling of wild gaiety and then by a faintness as though from loss of blood. 'What's the matter with me, in heaven's name?' And this Paris that he was walking through on his way home seemed quite new, seemed to have opened out and become larger, fairy-like, radiant.

Yes, at this hour when the beasts of night were unleashed and on the prowl, when the filth of the gutter was rising, swarming in the yellow gaslight, Sappho's lover, he who had been initiated into all the ways of lust, walked through the streets seeing Paris just as any young girl might see it on her way home from a ball, her head full of waltz-tunes that she repeated to the stars, all in the white shimmer of her jewellery—chaste Paris bathed in moonlight where virgin souls might open like flowers. And all at once, as he climbed the wide steps to the station, only such a short way now from his sordid home, he caught himself saying aloud: 'Oh, I love her! I love her!' And that was how he found out.

'Is that you, Jean? What are you doing?'

Fanny had waked up with a start, frightened by not finding him beside her. He should have gone and kissed her and told her lies and talked about the Foreign Office ball, all about the beautiful dresses and everyone he had danced with; but to escape that inquisition, and above all the caresses that he shrank from now that he was filled with memories of his new love, he made an excuse about having some urgent work to do, some drawings for Hettéma.

'The fire's gone out. You'll be cold.'

'No, no.'

'Leave the door open, anyway, so that I can see your lamp.'

He had to play out his pretence to the end, arranging the table and setting out the diagrams; then he sat down and stayed quite still, holding his breath, thinking, remembering. And to keep his dream fast he wrote it all down in a long letter to Césaire, while the night wind stirred the crackling, leafless branches. Now and then a train went rumbling past, and La Balue, disturbed by the light, fluttered about in his little cage, hopping from one perch to the other with hesitant cries.

He put it all down: the meeting in the woods, the other meeting in the train, his queer emotion on entering those drawing-rooms that had seemed so gloomy and tragic on the day of the consultation, with furtive whisperings going on in doorways, sad glances exchanged from chair to chair, and now, this evening, flung wide open, lively and bright with voices, all a long luminous gallery of rooms. And Bouchereau himself—no longer with that dour look, that dark, probing, disconcerting glance from under great bushy eyebrows—wore the calm, fatherly expression of a good citizen at peace with all the world and well pleased that people should be enjoying themselves in his house.

'Suddenly she came up to me and I didn't notice anything else after that. My dear fellow, her name is Irène, she is pretty, she has the kindest way, her hair is that golden-brown colour that English girls' hair often is, and her mouth is like a child's, always on the verge of laughing. Oh, not the cheerless laughter that makes some women so nerve-racking, but a real gushing up of youth and happiness. She was born in London, but her father was French and she speaks without an accent, only for an adorable way of pronouncing some words, for instance "Unclé," which always makes old Bouchereau's eyes soften. He adopted her to lighten the burden for his brother, who has a large family, and to replace Irène's sister, the eldest, who married his chief assistant two years ago. But she doesn't seem to care for doctors at all. She was so amusing about the idiocy of that learned young man, her brother-in-law, who insisted on his fiancée's entering into a formal, solemn agreement with him that they would both bequeath their bodies to the Anthropological Society! She herself is a bird of passage. She loves ships and the sea. The sight of a bowsprit turned seaward makes her heart leap. She told me all this quite frankly, all friendly directness, almost like an English girl, in spite of her Parisian grace. And I listened enchanted by her voice and her laugh and the way our tastes agree, feeling certain in my inmost heart that my whole life's happiness was there beside me, close to my hand, and that I only had to take hold of it and carry it far, far away, wherever my adventurous career may send me. . . .'

'Do come to bed, sweetheart.'

He started, stopped, and instinctively hid the letter that he had just been writing. 'Just a moment. Go to sleep, go to sleep!'

He spoke angrily and sat hunched up, listening for the woman's breathing to grow slow and sleepy again. They were very near to each other, and yet so far apart. . . .

'. . . Whatever happens, meeting her and falling in love with her will be the saving of me. You know how I have been living. Without our ever having talked about it, you have realized that things have gone on in the same old way. I wasn't able to break away. But what you don't know is that I was on the point of sacrificing my career, my whole future, all for the sake of this fatal habit that I was sinking a little deeper into with every day. Now I have found the strength, I have got the leverage I lacked before. And now, in order not to leave any loophole for my weakness, I have sworn not to go back there until I am free and on my own. To-morrow I escape!'

He did not escape the next day nor the day after that. He needed a way out, a pretext, the sort of quarrel that would end with a cry of: 'I'm going!' That was the only way to go once and for all. And Fanny was being as gentle and sunny-tempered as in those enchanted days of illusion when they had first lived together.

Should he write and tell her it was all over, without going into further explanations? But anyone of such violent temperament as Fanny would not resign herself to that, she would come raging to the door of his hotel, she would pursue him to his office. No, it would be better to make a frontal attack and convince her that this was really the final, irrevocable break, and give her all the reasons for it, without anger but without pity either.

But as he thought it over he began to feel a fear arising out of Alice Doré's suicide. Just opposite the house, on the other side of the road, was a little alley running downhill to a barrier that opened on to the railway line. When their neighbours were in a hurry they took this short-cut, walking along the rails to the station. In his imagination he began to have a picture of Fanny, after their final scene, rushing out into the road and down to the level-crossing and there flinging herself under the wheels of the train carrying him away. This fear so obsessed him that the mere thought of that wooden gate between two ivy-covered walls made him put off the final scene from day to day.

It would have been different if he had had a friend, someone who could look after her and help her over the first shock. But they had gone to earth like dormice, they were quite alone together, they knew nobody. And the Hettémas, those monstrous shiny-faced egoists, steeped in their own blubber and all the more bestial now as the time of their Eskimo-like hibernation drew on—they were not the people whom the unhappy woman could call upon for help in her abandon and despair.

And yet he must make the break, and he must do it quickly. In spite of the promise he had given himself, he had gone back to the Place Vendôme two or three times, each time more and more in love; and although as yet he had not spoken, the way old Bouchereau welcomed him with open arms, and Irène's attitude, which was a

mingling of reserve and some softer emotion, some special indulgence for him, a wistful waiting for the declaration, were a
warning that he must not let things go on like this much longer.
Then, too, there was the torment of lying to Fanny, the excuses that
he had to invent, and the sacrilege he felt it was to go from Sappho's
kisses to that other low-voiced, hesitant wooing. . . .

HE had still not made up his mind how to deal with the situation when, coming into his office one day, he found a card on his table and a message to say that a gentleman had already called twice that morning. The porter spoke in a tone of respect, for the card bore the following titles:

C. GAUSSIN D'ARMANDY
President of the Association of the Rhône Valley Submersionists,
Member of the Central Committee for Research and Vigilance,
District Delegate, etc. etc.

Uncle Césaire in Paris! The Rip a delegate, a member of a vigilantes committee! Jean had not recovered from his astonishment when his uncle appeared in person, looking the same as ever, as brown as a pine-cone, a mad look in his eyes, his face all wrinkled with laughter, and his beard still Henri Quatre style; but instead of his everlasting fustian jacket he wore a new cloth overcoat that fitted snugly over his paunch and gave the little man a truly presidential look of majesty.

And what had brought him to Paris? Why, the purchase of a new elevator-machine for the immersion of his new vines! He uttered the word 'elevator' with an earnestness that obviously made him feel grander than ever. And there was another thing, too: he was to have a bust of himself done, at the request of his colleagues, who wanted it to adorn the committee-room.

'As you see,' he added with affected modesty, 'they've made me president. My submersion idea is sweeping the South. And to think that it's me, The Rip, who is now saving France's vines! There's nothing like being a bit cracked, you see.'

But his journey's main object was the break with Fanny. Realizing that the thing was dragging on, he had come to lend a hand. 'Take it from me, I know the ropes. When Courbebaisse dropped his old flame to get married . . .' But before launching into the story he pulled himself up, unbuttoned his overcoat and produced a small bulging wallet.

'First of all, relieve me of this. Lord yes, money—liberating the territory—' and then, misunderstanding the gesture his nephew made and thinking that he was refusing out of compunction, he added: 'Take it! Go on, take it! It makes me proud to be able to repay the son something of what the father did for me. Anyway, Divonne wishes it. She knows all about the whole thing, and she's very glad you're thinking of getting married and getting out of that woman's clutches.'

Coming from Césaire, after what Fanny had done for him, Jean thought it was not quite fair to talk about 'that woman's clutches.' And there was a touch of bitterness in his voice as he replied:

'Put your wallet back in your pocket, uncle. You know better than anyone else how little these things matter to Fanny.'

'Ah yes, she was a good sort,' his uncle said, as though uttering an obituary. And solemnly winking, he added: 'Still, you keep the money! With all the temptations there are in Paris, I'd rather it was in your hands than in mine. And besides, you need money for breaking with women, the same as for fighting duels.'

At this point he got up, declaring that he was half-dead with hunger and that the main problem would be better discussed over luncheon, to the clatter of dishes. That was always the mocking, light-hearted Southern way of dealing with questions concerning women.

'Between ourselves, dear boy . . .' They were sitting at a table in a restaurant in the Rue de Bourgogne, and Uncle, with his napkin tucked under his chin, was warming up, while Jean picked at his food and felt his stomach tightening. 'Between ourselves, dear boy, I think you're taking the thing too tragically. Of course I know the first blow falls hard and it's a bore having it all out. But if you think you can't bear it, don't say anything, just do what Courbebaisse did. Right up to the morning of the wedding, la Mornas didn't know a thing about it. He used to leave his intended's house in the

K—S.

evening, go and fetch the singer from the place where she did her show, and take her home to her rooms. You may say it wasn't quite the right thing and not keeping very good faith. But when a man doesn't like scenes, and with terrible women like Paola Mornas —what can you do? For almost ten whole years that big fine fellow went in fear and trembling of that little blackamoor. The only way to get himself out of pawn, so to speak, was by cunning, by out-witting her. . . .' And this was how he had set about it.

On the day before the wedding—it was a holiday, the fifteenth of August—Césaire suggested that he and she should go up the Yvette and fish for their supper. Courbebaisse was to come along and join them for the meal and the three of them would return to Paris the next evening, when the smell of dust, burnt-out fireworks, and lamp-oil had evaporated. Well, that was all right. So there the two of them were, stretched out on the grass beside that little river that frisks and twinkles along between low banks, making the meadows so green and the willows so leafy. After they had fished for a while they had a bathe. It was not the first time they had gone swimming together, Paola and he, on equal terms, just two tom-boys together. But that day there was something about the little woman, something about her bare arms and legs, her smoothly moulded exotic form with the wet bathing-costume clinging to her skin—and perhaps too it was the thought that Courbebaisse had given him a free hand—ah, the little bitch! She turned round and looked him straight in the eye and said harshly:

'Now remember, Césaire, don't start that again!'

He desisted, for fear of spoiling his game, and said to himself: 'Must leave it till after dinner.'

And very gay the dinner was, out on the wooden balcony at the inn, between the two flags that the innkeeper had hung out in honour of the Fifteenth. It was hot, there was a sweet smell from the hay, and they could hear the drums and crackers and the voices singing in chorus all about the streets.

'Isn't it too bad of him, not coming till to-morrow!' la Mornas said, stretching her arms out, a flicker in her eyes from the cham-pagne. 'I feel like having some fun this evening.'

'Well, what about me?' He had come round to lean on the balustrade beside her. The wood was still hot from the sunshine of the day that was nearly over. Slyly, exploringly, he slid one arm round her waist. 'Oh, Paola, Paola!' he murmured. This time, instead of being annoyed, she burst out laughing, but so loudly and heartily that after a while he began to laugh too. Later in the evening, when they returned from dancing and playing for macaroons at the celebrations, a similar venture was similarly repulsed. And as their rooms were next door to each other, she sang through the partition-wall to him: 'You're too small, you're much too small!' with all sorts of unfavourable comparisons between him and Courbebaisse. He had a hard job to prevent himself retorting and calling her the Widow Mornas; but it was still too early. However, as they sat down to an excellent breakfast together and Paola began to be more and more impatient and anxious as time passed and her lover failed to arrive, it was with a certain satisfaction that he pulled out his watch and said solemnly:

'Noon. So that's over.'

'What is?'

'He's married.'

'Who's married?'

'Courbebaisse.'

Wham!

'Oh, my dear chap, what a slap that was! In all my affairs of the heart I never got the like of it. And then she wanted to start out instantly. But there wasn't a train till four o'clock. In the meantime the faithless man was dashing along in the P.L.M. *en route* for Italy, with his wife. And then—she was so furious, you see—she had another go at me, she went for me tooth and nail. What luck! To think I'd gone and locked us in together! Then she started throwing the dishes, too. And before long she was in the most awful hysterics you can imagine! It took five people to get her to bed and hold her down, while I—scratched all over, as though I'd been pulled through a briar hedge—I dashed off to get the doctor from Orsay. In cases of that sort it's the same as when you call someone out— you always need a doctor on the spot. You can imagine what it was like for me pelting down the lanes, on an empty stomach, and the sun blazing! It was night by the time I got back with him. As we got near to the inn we could hear a lot of shouting from a crowd that had gathered under the windows. God in heaven! I thought— Has she committed suicide? Has she killed someone? That was the more likely thing, with la Mornas. I rushed ahead—and what did I see? There was the balcony all decorated with Venetian lanterns, and the singer standing there, magnificent, her sorrows all forgotten, draped in one of the flags and bellowing the *Marseillaise*— bang in the middle of an Imperial holiday—and the crowd down below clapping and cheering her on.

'And that, dear boy, is how Courbebaisse's affair came to an end. I'm not going to say that it was all over and done with at one go. After ten years in chains, a little care is always needed. But after all, it was I who bore the brunt of it. And I'll take it on myself in your case too, if you want me to.'

'Ah no, Uncle, Fanny isn't the same sort of woman.'

'Get along with you,' Césaire said, ripping open a box of cigars that he had shaken close to his ear to make sure that they were dry. 'You're not the first one to leave her.'

'Yes, there's something in that.'

Jean found himself snatching with delight at an expression that would have wounded him deeply only a few months earlier. Actually his uncle and his uncle's comic story had reassured him a little, but what he could not face was months of such double disloyalty, the hypocrisy, the division of feeling; he would never be able to do it, and yet he had already let things drift too long.

'Well then, what are you going to do about it?'

While the young man was struggling with his own uncertainty, his uncle stroked his beard, tried out various smiling expressions, adopted various poses, held his head this way and that, and finally said with a careless air:

'Does he live far from here?'

'Who?'

'This artist, of course, this fellow Caoudal you told me about, for my bust. I thought we could go and see what he charges, while we're together.'

Renowned though he was, and a great spendthrift, Caoudal still kept the same studio in the Rue d'Assas where he had had his first successes. As they walked along Césaire sought for information about his calibre as an artist. He would make a stiff price, doubtless, but the gentlemen of the committee were bent on having a first-class work.

'Oh, you needn't worry about that, Uncle, if Caoudal will take the job on.' And he enumerated the sculptor's titles: Member of the Institute, Commander of the Legion of Honour, and a whole host of foreign decorations.

The Rip's eyes grew round. 'And you're friends?'

'Very good friends.'

'What a place Paris is! Wonderful, the people one gets to know!'

Jean was reluctant to admit that Caoudal was one of Fanny's old lovers and that it was she who had brought them together. However, it was almost as though Césaire had guessed as much, for he asked:

'So it was he who did the Sappho that we have at Castelet? Then he must know your mistress. He might be able to help you in making the break. The Institute, the Legion of Honour—all that sort of thing always impresses a woman.'

Jean did not reply. He had half-thought of using the first lover's influence.

'By the way,' his uncle went on, laughing heartily, 'the bronze isn't in your father's study any more, you know. When Divonne knew, when I unfortunately let slip that your mistress was the original, she wouldn't have it there any longer. With the consul being so set in his ways and making such a fuss about the slightest change, it wasn't too easy, especially as he mustn't suspect the reason. Ah, women, women! She contrived it so well that at this very moment it's Monsieur Thiers who presides on your father's mantelpiece, and poor Sappho is gathering dust in the windy room, among the junk and the broken furniture. In fact she even got a knock in transport, her bun was smashed and the lyre is loose. I suppose it was Divonne's grudge against her that brought her bad luck.'

They had reached the Rue d'Assas, that modest, hard-working artist quarter, all studios with numbered doors opening off each side of a long court, at the bottom of which there were the dreary-looking buildings of a parish school, from which rose the perpetual chanting of lessons. The sight made the president of the Submersionists' Association feel new doubts as to whether a man living in such humble surroundings could have much talent. But as soon as they were inside Caoudal's studio, he knew where he was.

'Not for a hundred thousand francs! Not for a million!' the sculptor roared, the moment Jean had broached the subject. And lifting his huge body from the divan where he lay sprawled among all the disorder and neglect of the studio, he went on: 'A bust! Ah yes! Quite so! But just look over there at all those crumbs of splintered plaster! That's the figure I was doing for the next Salon. I've just smashed it up with a mallet. That's the line I'm taking with sculpture now, and however tempting the sight of Monsieur——'

'Gaussin d'Armandy, President—' Uncle Césaire reeled off all his titles, but there were too many of them.

Caoudal cut him short, turning towards the young man. 'You're looking at me, Gaussin. Do you think I've aged?'

Indeed, he did look his age, here in the light coming down from the skylight, underlining the scars, furrows, and wrinkles in his face. It was the face of a man who had lived hard and worn himself out; his lion's mane looked as moth-eaten as an old carpet, his jowls were loose and flabby, and his moustache, which he no longer bothered to wax and curl, was the colour of tarnished metal. Why should he bother about anything? Cousinard, his little model, had just left him. 'Yes, my dear chap, with my moulder, a savage, a brute—but twenty!'

There was rage and irony in his voice as he walked up and down the studio, kicking at a stool that was in his way. Suddenly he stopped in front of the mirror with the florid brass frame over the divan and looked at himself, pulling a dreadful face. 'Look how ugly I am! What a wreck! Stringy as an old cow, and with these dewlaps!' He clutched at his throat, and then, in a melancholy and comical tone, with the foresight of the ageing dandy mourning his decay, he added: 'And to think that I shall look back on this with regret, a year from now!'

Uncle Césaire was thunderstruck. What an extraordinary way for an Academician to talk, pouring out the story of his low amours! Evidently there were crackpots everywhere, even at the Institute. And his admiration for the great man decreased in proportion as he began to feel sympathy with his weakness.

'How's Fanny? Are you still at Chaville?' Caoudal asked, suddenly calming down and coming to sit down by Gaussin, whom he clapped on the back in a friendly way.

'Oh, poor Fanny! We won't be living together much longer.'

'You're going away, are you?'

'Yes, quite soon. And I'm getting married first. I must leave her.'

The sculptor gave a ferocious guffaw. 'Splendid! I'm glad to hear it. Avenge us, dear boy, avenge us on the sluts! Leave them, deceive them, and let them weep, the wretches! You'll never do them as much harm as they have done to others.'

Uncle Césaire was triumphant. 'There you are, you see! Monsieur Caoudal doesn't take it as tragically as you do. What a simple-hearted boy it is—what's stopping him from going away is that he's afraid she'll kill herself!'

Jean quite frankly admitted what an impression Alice Doré's suicide had made on him.

'But that's not the same thing at all,' Caoudal said energetically. '*She* was a soft, sad creature with drooping hands, a poor doll without any stuffing. Déchelette was wrong to believe that she died for his sake. She committed suicide because she was tired, simply tired of living. Sappho, on the other hand—pooh! she wouldn't kill herself! She's too fond of making love, she'll burn away right to the end, down to the stub. She belongs to that species of *jeunes premiers* who never act any but the one part and end up without any teeth or eyebrows, but still *jeunes premiers*. Just look at me. Do I kill myself? However grieved I may be, I know I shall take another, I know I'll always have to have one. Your mistress will do the same as I do, just as she's always done. Only she isn't so young now, and it'll be harder.'

Uncle Césaire was more triumphant than ever. 'Well, now you know where you stand, eh?'

Jean said nothing, but his scruples were overcome and his mind made up. They were just leaving when the sculptor called them back to show them a photograph he had picked up out of the dust on his table. 'Look, there she is!' he said, wiping it on his sleeve. 'Lovely, isn't she, the wretch! Enough to make you get down on your knees. What legs, what breasts!' And there was something terrible in the contrast between his blazing eyes, and the passion in his voice, and the senile trembling of the thick splayed fingers, holding the smiling photograph of the girl Cousinard, the model with the dimpled charms.

'It's you! How early you're back!'

She had been walking up from the far end of the garden, her skirt full of fallen apples, and now came running up the steps, a little anxious at his mingled look of embarrassment and obstinacy.

'What *is* the matter?'

'Nothing, nothing. It's the weather, the sun. I wanted to make the most of the last fine day to go for a walk in the forest, just the two of us. What do you say?'

'Oh, goody!' she exclaimed, with the street-urchin cry of delight that would escape her when she was really pleased.

It was more than a month since they had been out together; the heavy rain and the wild winds of November had kept them indoors. It was not always so very amusing, living in the country; sometimes one might just as well have been in Noah's Ark with all the animals. She had a few orders to give in the kitchen, as the Hettémas were coming to dinner; and while he waited for her outside, in the Woodman's Walk, he looked at the cottage warm in this soft Indian summer light, the country road with the big paving-stones overgrown with moss, and saw it all with that last farewell gaze, like an embrace and endowed with memory, the look we bestow on places we are about to leave for ever.

The dining-room window was wide open, and he could hear the chirruping of the golden oriole, cut across by Fanny's voice giving orders to the servant. 'And don't forget, the main thing is—half-past six! Serve the guinea-fowl first. Oh, I must give you a fresh cloth!' Her voice rang out, clear and happy, above the quiet clatter from the kitchen and the little cries of the bird, singing away to himself in the sunlight.

And here was he, knowing that all this was only to last for another two hours, and these festive preparations made his heart bleed.

He almost went straight in and told her everything on the spot. But he was afraid of the way she would scream, of the appalling scene that everyone in the neighbourhood would hear, the uproar that would set all Chaville by the ears. He knew that once she let herself go she did not care in the least what she did. He stuck to his idea of taking her into the forest.

'Here I am!'

She came tripping lightly, took his arm, and warned him to speak quietly and walk fast past their neighbours' cottage, for fear that Olympe might want to come with them and spoil their little walk together. She was not easy in her mind until they had come to the end of the paved road, gone under the railway arch and turned to the left into the woods.

It was mild, sunny weather, the light muted by a silvery, drifting haze, floating everywhere in the air, clinging to the slopes, the trees standing there still with golden leaves on the twigs and, high above the ground, magpies' nests and clusters of green mistletoe. Somewhere a bird was uttering a long, continuous rasping cry, and there was the sound of beaks tapping on wood, the answer to the blows from the woodman's axe.

They walked slowly, leaving their footprints on ground softened by the autumn rains. Hot from hurrying, with bright cheeks and sparkling eyes, she stopped to take off the large light mantilla, a present from Rosa, that she had put over her head coming out—a fragile, costly remnant of past splendours. The dress she was wearing, a cheap black silk thing, split under the arms and at the waist, he had seen her in for three years; and when she picked up her skirts to avoid a puddle, going on ahead of him, he could see that the heels of her boots were walked over.

How light-heartedly she had taken to this semi-penury, without regrets or complaints, all her thoughts devoted to him and his welfare, and never happier than when she walked side by side with him, both her hands clasped over his arm. And seeing her suddenly so youthful again in this renewal of sunlight and love, Jean wondered what up-welling of vital force there must be in a being like her, what marvellous faculty of oblivion and forgiveness, that she could still have so much gaiety and careless good-humour after a life of passion, frustration, and tears; and though her face bore the marks of it, they vanished at the first bubbling up of gaiety.

'It's a real one. I tell you it's a real one,' she was saying.

She crept into the undergrowth, plunging knee-deep into dead leaves, and came back with her hair towsled and tangled by briars, showing him the tiny tracery on the mushroom that distinguishes the true cap from the false.

'You see, there's the frill on it!' she exclaimed in triumph.

He hardly listened, his thoughts far away. He was wondering: 'Is this the moment? Shall I do it now?' But he could not bring himself to do it. Either she was laughing too merrily or the place was not the right one; and so he drew her deeper and deeper into the forest, like a murderer brooding on the deed he is about to do.

He was on the point of speaking when they turned a corner in the path and saw someone coming towards them: it was Hochecorne, the keeper of the plantation, a man they sometimes met. The poor fellow lived beside the pool in the forester's cottage allocated him by the State, and there it was that two children and then his wife had died, one after the other, all of the same pernicious fever. At the time of the first death the doctor had declared the cottage unhealthy, too near to the water and the mists rising from it; but in spite of certificates and recommendations he had been left there for two and then for three years, in which time all his family died, with the exception of one little girl with whom he had at last moved to a new cottage on the edge of the woods.

Hochecorne had a stubborn Breton face, with clear, courageous eyes and a retreating forehead under his uniform cap. He was the very picture of loyalty and a superstitious sense of duty, with his gun slung over one shoulder; against the other rested the head of the sleeping child that he was carrying in his arms.

'How is she?' Fanny asked, smiling at the four-year-old girl, pale and thin from fever, now waking up, opening big red-rimmed eyes.

The woodman sighed. 'Not so good. I take her about everywhere with me, but it doesn't seem to do any good. She doesn't eat any more, there's nothing she has a fancy for. I suppose the change of air was too late and she'd taken the sickness already. She's so light, madame, look—no more than a leaf. One of these days she'll be away just like the others. Ah, dear God!'

This 'dear God!' murmured into his moustache was the only sign of his revolt against the cruelty of men in offices, the men with red tape.

'She's shivering. It looks as though she were cold.'

'It's the fever, madame.'

'Wait, we'll wrap her up warm.' She took the mantilla that she had hanging over her arm and wrapped it round the child. 'Yes, yes, leave it! It'll be her wedding-veil—some day.'

The father gave her a stricken smile and, as the child began to fall asleep again, wan as a little corpse in all this whiteness, he took her tiny hand and waved it as though in thanks to the kind lady. Then he walked on, murmuring 'dear God!' his last words lost amid the crackling of the branches under his feet.

Fanny's gaiety was gone. She clung to Jean with all the anxious tenderness of a woman whose emotion, whether it is sadness or joy, brings her yet closer to the man she loves. Jean thought to himself: 'What a good-hearted creature she is!' But he did not weaken in his determination; on the contrary, he felt himself grow firmer, for here was the place where the track went downhill; and here he re-membered meeting Irène, remembered the radiant smile that had captivated him from the very first instant, even before he knew her deeper charm, the inmost springs of her sweetness and sensibility. He reflected that he had waited until the last moment, for to-day was Thursday. 'Well, then, here goes,' he said to himself, and seeing a small clearing some way ahead, he set it as his furthest limit.

It was a glade in a hollow, with felled trees lying amid chips and torn shreds of bark, and faggots, and holes where fires had been made. A little farther on, glimpsed through the trees, they could see the pool, with a white mist hovering over it, and on the bank the abandoned cottage with the roof falling in, the smashed win-dows wide open, the Hochecornes' lazar-house. Beyond that again the woodland rose steeply towards Vélizy, a high hill thickly timbered with tall old trees, mournful, now all red foliage.

Jean stopped suddenly and said: 'How about resting for a while?'

They sat down on a fallen trunk, a huge, ancient, prostrate oak with only axe-wounds to show where the branches had been. The place was faintly warm, with a pale, luminous trembling in the air and a scent as of withering violets.

'How nice it is!' she said, drooping against his shoulder, searching for a place to kiss his neck.

He drew away slightly and took her hand.

Then, seeing his abrupt change of expression, the hard look on his face, she cried out in alarm: 'What's the matter? What has happened?'

'There's bad news, my poor darling. Hédouin—you know, the man who went away instead of me . . .' He spoke with difficulty, in a hoarse voice that surprised even himself, though it became firmer as he came nearer the end of the story he had thought out in advance: Hédouin had become ill on arriving to take up his post, and he, Jean, was appointed to replace him. It had seemed to him that it would be easier to put it that way; it would be less cruel than the truth. She heard him out without interrupting, her face ashen, her eyes staring.

'When do you leave?' she asked, pulling her hand away.

'Well—this evening—to-night.' And in an artificial, doleful tone he added: 'I shall stop at Castelet for twenty-four hours before embarking at Marseilles.'

'That's enough! Stop lying!' she exclaimed in a fierce rage that brought her to her feet. 'Stop lying! You can't do it! The truth is you're going to get married. Your family's been getting at you about it long enough. They're so terrified that I hold you back and stop you from going off to get typhus or yellow fever. I hope they're satisfied now! And I suppose the young lady's quite to your taste. When I think of the way I've tied your tie for you on Thursdays! I *was* stupid, wasn't I?'

She laughed a dreadful grievous laugh that twisted her mouth, revealing at one side a broken tooth that must have been something recent, for he had not seen it before; it spoilt the perfection of her beautiful pearly teeth, of which she was so proud, and the gap left by one tooth in this cadaverous, sunken, shocked face caused him a horrible pang.

'Listen to me,' he said, taking hold of her and forcing her to sit down beside him. 'Well, yes, I am getting married. My father was set on it, you know that. But what difference can it make to you, since I have to go anyway?'

She freed herself, wanting to keep her anger at white-heat. 'And it's to tell me this that you've made me come miles through the woods! You said to yourself: "Anyway nobody'll hear if she screams." Well, you see, I'm not making a sound. Not a tear! To start with, I've had my fill of the fine fellow you are and you can clear off for all I care, I won't lift a finger to make you come back. Be off to the tropics with your wife, your *little woman*, as they say in your part of the country. A nice piece your *little woman* must be— ugly as a gorilla, I suppose, or perhaps with a belly so big that any-one can see what month she's in. For you're as great a simpleton as those who've chosen her for you.'

She could not contain herself any longer. She plunged headlong into a stream of abuse and infamous slanders, until she reached the stage where she could only stutter words like 'coward—liar— coward,' right into his face, a provocation like a clenched fist.

It was Jean's turn to listen without saying a word, without making any effort to stop her. He liked her better this way, insulting and vile, a true daughter of old Legrand; it made the separation less cruel. And perhaps she caught a glimpse of this, for she was suddenly silent, fell on her knees before him, head and breast inclined towards the ground, and, with a great sob that shook her whole body, she began to moan, with little gasping cries: 'Forgive me, have pity on me. I love you, you're all I have. My love, my life, don't do this thing. Don't leave me. What do you think will become of me?'

He was stirred against his will. Oh, this was what he had feared! Seeing her so, in tears, he felt the tears rising to his own eyes, and he flung his head back to keep them from overflowing. He tried to quieten her with silly phrases, always with the same reasonable argument: 'But as I have to go away anyway . . .'

She pulled herself up with a cry that uttered her whole hope. 'Ah, but you wouldn't have gone away! I would have said to you: Wait a while, let me love you yet awhile. Do you think it happens to a man twice to be loved as I love you? You've plenty of time to marry, you're so young. I'll soon be finished. I shan't be able to go on much longer, and then we'll part as a matter of course.'

He wanted to get up. He found the strength to do so and to tell her that what she was doing was all in vain. But she clutched at him, dragging herself along on her knees, in the mud that was still left in this dip among the little hills, and forced him to sit down again. Kneeling before him, between his legs, the breath from her lips touching his face, her eyes glowing with voluptuous eagerness, with the flat of her hands, childishly, she caressed his stiff, shut face, she ran her fingers through his hair and across his lips, she did everything she could think of to fan the cold embers of their love. Under her breath she reminded him of all their past delights, the slack awakenings, their Sunday afternoons that were all a long embrace, oblivious of the world. All that was nothing compared to what she would give him now. She knew of other kisses, other intoxications, she would invent things for him. . . .

And while she was whispering those words that men hear in the doorways to low dens, there were great tears streaming down her face, which wore an expression of agony and terror. She struggled and cried out as though in a dream: 'Oh, don't let it happen! Say it isn't true that you're going to leave me!' And then there were more sobs, and moans, and cries for help, as though she were seeing him with a knife in his hands.

The executioner had scarcely more heart for this than his victim. He was no more afraid of her anger than of her caresses; but he had no defence against this despair, these deep cries like a stag's belling that rang through the woods, dying away on the stagnant, feverish waters in which a mournful red sun was sinking. . . . He had expected to suffer, but not with this intensity. And he needed all the dazzling rapture of his new love to help him resist, to stop him from putting out both hands and lifting her up and saying: 'I'll stay. Be quiet. I'll stay.'

How long had they been wearing each other out like this? There was nothing left of the sun but a streak, growing ever thinner, in the western sky; the pool faded to slate-grey, and its sickly vapours seemed to come creeping through the heathland and the woods and to go up the hills beyond. In the dusk gathering around them he could see nothing more than that pale face lifted to his, that open mouth wailing its undying anguish. A while later, when it was dark, the cries grew quieter. Now it was the sound of tears, an endless flood of tears, one of those long rains that set in after the great tumult of the storm. . . . And from time to time a deep, muffled 'Oh' was wrung from her, as though she were seeing some horrible thing that she kept driving off and that always returned.

Then there was nothing more. It was over. The living thing had died. A cold wind, rising, stirred in the branches and bore towards them the sound of a distant clock striking.

'Come along—come—don't stay there.'

He raised her gently and felt how limp she had become, as docile as a child, though shaken by great gasping sighs. She seemed to be overcome by fear and respect for the man who had shown himself so strong. She walked beside him, keeping step with him, but timidly, without taking his arm; and anyone seeing them like that, stumbling a little, dismal and in silence, coming along the paths with nothing to guide them but the yellow glimmer of the earth, might have thought they were a peasant couple going wearily home after the long, hard day in the open air.

At the outskirts of the wood a light shone out ahead. It came through Hochecorne's open door, showing the shadowy figures of two men.

'Is that you, Gaussin?' Hettéma asked, coming up with the wood-man. They had begun to be anxious when Jean and Fanny did not come back, and especially because of the moaning they had heard in the depths of the woods. Hochecorne was just going to take his gun and go out in search of them.

'Good evening, sir, good evening, madame. The little lass is very pleased with her shawl. I had to let her have it to go to bed with.'

The last thing they did together was that act of charity of a few hours earlier, their hands linked for the last time round the body of the dying child.

'Good-bye, good-bye, Hochecorne,' they said, and all ·three hurried towards the house, Hettéma still very puzzled to know what the clamour was that had echoed all through the woods. 'Sometimes it was high, and sometimes it was low,' he said. 'Like someone killing an animal. How on earth didn't you hear it?'

Neither of them replied.

At the corner of the Woodman's Walk Jean hesitated.

'Stay for dinner,' she said in a low voice, imploringly. 'You've missed your train. You can go on the nine o'clock.'

He went in with them. What was there to fear? Nobody goes through a scene like that twice over, and the least he could do was to give her that little consolation.

The dining-room was warm, the lamp burning brightly, and the sound of their footsteps had told the servant that they were coming, so that she had the soup already on the table.

'There you are at last!' Olympe said. She was sitting in her place with her napkin tucked under her short arms. She took the lid off the soup-tureen and suddenly broke off with a cry: 'My God, dear!'

Fanny was deadly pale. She looked ten years older, with swollen, red-rimmed eyelids, mud on her dress and even in her hair, in all the frantic disarray of a low prostitute who has been chased by the police. She drew a deep breath, her burning eyelids blinking in the bright light, and then gradually the warmth of the cottage and the sight of the gaily laid table woke memories of their good days and brought a new flood of tears, through which they heard the words:

'He's leaving me. He's getting married.'

Hettéma, and his wife, and the countrywoman who was serving at table, all looked at each other and then at Gaussin.

'Well, let's get on with dinner, anyway,' big, fat Hettéma said. It was obvious that he was terribly angry.

The sound of greedy gulpings mingled with the trickling of water in the next room, where Fanny was sponging her face. When she came back, her face almost blue with powder, and wearing a white woollen peignoir, the Hettémas scrutinized her in furtive

L—S.

dismay, expecting a fresh explosion at any moment; and they were amazed to see her sit down without a word and attack the food with the gluttonous eagerness of someone who has been wrecked and starving; it was as though she were filling in the pit of her grief and the abyss of her cries with everything she could lay hands on, bread, cabbage, a wing of guinea-fowl, apples. . . . She ate and ate. . . .

They talked at first with an air of constraint, and then gradually more freely. And since for the Hettémas the only things that counted were the thoroughly crude, material things, such as the best way of making pancakes to be served with jam, or whether horse-hair mattresses are better than feather-beds, they arrived without impediment at the coffee, which the fat couple sweetened with a caramel slowly sucked, elbows on the table.

It would have done anyone good to see the fine, trustful, tranquil looks exchanged by these ponderous stable-mates and bed-fellows. *They* had no desire to leave each other. Jean caught the look between them, and here, in the familiar warmth of this room that was so full of memories for him, every corner of it packed with old habit, he felt himself being overcome by a torpor of weariness and good digestion and well-being. Fanny, who had been watching him, quietly brought her chair closer, until her legs touched his, and slipped her arm under his.

'Look,' he said abruptly, 'nine o'clock. Quick, good-bye. I'll write.'

He was on his feet and outside and across the road, groping in the dark to open the barrier on the track to the station when two arms were flung round him and held him fast. He heard her say: 'At least kiss me.'

He felt her close against him, naked under the open peignoir, and was stirred by the smell and warmth of her flesh, overwhelmed by her farewell kiss, which left him with an after-taste of fever and tears in his mouth. And feeling his weakness, she breathed: 'One more night, only one. . . .'

On the railway line a signal went down. The train was coming!

He never knew how he found the strength to shake her off and go running and leaping up to the station, from where the lamps shone through the bare branches. He was still amazed as he sat down in a corner of the compartment, panting, and then leaned forward to peer through the glass at the lamp-lit windows of the cottage. There at the barrier was a white figure.... 'Good-bye! Good-bye!' he heard her calling. And the sound of her voice put an end to the silent terror that this bend of the line had inspired in him, as he looked back now and saw her standing where in his fantasies he had seen her lying dead.

With his head out of the window he watched their cottage receding into the distance, growing smaller, disappearing behind a rise in the landscape, its light at the last no more than the glimmer of a fallen star. Suddenly he felt enormous joy and relief. How freely he could breathe and how beautiful this whole Meudon valley was, these high black hills with a twinkling triangle of countless lights springing up against the darkness, away in the distance, strung out in long ribbons down towards the Seine! There Irène was waiting for him and he was going to her as fast as the train would carry him, with all his love and longing, with all that was in him driving towards that straight young life.

Paris!... He hailed a cab, meaning to drive to the Place Vendôme. But in the gaslight he saw his clothes and shoes—plastered with thick, heavy mud, all his past still clinging to him, a dead weight of something soiled. 'Oh no, not this evening,' he thought to himself and went to his old hotel in the Rue Jacob, where The Rip had taken a room for him next to his own.

❧ 13 ❧

THE next day Césaire took on the delicate job of going to Chaville to collect his nephew's clothes and books, to complete the break by moving these things out. He came back very late, when Jean was beginning to wear himself out with all sorts of wild and dreadful surmises. At last a double-decker cab came round the corner of the Rue Jacob, ponderous as a hearse, loaded up with rope-bound boxes and a vast trunk that Jean recognized as his own. His uncle came in looking mysterious and heart-sick.

'It's taken me a long time, for I wanted to take the whole lot at one go and not have to go back again,' he said. And then, pointing to the boxes, which two porters were putting down all over the room: 'That's linen, that's clothes, those are your papers, and these are your books. The only thing that's missing is your letters. She begged me to let her keep them awhile to read them over again, to have something to remind her of you. I thought there couldn't be any harm in it. She's such a good soul.'

He gave a long puff of weariness as he sat on the trunk and mopped his forehead with an unbleached silk handkerchief as big as a napkin. Jean had not the heart to ask for details as to the state he had found her in; and his uncle gave none, from fear of depressing him. And so they filled the uneasy pause, heavy with things unsaid, with remarks about the sudden change in the weather since the day before. How cold it had turned, and how wretched that leafless and deserted district looked, there on the outskirts of Paris, with its groves of factory chimneys and those enormous cast-iron water tanks used by the market gardeners. Then after a while Jean asked:

'So she didn't give you anything for me, Uncle?'

'No. You needn't worry. She won't bother you. She's accepted her lot in a very resolute and dignified way.'

Why did Jean read into these few words an intention to blame him, to reproach him for his rigorous stand?

'It's all very well,' his uncle went on, 'but weighing up one bad business against another, I'd rather face la Mornas' claws than that poor woman's despair.'

'Did she cry a great deal?'

'Oh, my dear chap! She seemed to be crying her heart out, and it reduced me to tears too, so that I hadn't even the strength to . . .' He became confused and then suddenly shook his emotion off, tossing his head like an old goat. 'After all, what can be done about it? It isn't your fault. You couldn't spend your whole life like that. Everything's been done very properly, you've left her with money and the furniture. . . . And now off with the old loves! Try and make the right thing of your marriage. Bless me, these are things too serious for me to deal with! This is where the consul will have to take a hand. I'm just the chap for settling up the little irregularities. . . .' And all at once he was seized by another fit of melancholy, pressing his forehead to the window-pane and looking out at the lowering sky and the rain pattering on the roofs. 'It's all very well, but the world's growing a sad place. In my day people parted more light-heartedly than this.'

When The Rip had gone, followed by his elevator-machine, Jean missed his bustling, talkative good humour. The week seemed to pass very slowly; everything felt desolate and lonely, with all the blank gloom of bereavement. In such cases, even if there is no true passion to be mourned, each man seeks his counterpart, the missing half of himself; for living together, the sharing of bed and board, creates a web of invisible and subtle bonds whose strength becomes apparent only in the pain and stress of tearing apart. Contact and habit have an influence so miraculously pervasive that two people living the same life together end up by resembling each other.

The five years he had spent with Sappho had not succeeded in moulding him to that point; yet his body still bore the marks of the chain, still felt the heavy dragging of it. And just as his footsteps had several times turned of their own accord towards Chaville when he came out of his office, so too in the morning he would sometimes look at the pillow beside him, expecting to see those heavy drifts of black hair, fallen free of the comb, which he had always kissed on waking.

Above all it was the evenings that seemed endless. The hotel room reminded him of the early days of their liaison and the presence of a mistress so different, sensitive, and with quiet ways, whose little visiting-card gave the mirror an elusive perfume, like the mystery of her name: Fanny Legrand. At such times he would go out and walk himself tired, or stupefy himself with the brassy music and glaring lights of some little theatre, until the time when old Bouchereau gave him the right to spend three evenings a week in his fiancée's company.

For they did come to an understanding. Irène loved him, and *Unclé* was all in favour of it; they were to be married at the beginning of April, when his course was over. Before them were three winter months in which they would gaze at each other, get to know each other, and desire each other, weaving fond, beguiling variations on that first soul-linking glance and the first soul-troubling confession.

Coming home without the least desire to sleep, after the evening when their engagement was formally settled, Jean felt an impulse to make his room tidy and neat, a place to work in; it was a natural instinct to make outer things correspond to an inner attitude. He arranged his table and his books, which had not yet been unpacked, but were piled up at the bottom of one of those hurriedly packed boxes, law books jumbled between a pile of handkerchiefs and a gardening jacket. A dictionary of commercial law, the book he referred to most, flopped open, and out fell a letter without an envelope, in Fanny's handwriting.

She had left it to luck and to his future work, mistrusting Césaire's momentary sentimentality and thinking this the best way to make sure it would arrive. At first he did not want to open it, but he gave way at the sight of the first words, very gentle, very reasonable as they were, the writer's emotion apparent only in the unsteadiness of the pen and the uneven sloping of the lines. She asked for only one act of grace, one thing only: that he would come back from time to time. She would not say anything, she would not reproach him for anything: neither for his marriage nor for this separation, which she recognized as absolute and final. She only wanted to see him. . . .

'Remember, it's a terrible blow for me, and so unexpected, such a shock. It's like after someone has died or there has been a fire, I don't know what to do with myself. I cry a lot, I keep waiting for you, I look round the place where I have been so happy. There is nobody but you who can make me get used to this new situation. It would be a kindness—come and see me, so that I don't feel so alone. I'm afraid of what I may do.'

These supplications, this imploring cry, recurred all through the letter, summed up each time in the same word: 'Come. . . .' It almost seemed to him that he was in that clearing deep in the woods with Fanny at his feet, in the ashy, violet light of evening, with that despairing face looking up at him all streaked and soft with tears, the open mouth a pool of darkness, an unuttered cry. It was this that haunted him all night long, troubling his dreams, while the blissful enchantment in which he had come home had faded. It was that ageing, worn face that he kept on seeing, in spite of all his efforts to put another face between it and himself: Irène's face with its pure contours and the freshness of a flowering pink, the candour of her love lighting her cheeks with tiny flames of colour.

The letter was a week old. For a week that unhappy woman had been waiting for a word or a visit, something to hearten her in her resignation, as she had asked him. But how was it that she had not written since? Perhaps she was ill, he thought, his old fears quickening again. It occurred to him that Hettéma would be able to give him news and, relying on the regularity of his habits, he went to the Artillery Museum to meet him.

The last stroke of ten was striking from the belfry of St. Thomas Aquinas's as the big fat man came round the corner into the little square, his collar turned up and his pipe clenched between his teeth, both hands clasped round the bowl to warm his fingers. Jean watched him from a distance, deeply moved at the thought of all this reminded him of. But Hettéma greeted him with hardly concealed ill-humour. 'Oh, it's you! We haven't exactly been blessing

you this week! To think we went to the country for peace and
quiet!'

And standing in the doorway, finishing his pipe, he told Jean
that the previous Sunday they had invited Fanny to dine with them
and bring the child, whose day out it was. They wanted to try and
distract her from her gloomy thoughts. And indeed they had quite
a cheerful meal and she even sang them a bit of a song over dessert.
They took leave of each other about ten o'clock and the Hettémas
were just going to cuddle into their warm, soft bed when there was
a banging on the shutters and little Josaph called out in a frightened
voice: 'Come quick, Mother's going to poison herself!' Hettéma
rushed into the other house just in time to wrench the laudanum
bottle out of her hands. He had to struggle with her, holding her
firmly round the body while she butted him with her head and
scratched his face with her comb. The bottle was smashed in the
struggle, laudanum poured all over the place, and all he got out of
it was clothes stained and smelling of poison. 'But I don't have to
tell you that scenes like that and all that sort of melodrama isn't
just the thing for quiet people. So we've finished with it, I've given
notice and we're moving out next month.' He put his pipe away
in its case, and with a thoroughly unperturbed good-bye to Jean
vanished under the low arches of a small courtyard, leaving Jean
overwhelmed by what he had heard.

He imagined the scene in the room that had been their bedroom,
the terrified child running for help, the violent struggle with that
big man; and he could almost feel the opiate taste, the sleepy bitterness of the spilt laudanum. The horror of it remained with him all
day, heightened by his awareness of the complete solitude in which
she would soon be left. Once the Hettémas were gone, who would
restrain her from another attempt?

A letter came, reassuring him slightly. Fanny thanked him for
not being as harsh as he seemed, since he still took some interest in
the wretched woman whom he had abandoned.

'They've told you, haven't they? I wanted to die. I felt so alone!
I tried, but I couldn't, they stopped me. Perhaps my hand shook too

much. And being frightened of pain, frightened of being ugly. . . . Oh, how did the Doré woman have the courage? After the first shame of having failed, it was a joy to think that I would be able to write to you and love you from a distance and see you some day again. For I don't give up hope that you will come some time, just as people go to see a friend in trouble, in a house of mourning, from pity, simply from pity.'

From that time on a random series of letters came from Chaville, one every two or three days, some long, some short, a record of grief that he had not the strength to send back; and so they made larger the raw wound in his over-sensitive heart, filling him with pity that was not love, pity not for his former mistress but for a human being suffering on his account.

One day she wrote to him about the departure of their neighbours, those witnesses of her past happiness who would take so many memories away with them. All she had to remind her of him now was the furniture, the cottage itself, and the maidservant, a half-witted boorish creature who took no more interest in things than did the golden oriole, shivering in this winter weather, sadly ruffling up his feathers as he cowered in a corner of his cage.

Another day, when a pale gleam of sunlight had fallen on the window-pane, she had waked up with the joyous conviction that he would come that day. Why? Oh, it was only an idea. . . . At once she set about putting the house in order, making herself look her best in her Sunday dress and with her hair done the way he liked it. Then as evening drew on and the last light fled she watched the trains from the dining-room window, believed she heard his footsteps coming along the Woodman's Walk. . . . She must be crazy!

Sometimes she sent no more than a line: 'It's raining, it's quite dark. I'm all alone, crying for you.' Once she did no more than put a flower into the envelope, a pathetic little flower stiff with frost, the last bloom from their tiny garden. More than all her lamentations this flower picked in the snow spoke to him of winter, solitude and desolation; he could see the place at the end of the road, and against the background of the flower-beds a woman's skirt, the hem wet through, coming and going as she walked up and down alone.

This pity tearing at his heartstrings meant that he was still living with Fanny in his thoughts, even though he had separated from her. He thought of her continually, had her in his mind's eye at every other moment; but by some strange trick of memory, although it was only five or six weeks since their separation and he remembered the smallest details of the cottage rooms, from La Balue's cage hanging opposite a wooden cuckoo-clock, won at a country fair, to the hazel branches that tapped against the bathroom window whenever there was the slightest breath of wind, the woman herself never appeared distinctly. He saw her at a remove, in a mist, only one detail of her face quite clear, emphatic and distressing: the twisted mouth, the smile showing the gap left by the broken tooth.

Now that she had aged so much, what was to become of her, this poor creature with whom he had slept side by side for so long? When the money he had left her came to an end, where would she go, to what depths would she sink? And suddenly there loomed up a memory of that miserable woman of the streets whom he had encountered one evening in an English tavern, who had been dying of thirst as she ate her plateful of smoked salmon. That was what Fanny would become, Fanny whose loving care, faithful and passionate devotion he had for so long taken for granted. The thought of it reduced him to despair. And yet what was he to do? Because he had had the misfortune to meet this woman and to live with her for a while, was he condemned to keep her for ever and sacrifice his happiness to her? Why he, and not the others? What justice was there in that?

Even while he still would not let himself go and see her, he began to write to her; and his deliberately downright, matter-of-fact letters betrayed something of his emotion in spite of the advice he gave her about being sensible and calming down. He urged her to take Josaph away from the place where he was boarded out and have him with her, to give her something to do, something to take an interest in. But Fanny refused. What was the good of bringing the child home to see her grief and discouragement? It was quite bad enough on Sundays when he prowled from chair to chair or wandered out into the garden, guessing that some great misfortune had caused this air of mourning in the house and never daring to ask for news of 'Papa Jean' since being told, in tears, that he had gone away and would not ever come back again.

'So all my papas go away,' he had said.

And this saying of the little waif's, which she told him of in a heart-rending letter, weighed heavily on Gaussin's heart. Soon it became so unbearable to know that she was at Chaville that he advised her to come back to Paris and go about and see people. With her sordid experience of men and separations, Fanny saw nothing in this suggestion but an appalling egoism, a wish to get rid of her for ever by means of one of those sudden infatuations that she knew so well. And she came out with it quite frankly and sincerely:

'You know what I told you a long time ago. I shall always be your wife, in spite of everything—your loving, faithful wife. Here in our cottage your presence is all around me, and I wouldn't leave it for anything in the world. What should I do in Paris? I loathe my past, which takes you away from me. And just think what you would be exposing us to. You think you're so strong-minded, do you? Then come, you cruel man, just once, one single time. . . .'

He did not go. But one Sunday afternoon, when he was alone, working, he heard a little double knock at his door. He started, recognizing her old way of telling him that she was there. Afraid of being turned away with an excuse by the concièrge, she had come running straight up the stairs without asking for him at all. He went over to the door quietly, his footsteps muffled by the carpet, and heard her breathing through the keyhole:

'Jean? Are you there?'

Oh that humble, broken voice! And once more, though fainter now, it came: 'Jean! . . .' Then there was a moaning sigh, the rustle of a letter being slipped under the door, and the faint sound of a last blown kiss.

He heard her going slowly down the stairs, lingering on each step, as though she were expecting to be called back. Only when she had quite gone did he pick the letter up and open it. That morning the Hochecorne child had been buried at the Children's Hospital. She had gone with the father and several people from Chaville, and she had not been able to stop herself from going up to see him or at least to leave these lines written in advance. 'I told you, didn't I? If I lived in Paris I'd be on the stairs outside your room all the time. Good-bye, sweetheart, I'm going home to our house now.'

And as he read, his eyes misty with tears, he remembered the same scene in the Rue de l'Arcade, the cast-off lover's agony, the letter slipped under the door, and Fanny's heartless laughter. So she loved him more than he loved Irène! Or was it only that men, being more involved than women in the battle of life and affairs, did not give themselves so exclusively to love and had not the same capacity for forgetting or neglecting everything but one all-absorbing passion?

This torment, this aching pity that consumed him, ceased only when he was with Irène. Only then did the anguish slacken, melting in the gentle beam of her blue eyes. There was nothing left but a great weariness, a longing to put his head on her shoulder and stay like that, not speaking, not moving, safe at last.

'What is the matter?' she would ask him. 'Are you not happy?'

Oh yes, he was very happy. But why was his happiness made up of so much sadness, so many tears? And there were times when he almost began to tell her the whole story, treating her as a kind, sensible friend; poor fool, he did not stop to think of the distress that such confidences cause in young minds and the incurable wounds that may be dealt to trust and affection. If only he could have carried her off, if only he could have run away with her! He could feel that then his torment would be over. But old Bouchereau would not let the wedding take place an hour earlier than the appointed time. 'I'm old,' he said, 'I'm a sick man. I shall not see my girl again. So you mustn't deprive me of these last days.'

Under his apparent sternness the great Bouchereau was the best of men. Although he was constantly in pain from the heart disease that he himself observed, following the course of it and speaking of it with astonishing calm and coolness, he continued to practise and teach, often in agonies while examining patients less ill than himself. The only weakness that this great mind had, and one characteristic of his peasant origins in Tourangeau, was his respect for titles and the nobility. And the recollection of the turrets at Castelet, and the old name d'Armandy, had not been without influence in making him so willing to accept Jean as a husband for his niece.

The wedding was to take place at Castelet, to avoid having to move the poor invalid mother, who wrote to her future daughter once a week, warm-hearted, loving letters that she dictated to Divonne or one of the little sisters from Bethany. And it was a very sweet joy for Jean to talk to Irène about his family, gathering Castelet about him in imagination there in the Place Vendôme, the threads of all his affections drawn together round the dear girl to whom he was engaged.

There was only one thing that frightened him—that he felt so old and tired compared with her, watching her taking a child-like pleasure in things that no longer amused him and looking forward to the delights of life shared in common, which were already discounted for him. So it was for instance with the list that had to be made of all the things they would need to take with them going abroad, and the furniture and materials to be chosen. He was going through it one evening when he suddenly stopped, his pen hovering, and was appalled to realize that he was going through exactly the same things as when he had set up house in the Rue d'Amsterdam; it was an inevitable repetition of so much joyful excitement, and his capacity for such happiness was worn out, finished by those five years spent with that other woman in a travesty of real marriage.

⇛ 14 ⇚

'Yes, my dear chap—died in Rosa's arms last night. I've just taken him to be stuffed.'

The composer de Potter, whom Jean had met coming out of a shop in the Rue du Bac, attached himself to him in an obvious desire to pour out his feelings, which did not go with his imperturbable, hard face, the face of a business man. He told Jean the whole story of poor Bichito's end: he had been killed by the Paris winter, had simply shrivelled up in the cold, in spite of all the cottonwool and the wick soaked in spirits of wine that had been kept under his little nest for the last two months, as people did with prematurely born babies. But nothing they could do made any difference; he went on shivering. And the previous night while they all gathered round him he was shaken from head to tail by a last shudder and died a good Christian death, thanks to the floods of holy water that Mother Pilar sprinkled on his rough-grained skin from which the life ebbed in prismatic wavy lines as of watered silk, with the old woman muttering over him: '*Dios loui pardonne!*'

'It makes me laugh, but my heart is heavy all the same, particularly when I think of my poor Rosa's grief. I left her at home in tears. Luckily there's Fanny with her.'

'Fanny?'

'Yes. It's a long time since we saw her. She turned up this morning just in the middle of the whole excitement, and the good soul stayed on to comfort Rosa.' And without noticing the effect that his words had had on Jean, he added: 'So it's all over? You're not living together any more? Do you remember the talk we had on the lake at Enghien? At least you make some use of the lessons you're given.' And there was a trace of envy in his approval.

Jean frowned. He felt genuinely uneasy at the thought that Fanny had gone back to Rosario; but he was annoyed with himself for his weakness, since after all he had neither rights nor responsibilities now where her life was concerned.

Outside a house in the Rue de Beaune, a very old street in what was once the aristocratic part of Paris, a short distance from where they had met, de Potter stopped. Here it was that he lived or was supposed to live, for the sake of convention, in the eyes of the world; for actually his time was spent either in the Avenue de Villiers or at Enghien and he only put in an appearance at his conjugal dwelling from time to time in order that his wife and child should not seem altogether abandoned.

Jean was about to go on his way and had begun to say good-bye, but de Potter kept his hand in his own two long, hard hands and said without any embarrassment, like a man who has given up being ashamed of his vice:

'Do me a favour and come in with me. I was supposed to dine with my wife to-day, but I really can't leave my poor Rosa all alone in her sorrow. You can be my excuse for going out again, so that I won't have to go through a tiresome explanation.'

The composer's study, in a superb, chilly apartment on the second floor, had the atmosphere of desolation typical of such a room when nobody works there. Everything was far too tidy; there was no disorder, none of the active little fever that takes hold of objects, even of furniture. There was not a book, not a sheet of paper on the desk, which was majestically adorned with an enormous bronze ink-stand, empty and shining as though in a shop window. There was no music on the old spinet-shaped piano on which he had composed his first works. On the mantelpiece over the empty grate was a white marble bust of a delicate-featured young woman with a sweet expression, pallid in the failing light, making the fireplace seem more bleak than ever and gazing sadly at the walls on which hung gilded and beribboned laurel wreaths, medals, commemorative rolls, all the trappings of fame and worldly vanity, now generously left to the wife as some sort of compensation and by her kept there like everlasting flowers on the grave of her happiness.

They had only just come in when the study door opened and Madame de Potter appeared, asking:

'Is that you, Gustave?'

She had thought he was alone and stopped, visibly disturbed, at the sight of a strange face. She was a beautiful and elegant woman, dressed with sensitive good taste; she seemed more rarefied than the bust showed her, the sweetness of her face transformed into something resolute that was a combination of courage and nervous energy. In society there was a division of opinion as to what she was really like. Some people blamed her for putting up with her husband's glaring neglect, the insult of his long-standing bare-faced affair with another woman; others admired her silent resignation. The general view was that she was a quiet person who valued peace above all else and found adequate compensations for her semi-widowhood in the affection of her lovely child and the joy of bearing a great man's name.

But while the composer was introducing his companion and mumbling some excuse for not dining at home, a quiver passed over the young woman's face and her eyes became blank and staring; she obviously ceased to hear what he was saying, as though quite absorbed in her distress. Watching her, Jean realized that a great sorrow was buried alive under that socially correct exterior. She seemed to accept her husband's excuses, which she did not believe, merely saying gently:

'Raymond will cry. I promised him that we would have dinner at his bedside.'

'How is he?' de Potter asked absently, impatiently.

'He's better, but he still coughs. Aren't you coming in to see him?'

He muttered something into his moustache, pretending to be looking about the room for something. 'Not now—great hurry—appointment at the club—six o'clock.' The one thing he dreaded was to be left alone with her.

'Then good-bye,' the young woman said, suddenly tranquil, her features smooth as a pool of clear water closing over again where a stone has dropped to the bottom. She inclined her head and withdrew.

'Let's clear out!' de Potter exclaimed in relief, and dragged Jean away.

Jean followed him down the stairs, gazing at this stiff, correct figure in the long, close-fitting English-style overcoat, this man with his dreadful passion, so upset by having to take his mistress's chameleon to be stuffed, and going away without a kiss for his sick child.

'All this, my dear fellow,' the composer said as though in answer to what his friend was thinking, 'all this is the fault of the people who married me off. What a favour they did me and that poor woman! What madness to try turning me into a husband and father! I was Rosa's lover and I still am, and it will always be the same till one of us dies. Do you think a vice that's got you at the right moment and has a firm hold on you is something you ever shake off? And how about yourself? Are you sure that if Fanny had wanted . . .?'

He hailed an empty cab that was passing and got in.

'Talking about Fanny,' he concluded, 'have you heard the news? Flamant has been pardoned and let out of jail. It was Déchelette's petition that did it. Poor Déchelette! So he has done good even after his death.'

Standing quite still, with a mad desire to run and catch hold of the wheels that were jolting away at full speed down the dark street where the gas had just been lit, Jean was amazed at how deeply moved he was. 'Flamant pardoned and out of jail . . .' he murmured to himself, seeing the reason for Fanny's silence in the last few days. Her lamentations had broken off so suddenly because she was enjoying the consoler's caresses; for of course the wretched man's first thought, the moment he was free, must have been for her.

He remembered the exchange of love-letters that had gone on while Flamant was in jail, and Fanny's obstinacy in defending Flamant, and him alone, while holding the others so cheap; and instead of congratulating himself on an event that logically rid him of all anxiety and all remorse, an indefinable misery kept him feverishly awake for part of the night. Why? He did not love her; but he thought of his letters, which she still had, which she might read to the other man, or even—how could he be sure of anything?—some day under an evil influence might use to trouble his peace, his happiness.

M—S.

Whether this was true or false, or whether, without his knowing it, it concealed some other worry, this preoccupation with his letters made him decide on a rash move: he would make the visit to Chaville that he had always stubbornly refused to make. To whom, after all, could he entrust so intimate and delicate a mission? One February morning he took the ten o'clock train, very calm in mind and heart, with only the one fear that he might find the house shut and the woman already gone off in company with the ex-convict.

The moment the train came round the bend he saw the open shutters and the curtains on the windows and was reassured; and remembering his emotion when he had watched the little light disappear, a glow-worm in the darkness, he mocked at himself and the instability of his feelings. Coming back now, he was no longer the same man and undoubtedly he would not find the same woman. Yet it had happened only two months ago. The trees alongside the railway-line had not yet put out new leaves; they were still flecked with the rust-red patches that had been there on the day of the great break, when the woods had echoed with her cries.

He was the only person to get out at the station, in a chill, penetrating mist, and he set off along the lane, slippery with hardened snow, and passed under the railway arch. He met nobody until he came to the Woodman's Walk, where he saw a man and a child come round the corner, followed by a porter pushing a barrow loaded with suitcases.

The child, muffled up to the eyes, with his cap pulled down over his ears, stifled a cry as they passed Jean. 'It's Josaph!' he said to himself, faintly surprised and hurt by the little boy's ingratitude; and, turning round, he met the gaze of the man walking hand in hand with the child. That fine, intelligent face, pale from lack of fresh air, those reach-me-down clothes obviously bought only the previous day, the fair beard just sprouting on the chin, not having had time to grow since prison. . . . Flamant, of course! And Josaph was his son.

It was a flash of revelation. He saw it all, understood it all, from the letter in which Flamant had asked Fanny to look after the child he had in the country, down to the little boy's mysterious arrival, Hettéma's air of embarrassment in speaking of the adoption, and the glances between Fanny and Olympe; for they had all conspired to get him to support the forger's son. Oh, a nice fool he had been! How they must have laughed at him! He felt a wave of disgust with all that shameful past and a desire to hurry away as fast and as far as possible. But he was worried by things that he wanted to find out. The man and the child had gone—why had she not gone too? And then there were his letters. He must have his letters; he must not leave anything of himself in this den of stained honour and unhappiness.

'Madame! Here is monsieur!'

'Monsieur who?' a voice asked ingenuously from inside the room.

'It's me. . . .'

There was a cry, the sound of someone leaping to the floor, and then: 'Wait a moment! I'm getting up! I'm coming!'

Still in bed after midday! Jean had his own suspicions of the reasons why, for he knew the causes of these shattered, exhausted mornings. And while he waited in the dining-room the tiniest familiar things, the whistle of the train coming up the hill, the tremulous ma-a-a! of a goat in a neighbouring garden, the few dishes on the table, all took him back to mornings in the past and the hasty breakfast before going to catch the train.

Fanny came in, eagerly dashing towards him. Then, at his chilly manner, she stopped short. For a moment they both stood astonished, wavering, not knowing what to make of this encounter after the breaking off of their intimacy; they were like two people standing on opposite banks of a river, the bridge broken, and between them the immense stretch of the fathomless running waters.

'Good morning,' she said in a low voice, not moving.

To her he seemed changed, pale. He was surprised to find her looking so young, only rather fatter and not as tall as he had been imagining her, but drenched in that special radiance, with that brilliance in her skin and eyes, that softness as of a fresh, grassy meadow, which she always had after nights of the deepest passion. So she had stayed in the woods, at the bottom of the ravine full of dead leaves, while he had been eaten up with pity for her.

'Late rising seems to be the thing in the country,' he said sardonically.

She made excuses, pretending that she had had a headache, and like him used impersonal turns of phrase, speaking only in the third person. Then, as he raised his eyebrows in silence, glancing at the remains of the meal, she said: 'It's the child. He had breakfast here this morning before going away.'

'Going away? Where is he going?' He affected a supreme indifference, as though nothing could possibly matter less; but the gleam in his eyes betrayed him.

'His father came for him,' Fanny said. 'He's taken him away.'

'On being let out of jail, I suppose?'

She started, but she did not attempt to lie. 'Well, yes. I had promised and I did it. Time and again I wanted to tell you, but I didn't dare to, I was afraid you would send him away, poor little thing.' And she added timidly: 'You were so jealous.'

He gave a great mocking laugh. Jealous! He jealous of that criminal! It was too absurd! Then, feeling his anger rising, he broke off short and told her sharply what he had come for. His letters! Why had she not given them to Césaire? It would have spared them an interview painful to both.

'That's true,' she said, still very quiet and gentle. 'But I'm going to give them to you, they're here.'

He followed her into the bedroom, saw the unmade bed, the clothes hastily drawn up to the two pillows, and breathed in that odour of cigarette-smoke mingled with perfumes of cream and powder, and knew it all again just as he knew the small mother-of-pearl box on the table. And the same thought came to them both.

'It isn't so much this time,' she said, opening the box. 'There's no danger that we'll set anything on fire.'

He was silent, uneasy, dry-mouthed, hesitating to go nearer to that tumbled bed where she was standing, leafing through the letters for the last time. She stood with her head bent, the nape of her neck firm and white under the upswept, coiled hair, her figure somewhat thickened, flabby in the loose folds of the woollen robe she was wearing, all slackness and neglect.

'There! That's the lot!'

He took the bundle and stuffed it hastily into his pocket, already thinking of something else. Then he asked:

'So he's taken his child away? Where are they going?'

'He's going back to Morvan, to his own part of the country, to hide. He'll do his engravings and send them to Paris under another name.'

'And you? Do you mean to stay here?'

She averted her eyes to avoid meeting his, stammering that it would be very dismal. So she thought—she thought she might go away soon—go on a short journey.

'To Morvan, I suppose? To the family!' And unleashing all his jealous fury, he exclaimed: 'You might as well admit at once that you're going to join this thief of yours, you're going to live with him. You've been wanting to do it long enough. Go on then! Go back to your sty! A whore and a forger together make a pretty pair. What a fool I was to try pulling you out of the mud!'

She was still silent and motionless, but there was a triumphant glitter under her lowered lids. And the more he lashed her with ferocious and outrageous irony, the prouder she seemed and the more the trembling at the corner of her mouth increased. Now he was talking of his own happiness, that pure, young love, the only love. Oh, how sweet it would be to sleep pillowed on a decent woman's heart! Then swiftly, dropping his voice as though he were ashamed, he asked:

'I passed your Flamant in the road. Did he spend the night here?'

'Yes, it was late, it was snowing. We made him up a bed on the couch.'

'You're lying! He slept *there*! I've only got to see the bed, I've only got to look at you!'

'And what if he did?' She brought her face close up to his, her big grey eyes lit with voluptuous fire. 'Could I know you were coming?

And after I'd lost you what could anything else matter? I was miserable, lonely, sick of everything. . . .'

'And then the prison smell! After living with an honest man for so long it was an interesting change, was it? The two of you must have had your fill of—ah, the filth of it! There!'

She saw the blow coming and did not try to dodge. It struck her full in the face. Then with a stifled groan of pain, joy, and victory she flung herself on him, hugging him in her arms, and cried out: 'Sweetheart! Sweetheart! You still love me!' And they fell on to the bed, locked in each other's arms.

The roar of a passing express woke him up with a start, towards evening. For a few minutes he lay with open eyes, not knowing where he was, alone in the depths of this big bed where his limbs—aching as though after long hours of walking—seemed to lie in a senseless jumble, apparently not belonging to his body. There had been a heavy fall of snow during the afternoon. The profound silence was interrupted only by the sound of the snow trickling and slithering against the walls, along the panes, dripping from the eaves, and sometimes down the chimney on to the coke fire, where it made a sizzling splash.

Where was he? What was he doing there? Little by little the light reflected from the snow outside in the small garden showed him the room, all white, lit from below, the big portrait of Fanny on the wall opposite him; and the memory of his fall came back to him, without any shade of surprise. From the moment of entering this room and seeing the bed he had felt the spell descend and known he was lost; the sheets had drawn him like a chasm, and he had said to himself: 'If I fall, it will be irreparable and for ever.' Now it had happened, and mingled with a bleak feeling of disgust at his feebleness there was something like relief at the thought that he would never get out of this mire. It was the pitiable sense of comfort that a wounded man might have, with his blood draining away, his wound gaping open, as he collapsed on to a dunghill to die there—tired of pain, tired of struggling, his veins open, exquisitely sinking into that soft, fetid warmth.

What remained to be done now was horrible, but very simple. He could not go back to Irène after this betrayal and risk entering on a life like de Potter's. However low he had fallen, he had not come to that. He would write to Bouchereau, the great physiologist who had been the first to study and describe maladies of the will, and lay a terrible case before him: the story of his life from the first meeting with this woman when she had laid her hand on his arm, down to the day when, thinking himself saved, in the full intoxication of his happiness, he fell a victim to her once again, ensnared by the magic of the past, that horrible past in which love had so little place, only cowardly habit and vice that had entered into the very bone.

The door opened. Fanny came into the bedroom very quietly in order not to wake him. Between half-closed lids he watched her, lithe and energetic, years younger, sitting at the fire to warm her feet, which were wet from the snow in the garden, and now and then turning towards him with the little smile that she had worn that morning during their quarrel. She went over and got her packet of Maryland from the usual place, rolled herself a cigarette and was about to leave the room, when he stopped her.

'I thought you were asleep,' she said.

'No. Sit down here—let's have a talk.'

She sat on the edge of the bed, slightly surprised by his gravity.

'Fanny—we're going away.'

At first she thought he was joking, testing her. But the very precise details that he gave soon made her change her mind. There was a post vacant at Arica and he was going to apply for it. It would take about a fortnight to settle, which would just give them time to pack.

'What about your marriage?'

'Don't ever speak of it. What I've done can't be undone. I see plainly that it's over. I couldn't give you up again.'

'Poor baby,' she said with mournful gentleness, a shade contemptuously. Then, after two or three puffs at her cigarette, she asked: 'Is it a long way—the place you said?'

'Arica? A very long way. It's in Peru.' And in a low voice he added: 'Flamant won't be able to follow you there.'

She sat looking dreamy and mysterious in a cloud of cigarette-smoke. He kept her hand in his and stroked her bare arm and, lulled by the trickling of water all round the cottage, he closed his eyes and sank quietly deeper into the ooze.

NERVOUS, trembling, with steam up, already on his way, like everyone just on the eve of a journey, Jean had been in Marseilles for two days. Here Fanny was to join him and set out with him. Everything was ready. Their tickets were bought; two first-class cabins were booked for the Arican vice-consul and his sister-in-law, who was travelling with him; and now here he was pacing up and down the worn red carpet of the hotel bedroom, in a double fever of suspense, waiting for his mistress and waiting to get under way.

He had to walk about and swing his arms where he was, because he did not dare to go out. Being in the streets made him as uneasy as a criminal, a deserter; for in these variegated, swarming streets, here in Marseilles, it seemed as if at every corner either his father or old Bouchereau would loom up at any moment to lay a hand on his shoulder, take possession of him and carry him back again.

So he shut himself up in his room and had his meals there, not even going down to the table d'hôte; he read without seeing the print on the page; he threw himself on his bed, trying to distract himself in his vague siestas by staring at the fly-blown pictures on the walls, *The Wreck of the Pérouse* and *The Death of Captain Cook*; or for whole hours on end he would lean on the worm-eaten balcony railing, in the shade of a yellow awning as patched as a fishing-boat's sails.

His hotel, called the Young Anacharsis, a name picked at random out of Bottin's guide for its tempting sound when he was arranging with Fanny where they would meet, was an old inn, neither very comfortable nor even very clean, but overlooking the harbour, right down among the ships, itself almost travelling out to sea. Just under the windows was a bird-catcher's stall with an array of cages, parrots, cockatoos, and humming-birds that hailed the dawn with tumultuous jungle cries. And then, as daylight increased, this noise was gradually lost in the greater uproar of work in the harbour, over which the great bell of Our Lady of Succour tolled the passing hours.

There was a babel of oaths, watermen's cries, porters' cries, shellfish-vendors' cries, and hammerings from the repair dock, the squeaking of cranes, the clangour of the great weighing-scales banging on the ground, ships' bells, machines whistling, the rhythmic clatter of pumps and capstans, bilge-water running out, steam escaping, the whole turmoil multiplied and flung back by the sea acting as a sounding-board, whence every now and then a hoarse bellowing went up, the roar of some marine monster, some great ocean-going ship standing out to sea.

And the smells, too, evoked distant countries, sunnier and hotter wharves than these. There were sandalwood and logwood being unloaded, and lemons, oranges, pistachios, beans, ground-nuts, all of them giving off a sharp smell that rose into the air in eddies of tropical dust, the whole atmosphere reeking of brine water, burnt herbs, and smoking fats from the galley.

As night fell, so the noise grew less and the air gradually cleared; and while Jean, feeling safer in the darkness, lifted his blind and looked out on the black, sleeping harbour with all that criss-cross hatching of masts, yards, and bowsprits, and nothing broke the silence but the dipping of an oar or the distant barking of a dog on board a ship, there—out to sea, right out to sea—was the Planier lighthouse throwing out its revolving beam, a long red or white flame slicing the darkness, a lightning-flash showing up the islands, forts, and rocks. And this luminous eye guiding thousands of lives to the horizon was another symbol of the voyage that was inviting and beckoning him, calling to him in the voice of the wind and the high seas' swell and the raucous clamour of a steamer groaning and gasping somewhere out in the roadstead.

There was still another twenty-four hours of waiting. Fanny was not to join him until Sunday. These three days by which he was too early at their meeting-place he had intended to spend with his family; he had meant to give them to those dearly loved people whom he would not see again for years and not all of whom he might ever see again. But on the evening of his arrival at Castelet, when his father learnt that the marriage was broken off and when he had guessed at the reasons, a violent and terrible scene took place.

What are we human beings, after all, and what are our tenderest affections, the affections closest to our hearts, that a wave of anger breaking between two beings of the same flesh and blood can tear and twist their tenderness and natural feelings, wrenching out their deep and subtle roots, and sweep it all away? Such angers have the blind, irresistible violence of one of those typhoons in the China seas which the hardiest sailors do not care to remember, turning pale and saying: 'Don't let us talk of that.'

He will never talk of it, but all his life he will remember that dreadful scene on the terrace at Castelet, his happy childhood home, looking out on that calm and splendid horizon, those pines and myrtles and cypresses clustered silent, shivering in the breeze, while his father cursed him. He will always see that tall old man, with jaws working convulsively, walking up to him, hate contorting his mouth and glaring in his eyes, and uttering words that could never be forgiven, driving him from the house and from honour: 'Go away, go! Go with your trollop! You are dead to us!' And the little twins crying, kneeling on the stone terrace, asking pardon for their big brother. . . . And Divonne white-faced, without a look, without a word for him. . . . And upstairs his mother peering through the pane, her face mild and anxious, wondering why there was so much noise and why her boy was going away so quickly, without kissing her good-bye.

The thought that he had not kissed his mother made him turn round half-way to Avignon; he left Césaire there at the bottom of the hill, with the carriage, and went cross-country through the fields and the vineyards, like a thief, to Castelet. The night was dark; he stumbled in the dead vine-stumps and in the end even lost his sense of direction completely, searching for the house in the blackness, already a stranger in his home. In the end it was the glimmering whiteness of the rough-cast walls that guided him; but he found the door to the terrace locked and all the windows darkened. Should he ring or call out? He did not dare, for fear of his father. He walked round the house two or three times, hoping to find some shutter not properly fastened. But Divonne with her lantern had passed by each of them, as every other night. After a long gaze up at his mother's room, a heartfelt farewell to his childhood home now locked against him, he hurried away in despair, already haunted by a remorse that would never leave him.

It was usual when someone was going away for a long period, and making a long journey with all the risks of wind and water, that parents and friends should prolong their leave-taking until the final embarkation. The last day would be spent together and visits paid to the ship and to the traveller's cabin, in order to follow him, in imagination, on his journey. Several times a day Jean saw such affectionate good-byes taking place outside the hotel. Sometimes they were noisy; sometimes there was a whole crowd of people. What moved him most was a family staying on the floor above him. There were an old man and an old woman, country people apparently in comfortable circumstances, dressed in serge and yellow cambric, who had come to see their son off, staying with him until the moment that his ship left; and the three of them could be seen leaning out of the window, in the idle hours of waiting, arm in arm, pressed close to each other, the sailor in the middle. They did not talk; they only pressed close together.

Watching them, Jean thought of the grand leave-taking he might have had—his father and his little sisters and, with one gentle, tremulous hand laid on his arm, that other, she whose lively spirit and adventurous soul had responded to the call of the bowsprits turned seaward. . . . How barren these regrets were! The crime was done, his destiny was going its course, and there was nothing for him to do but go away and forget. . . .

How slow and cruel the hours of that last night seemed! He turned this way and that on his hotel bed, watching the windowpane to see the daylight come, the slow fading from black to grey and then to the white of dawn, the lighthouse beam still sending a faint red spark across the face of the rising sun.

It was only then that he fell asleep, to be suddenly awakened by a flood of sunlight in his room and the confused cries rising from the bird-cages, mingled with the innumerable chimes of Marseilles's Sunday morning bells flung out over the widening quays, all the machines now still, the pennants fluttering at the mastheads. . . . Ten o'clock already! And the Paris express was due at midday. He dressed quickly, to go and meet Fanny. They would have lunch together looking out on the sea, then the luggage would be taken on board, and at five o'clock the siren would blow.

It was a wonderful day. Across the deep blue sky the gulls wheeled, white specks. The sea was even darker blue, a mineral blue against which everything stood out clearly even to the sky-line— sails, smoke, everything—all sparkling and dancing. And like the natural song of this sunny shore with its transparent air and water there rang out the sound of harps playing under the hotel windows, a divinely facile Italian air with sharpened, long-drawn plucking of the strings that wrung the nerves. It was more than music; it was the winged symbol of all that Southern gladness, that overflowing abundance of life and love, brimming over in tears. And the memory of Irène passed into the melody, vibrating and sobbing. How far away it was! What fair lost land! What everlasting regret for things irreparably broken!

And now it was time to go.

Just as he was going out of the door a waiter came up to him, saying: 'A letter for the Consul. It came this morning, but Monsieur le Consul was so fast asleep.' First-class travellers were rare at the Young Anacharsis Hotel, and so the worthy Marseillais took every opportunity to trot out the Consul's title. Who could be writing to him? Nobody knew his address, unless Fanny. . . . And looking closer at the envelope he had a feeling of dread and suddenly understood.

'Well, there it is. I'm not going. It's too big a thing, too utterly mad, and I feel I haven't the strength for it. For things of that sort, you know, poor sweetheart, people need to be young, and I'm not so young any more. Or they need to be blinded and mad for love, and neither of us is. Five years ago, in our good times, if you had raised a finger I would have followed you to the ends of the earth, for you can't deny that I loved you passionately. I gave you everything I had. And when I had to tear myself away from it I suffered as I never did over any other man. But love like that wears a person out, you see. Seeing you always so handsome and young, always being in fear and trembling, with so much to fight for! Now I can't do it any more. You made me live too hard and suffer too much and I'm finished now.

'In these conditions the prospect of a long voyage and starting a completely new life frightens me. I'm so fond of staying in one place. I've never been farther than Saint-Germain in my life! And then, women age too fast in the sun, and you would hardly be thirty and I would be yellow and wrinkled as Mother Pilar. As sure as anything you would bear me a grudge for the sacrifice you had made and poor Fanny would take the rap for everyone. Listen—there's an Oriental country, I read about it in one of your magazines, and when a woman there deceives her husband she's tied up with a cat in a raw hide and then the bundle is left on the beach, yelling and leaping about in the sunlight. The woman shrieks, the cat scratches, the two of them tear each other to pieces while the skin shrinks and shrivels round the captives' horrible battle, till the last gasp, the last quiver of the bag. That's the sort of torture that would be waiting for us out there. . . .'

He stopped a moment, staggered, stunned. For as far as the eye could see the blue water sparkled. *Addio* sang the harps, *addio* sang a voice as warm and passionate as the strings. And the abyss of his ruined, ravaged life, all tears and devastation, opened up before him and he saw the shorn field and the harvest reaped beyond all hope of a return, and all for this woman who had slipped between his fingers. . . .

'I should have told you sooner, but I didn't dare, seeing you so worked up, so determined. Your exaltation infected me. And then too there was a woman's vanity, the natural pride of having won you back after we had parted. Only right at the bottom of my soul I felt it wasn't the same any more, there was a crack in it, it was finished. It was only to be expected, after all, after all we went through. . . . And you needn't think it is because of poor unhappy Flamant. For him or for you and for all the others, it's done with, my heart is dead. But there is still the child, I can't do without him now, and that takes me back to the father, poor man, who ruined himself for love and came back to me from jail as eager and loving as the first time we met. Just think, when we saw each other again he spent the whole night weeping on my shoulder. You see there wasn't so much for you to get excited about.

'I told you, my darling boy, I have loved too much and I'm a wreck. Now I need someone to love me instead, someone who will make a fuss of me and admire me and rock me in his arms. He will be on his knees to me, he will never see my wrinkles or white hair. And if he marries me, as he means to do, I shall be doing him an infinite kindness. Compare the two situations. . . . Above all, don't do anything crazy. I've taken precautions to stop you from finding me. From the little café by the station where I am writing, through the trees I can see the cottage where we had such good and lovely times, and such bitter times, and the sign swinging over the door till new tenants come. Well, now you're free. You will never hear of me again. Good-bye—one last kiss on your neck—sweetheart. . . .'

Also published by The Soho Book Company:

MY HEART LAID BARE,
by CHARLES BAUDELAIRE

Charles Baudelaire was born in Paris in 1821. His passionate and almost unnatural love for his young widowed mother was shattered when she married General Aupick in 1828. He came to see Aupick as a symbol of the respectability and authority he loathed, and his loss of the love of his mother as a symbol of his destiny in the world. His parents opposed his determination to become a poet and embarked him for India but Baudelaire left the ship at Reunion and returned to Paris. He set up an apartment on the Ile Saint-Louis, which he furnished in decadent style, filling it with gilt and damasks and paintings by Delacroix. Here he set out to embody his ideal of the Dandy. He contracted dangerous debts and his life of desperate excess soon became depraved and sordid when he began the disastrous liasion with the mulatto actress Jeanne Duval, the *Venus Noire* of his poems. In 1857 he published *Les Fleurs du Mal*. He was prosecuted and fined for offences to public morals and a ban was imposed on the more obscene poems in the work which was not lifted until 1949. By 1864, Baudelaire's resources were exhausted and he fled to Brussels where his ruined constitution finally gave way. He was brought back to Paris in 1866 suffering from general paralysis and lingered on until 31 August 1867, when he died.

A characteristic theme of Baudelaire's is "l'horreur et l'extase de la vie." He found inspiration in the streets and the mysterious hidden life of Paris, and also in the spirit of evil itself. A sense of damnation provoked him to blasphemy; "*Enfer ou Ciel, qu'importe?*" he wrote. Beauty, to him, already contained the elements of its own corruption. *My Heart Laid Bare* and the other prose works published in this volume exhibit all Baudelaire's characteristic themes and are written with a disturbing blend of intellectual precision and romantic beauty, and with a sarcasm which merges into squalid decadence.

ISBN 0948166 07 X   £5.95

Please ask for these books at your local bookshop. If unavailable they can be ordered direct from The Soho Book Company, Orders Department, 1/3 Brewer Street, London W1R 3FN. Please enclose £1 extra for each complete order to cover postage and packing.

Also published by The Soho Book Company:

DOMINIQUE, by EUGENE FROMENTIN

Eugene Fromentin was born at La Rochelle, on the Atlantic coast of France, in 1820. His family owned considerable properties in the area and his father was the superintendent of a mental hospital. He was sent to Paris to read for the bar but gave up law for painting. He was a successful artist of the school of Delacroix, and was highly esteemed by his contemporaries for his paintings of North Africa, which he visited several times during the 1840's and 1850's. *A Summer in the Sahara* (1857) and *A Year in the Sahel* (1859) are accounts of his wanderings there which at once established him as a literary artist of the first order. After the publication of *Dominique* he felt unable to satisfy his high literary standards and returned to painting. Shortly before his death he published *The Old Masters of Belgium and Holland* (1876), essays on the Dutch and Flemish painters. He died prematurely of an anthrax infection in 1876.

Dominique, his masterpiece, first appeared in 1862. The touching freshness of its landscapes would alone render it valuable, but it is remarkable as a sober analysis of delirious passion. While still at school M. Dominique de Bray falls in love with Madeleine d'Orsel, who is a few years older than him. She discovers this only after her marriage, and elects to cure him, but falls in love herself. Their moral distress rises to a climax when by accident, Dominique discovers this. The book offers a vision of chastity and pain which hints at the dark side of life, suggesting that there are other ends to existence besides mere happiness.

ISBN 0948166 06 1   £4.95

Please ask for these books at your local bookshop. If unavailable they can be ordered direct from The Soho Book Company, Orders Department, 1/3 Brewer Street, London W1R 3FN. Please enclose £1 extra for each complete order to cover postage and packing.

Also published by The Soho Book Company:

TO THE HAPPY FEW
SELECTED LETTERS OF STENDHAL

Stendhal was one of the many pen-names used by Henri Beyle. He was born at Grenoble in 1783, and educated there. His mother died when he was seven; he detested his father and the rest of his family, and the devout, Royalist atmosphere in which they lived. In Paris by 1799, he procured an army commission in 1800 which took him to Milan. In Italy, he fell in love and discovered his spiritual home. Between 1806 and 1813 the victualling of Napoleon's armies in Germany, Russia and Austria constituted much of his work. He left the army at the end of this period, his health impaired largely through his own excesses. He refused office under the Bourbons and spent seven years in Italy, absorbed by a shattering unrequited passion which was the main event of his life. Unjustly accused of spying, he was forced to leave and from 1821 to 1830 he was mostly in Paris, living frugally, writing, and frequenting literary *salons*. He published *Of Love* (1822) and *The Red and the Black* (1830) during this period. Under the July monarchy he was appointed French consul at Trieste, but was soon transferred to Civitavecchia, a dreary, unhealthy port, 45 miles outside Rome. He held this office until his sudden death from apoplexy, in a Paris street in 1842. His masterpiece *The Charterhouse of Parma*, which he wrote in 52 days, appeared in 1839. Stendhal was not a conscious stylist, and was prepared to sacrifice harmony and rhythm to the lucidity with which he expressed his often complicated ideas. He had an ironical attitude to life, and the behaviour of his characters, and even their virtue, springs from their passions. His ideal was what he called Beylism; a worship of magnificent, all-conquering energy in the pursuit of happiness.

Stendhal's life resembled that of his novels. If his heroes were on the whole younger and better looking than he was, they were less mature; in many of these letters it is the poet who did not die young who writes, in a poetry of ideas. The three persistent themes of the novels, the love affairs, the life of action, and the precise analysis of the various forms of passion he distilled from these, are also the persistent themes of his correspondence. Here Stendhal courts Metilde, delineates the anatomy of love and struggles through the snow, retreating from Russia.

ISBN 0948166 09 6

£6.95

Please ask for these books at your local bookshop. If unavailable they can be ordered direct from The Soho Book Company, Orders Department, 1/3 Brewer Street, London W1R 3FN. Please enclose £1 extra for each complete order to cover postage and packing.

ARMANCE, by STENDHAL

Stendhal was one of the many pen-names used by Henri Beyle. He was born at Grenoble in 1783, and educated there. His mother died when he was seven; he detested his father and the rest of his family, and the devout, Royalist atmosphere in which they lived. In Paris by 1799, he procured an army commission in 1800 which took him to Milan. In Italy, he fell in love and discovered his spiritual home. Between 1806 and 1813 the victualling of Napoleon's armies in Germany, Russia and Austria constituted much of his work. He left the army at the end of this period, his health impaired largely through his own excesses. He refused office under the Bourbons and spent seven years in Italy, absorbed by a shattering unrequited passion which was the main event of his life. Unjustly accused of spying, he was forced to leave and from 1821 to 1830 he was mostly in Paris, living frugally, writing, and frequenting literary *salons*. He published *Of Love* (1822) and *The Red and the Black* (1830) during this period. Under the July monarchy he was appointed French consul at Trieste, but was soon transferred to Civitavecchia, a dreary, unhealthy port, 45 miles outside Rome. He held this office until his sudden death from apoplexy, in a Paris street in 1842. His masterpiece *The Charterhouse of Parma*, which he wrote in 52 days, appeared in 1839. Stendhal was not a conscious stylist, and was prepared to sacrifice harmony and rhythm to the lucidity with which he expressed his often complicated ideas. He had an ironical attitude to life, and the behaviour of his characters, and even their virtue, springs from their passions. His ideal was what he called Beylism; a worship of magnificent, all-conquering energy in the pursuit of happiness.

Armance, his earliest novel, appeared in 1827. It exemplifies Stendhal's style and attitude to life. Set in contemporary Paris, this charming love story conceals a powerful study of nobility of spirit. Armance and Octave are secretly in love: as clouds of passionate tension gather we are compelled to ask whether destiny will allow them to meet, and honour allow them to be happy.

Translated by C. K. Scott Moncrieff.

ISBN 0948166 03 7   £5.95

THE ENCHANTED WANDERER,
by NICOLAI LYESKOV

Nicolai Semyonovich Lyeskov (or Leskov) was born in a small village in Central Russia in 1831. His mother was of aristocratic birth and his father was a famous criminal investigator of seemingly supernatural abilities, who ruined himself by turning to farming. Lyeskov himself was brought up with the children of serfs. Both his parents died when he was sixteen and he was then looked after by his aunt, a quaker convert married to an Englishman. English influences, combined with the lessons of his early impoverishment and extensive travels through Russia can be detected in his work. As a minor official in the Orel penal court, he became thoroughly acquainted with the severities and inefficiencies of the penal system under Nicholas I. He went to St Petersburg in 1862, where he became a journalist and published several novels. It was during this period that he wrote his remarkable series of tales, including *Lady Macbeth of Mtensk* (1865) and *The Enchanted Wanderer* (1873), and culminating in *The Left-Handed Smith, The Lady and the Slut,* and *The Mountain.* His later tales became increasingly religious. Lyeskov refused to align himself with any political faction and was ill-treated by his critics. His reading public was large. Tolstoy wrote of him that "he has long followed the road which I am now travelling", and Maxim Gorky recognised him "as a literary artist, assuredly worthy of being placed on a level with such masters of Russian literature as Tolstoy, Gogol, Turgenev and Goncharov." He died of a heart attack in 1895 and was buried at St Petersburg.

The Enchanted Wanderer has been described as the high water mark of Lyeskov's narrative power, providing a Quixotic account of the Russian people through the eyes of an illiterate sage. As this wanderer travels from place to place, he recounts his restless history in a series of rustic episodes describing the essence of life under the Tsars. The adventures follow each other in breathless succession, and they are saturated with expressive and picturesque detail. They provide the reader with a delightful portrait of the Russia of the time, as well as a more sombre portrait of a strong and unschooled character searching for truth.

Translated by A. G. Paschkoff.

ISBN 0948166 04 5   £5.95

Also published by The Soho Book Company:

NAPOLEON'S MEMOIRS,
edited by SOMERSET DE CHAIR

Napoleon Bonaparte, the Emperor Napoleon I, appeared unexpectedly in a Corsican drawing room during the feast of the Assumption of 1769. He was born, he claimed, 'on an old carpet, on which were worked large designs.' He climbed rapidly in the French Revolutionary Armies and by 1796, aged 27, he commanded the Army of Italy which he led to victory against Austria. In 1798 he conquered Egypt but was thwarted in his hopes of destroying British Power in India by Nelson's naval victory at Aboukir Bay. In 1799 Napoleon took advantage of a political crisis in Paris to return there. His popularity was still high and he engineered the *coup d'etat du 18 Brumaire* from which he emerged as First Consul, effectively a dictator. In 1802 he was elected consul for life and was constituted emperor by the *senatus-consulte* of 18 May 1804, confirmed by plebiscite. He and his wife Josephine were crowned at Notre-Dame in the presence of Pope Pius VII.

He had no children by Josephine, and divorced her in 1809 to marry the archduchess Marie-Louise of Austria, who bore him a son. He restored order and civil unity to France and reconstructed the financial, educational, judicial, executive and legislative systems. At the same time he ruthlessly suppressed conspiracies and destroyed the freedom of the press. By 1810 his empire covered most of Europe, excluding Russia, but following his disastrous Russian campaign (1812) and defeat at Leipzig (1813) the allies invaded France in 1814. Napoleon abdicated unconditionally, and was granted sovereignty of Elba, a small island to which he was confined off the Mediterranean coast. Ten months later he escaped on the brig *L'Inconstant* and landed with 700 soldiers at Juan les Pins. Louis XVIII fled to Belgium and Napoleon made his way to Paris amidst scenes of exultation. The allied coalition regathered in order to destroy him, and he was narrowly defeated at Waterloo (1815). He abdicated for a second time and considered sailing for America, but finally gave himself up to the British government. He spent the rest of his life interned on the Atlantic Island of St Helena, where he dictated and corrected his memoirs. He died in 1821, probably of stomach cancer, but possibly of Arsenic poisoning.

Somerset de Chair (1911–) was a member of the House of Commons (1935–45, 50–51) and parliamentary private secretary to the Minister for Production (1942–44). During the war he served in the British Army in the Middle East in the Royal Horse Guards (1938–42). He is an author and poet.

ISBN 0948166 10 X   £7.95

Please ask for these books at your local bookshop. If unavailable they can be ordered direct from The Soho Book Company, Orders Department, 1/3 Brewer Street, London W1R 3FN. Please enclose £1 extra for each complete order to cover postage and packing.

Also published by The Soho Book Company:

SELECTED LETTERS of FRIEDRICH NIETZSCHE

Friedrich Wilhelm Nietzsche was born near Leipzig in 1844, the son of a Lutheran pastor. His upbringing was very pious. He went to the famous grammar school of Pforta, and then to the universities of Bonn and Leipzig where he was powerfully influenced by his reading of Schopenhauer. His brilliance as a philologist was such that he was appointed to the chair of classical philology at the University of Basel at the age of 24, before he had taken his degree. While at Basel he made and broke his passionate friendship with the composer Richard Wagner and took part as an ambulance orderly in the Franco-Prussian war. Plagued by ill health, he was obliged to retire from the University in 1879. After this he lived a reclusive life in Switzerland, France and Italy, until in 1889 he became paralysed and went mad. He died in 1900.

Nietzsche became famous with *The Birth of Tragedy* (1872) which was of revolutionary importance, challenging the accepted tradition of classical scholarship. He achieved lasting fame with *Thus Spake Zarathustra*, mostly written between 1883 and 1885. His other works include *Untimely Meditations* (1873–6); *Human, All Too Human* (1878–9); *The Wanderer and his Shadow* (1880); *The Dawn* (1881); *The Gay Science* (1882 & 1887); *Beyond Good and Evil* (1886); *Towards a Genealogy of Morals* (1887); and, at the end of his working life, *The Twilight of the Idols, The Anti-Christ* and *Ecce Homo*. In seeking to analyse and redefine morality, Nietzsche was led to reject Christian ethics and affirm the "Superman" and the doctrine of power. His influence on modern German literature has been enormous.

This selection of his letters by Oscar Levy, the Nietzschean scholar, contains the essence of a vast correspondence spanning Nietzsche's life and work. It includes confessional letters to his mother and sister, alongside impassioned correspondence with great figures of the time, such as Strindberg, Burckhardt and Taine. In it we see "a writer of the most forbidding aspect, a prophet of almost superhuman inspiration, a hermit inabiting a desert of icy glaciers, coming down, so to say, to the inhabited valley, to the familiar plain, where he assumes a human form and a human speech." (O. Levy)

Translated by A. N. Ludovici. Edited with an introduction by O. Levy.

ISBN 0948166 01 0   £6.95

Please ask for these books at your local bookshop. If unavailable they can be ordered direct from The Soho Book Company, Orders Department, 1/3 Brewer Street, London W1R 3FN. Please enclose £1 extra for each complete order to cover postage and packing.

AXEL, by VILLIERS de l'ISLE-ADAM

Philippe-Auguste, Comte de Villiers de l'Isle-Adam was born at St Brieuc, Britanny, in 1838. He came of an ancient, impoverished and eccentric family, fervently Catholic and steeped in chivalric tradition. He lived mostly in Paris, making literature the sole object of a vagabond existence, and suffered atrocious poverty until his death in 1889. His writing has a powerful poetic quality, concealing a mystical philosophy beneath an ornate and extravagantly decadent romantic style.

Axel is the epitome of symbolist drama, and gave its name to the definitive work on decadence and symbolism, Edmund Wilson's *Axel's Castle*. "Count Villiers de l'Isle-Adam," wrote W. B. Yeats, "swept together words behind which glimmered a spiritual and passionate mood, as the flame glimmers behind the dusky blue and red glass in an Eastern lamp." Villiers started Axel at about the time he became acquainted with Wagner, in 1869, and worked on it during nearly two decades. Over this period his own metaphysical enthusiasms moved from occultism, through more orthodox idealisms and back to Catholicism, which he had never ceased to practice. Each of these positions is examined in turn by Axel, Count of Auersperg and by Sara, an escaped nun of heartbreaking beauty whom he discovers in the vaults of his storm-swept castle. Each is rejected and it is with the dramatic discovery of the highest ideal, amidst tumbling cascades of gold and jewels, that the work ends.

ISBN 0948166 05 3   £4.95

Also published by The Soho Book Company:

THE DEAD SEAGULL, by GEORGE BARKER

George Barker was born in Essex in 1913 of an English father and an Irish mother. At an early age he came to London, where he set up a printing press in Shepherd's Bush (The Phoenix Press). His first poems were printed there. He was soon noticed as an extravagant figure around town and his work attracted the practical encouragement of T. S. Eliot and the admiration of W. B. Yeats. *Thirty Preliminary Poems* were published in 1933, followed by *A Vision of Beasts and Gods, Eros in Dogma* (1944), *News of the World* (1950), *The True Confession of George Barker* (1950), *Calamiterror* and other works. His *Collected Poems* were first published by Faber & Faber in 1957. His more recent works include *In Memory of David Archer* (1973), *Villa Stellar*, and *Anno Domini* (1983). Apart from verse, George Barker has written three books for children. He has lived in the United States, Japan and Italy, and now lives in Norfolk.

His novel, *The Dead Seagull*, was first published in 1950. It is recognisably the work of a poet being short, lyrical and strong. It is the closely-observed story of a love affair, sometimes brutally scathing, sometimes almost pornographical; above all it is an unparalleled description of the power of sexual love.

'I warn you that as you lie in your bed and feel the determination of your lover slipping its blade between your ribs, this is the real consummation. "Kill me, Kill me," you murmur. But it always surprises you when you die.'

ISBN 0948166 00 2   £4.95

Please ask for these books at your local bookshop. If unavailable they can be ordered direct from The Soho Book Company, Orders Department, 1/3 Brewer Street, London W1R 3FN. Please enclose £1 extra for each complete order to cover postage and packing.

MARIUS THE EPICUREAN,
by WALTER PATER

Walter Horatio Pater was born in 1839 into a family of Dutch descent. He spent his entire working life at Oxford, where he received his B.A. from Queen's College in 1862. In 1864 he became a fellow of Brasenose College. He became associated with the Pre-Raphaelites, particularly Swinburne, in 1869. A volume of collected essays entitled *Studies in the History of the Renaissance* (1873) first brought Pater fame. It was followed by other collections: *Imaginary Portraits* (1887); *Appreciations* (1889), containing his judgements of Shakespeare, Wordsworth and other English writers; *Plato and Platonism* (1893); and two posthumous collections issued in 1895. *Gaston de LaTour* (1896), a story of the France of Charles IX, was left unfinished at Pater's death in 1894. It was as a critic and a humanist that he became a powerful influence on his own and succeeding generations, claiming disciples as diverse as Virginia Woolf and Ezra Pound.

Marius the Epicurean stands apart from the rest of his work, enshrining its values and presenting them in a more rounded and complete form. It has been described as "the most highly finished of all his works and the expression of his deepest thought." He gave up a considerable period, between 1880 and 1885, to its composition. It is the story of the life, at the time of the Antonines, of a grave and thoughtful man. Pater traces the reactions of Marius to the spiritual and philosophical influences to which he is subjected. These range from the *Golden Book* of Lucius Apuleius to the stoicism of Marcus Aurelius, and from the tranquil beauties of the old Roman religion to the lurid horrors of the Christian persecution. An excuse for the detailed examination of a series of human ideals, the book was written to illustrate the highest aim of the aesthetic life.

ISBN 0948166 02 9 £7.95